The Diary of a Superfluous Man and Other Stories

Ivan Turgenev

Contents

THE DIARY OF A SUPERFLUOUS MAN AND OTHER STORIES

BY

Ivan Turgenev

THE DIARY OF A SUPERFLUOUS MAN

VILLAGE OF SHEEP'S SPRINGS, *March* 20, 18--.
The doctor has just left me. At last I have got at something definite! For all his cunning, he had to speak out at last. Yes, I am soon, very soon, to die. The frozen rivers will break up, and with the last snow I shall, most likely, swim away ... whither? God knows! To the ocean too. Well, well, since one must die, one may as well die in the spring. But isn't it absurd to begin a diary a fortnight, perhaps, before death? What does it matter? And by how much are fourteen days less than fourteen years, fourteen centuries? Beside eternity, they say, all is nothingness--yes, but in that case eternity, too, is nothing. I see I am letting myself drop into metaphysics; that's a bad sign--am I not rather faint-hearted, perchance? I had better begin a description of some sort. It's damp and windy out of doors.

I'm forbidden to go out. What can I write about, then? No decent man talks of his maladies; to write a novel is not in my line; reflections on elevated topics are beyond me; descriptions of the life going on around me could not even interest me; while I am weary of doing nothing, and too lazy to read. Ah, I have it, I will write the story of all my life for myself. A first-rate idea! Just before death it is a suitable thing to do, and can be of no harm to any one. I will begin.

I was born thirty years ago, the son of fairly well-to-do landowners. My father had a passion for gambling; my mother was a woman of character ... a very virtuous woman. Only, I have known no woman whose moral excellence was less productive of happiness. She was crushed beneath the weight of her own virtues, and was a source of misery to every one, from herself upwards. In all the fifty years of her life, she never once took rest, or sat with her hands in her lap; she was for ever fussing and bustling about like an ant, and to absolutely no good purpose, which cannot be said of the ant. The worm of restlessness fretted her night and day. Only once I saw her perfectly tranquil, and that was the day after her death, in her coffin. Looking at her, it positively seemed to me that her face wore an expression of subdued amazement; with the half-open lips, the sunken cheeks, and meekly-staring eyes, it seemed expressing, all over, the words, 'How good to be at rest!' Yes, it is good, good to be rid, at last, of the wearing sense of life, of the persistent, restless consciousness of existence! But that's neither here nor there.

I was brought up badly and not happily. My father and mother both loved me; but that made things no better for me. My father was not, even in his own house, of the slightest authority or consequence, being a man openly abandoned to a shameful and ruinous vice; he was conscious of his degradation, and not having the strength of will to give up his darling passion, he tried at least, by his invariably amiable and humble demeanour and his unswerving submissiveness, to win the condescending consideration of his exemplary wife. My mother certainly did bear her trial with the superb and majestic long-suffering of virtue, in which there is so much of egoistic pride. She never reproached my father for anything, gave him her last penny, and paid his debts without a word. He exalted her as a paragon to her face and behind her back, but did not like to be at home, and caressed me by stealth, as though he were afraid of contaminating me by his presence. But at such times his distorted features were full of such kindness, the nervous grin on his lips was replaced by such a touching smile, and his brown eyes, encircled by fine wrinkles, shone with such love, that I could not help pressing my cheek to his, which was wet and warm with tears. I wiped away those tears with my handkerchief, and they flowed again without effort, like water from a brimming glass. I fell to crying, too, and he comforted me, stroking my back and kissing me all over my face with his quivering lips. Even now, more than twenty years after his death, when I think of my poor father, dumb sobs rise into my throat, and my heart beats as hotly and bitterly and aches with as poignant a pity as if it had long to go on beating, as if there were anything to be sorry for!

My mother's behaviour to me, on the contrary, was always the same, kind, but cold. In children's books one often comes across such mothers, sermonising and just. She loved me, but I did not love her. Yes! I fought shy of my virtuous mother, and passionately loved my vicious father.

But enough for to-day. It's a beginning, and as for the end, whatever it may be,

I needn't trouble my head about it. That's for my illness to see to.

March 21.

To-day it is marvellous weather. Warm, bright; the sunshine frolicking gaily on the melting snow; everything shining, steaming, dripping; the sparrows chattering like mad things about the drenched, dark hedges.

Sweetly and terribly, too, the moist air frets my sick chest. Spring, spring is coming! I sit at the window and look across the river into the open country. O nature! nature! I love thee so, but I came forth from thy womb good for nothing--not fit even for life. There goes a cock-sparrow, hopping along with outspread wings; he chirrups, and every note, every ruffled feather on his little body, is breathing with health and strength....

What follows from that? Nothing. He is well and has a right to chirrup and ruffle his wings; but I am ill and must die--that's all. It's not worth while to say more about it. And tearful invocations to nature are mortally absurd. Let us get back to my story.

I was brought up, as I have said, very badly and not happily. I had no brothers or sisters. I was educated at home. And, indeed, what would my mother have had to occupy her, if I had been sent to a boarding-school or a government college? That's what children are for--that their parents may not be bored. We lived for the most part in the country, and sometimes went to Moscow. I had tutors and teachers, as a matter of course; one, in particular, has remained in my memory, a dried-up, tearful German, Rickmann, an exceptionally mournful creature, cruelly maltreated by destiny, and fruitlessly consumed by an intense pining for his far-off fatherland. Sometimes, near the stove, in the fearful stuffiness of the close ante-room, full of the sour smell of stale kvas, my unshaved man-nurse, Vassily, nicknamed Goose, would sit, playing cards with the coachman, Potap, in a new sheepskin, white as foam, and superb tarred boots, while in the next room Rickmann would sing, behind the partition--

Herz, mein Herz, warum so traurig?
Was bekuemmert dich so sehr?
'Sist ja schoen im fremden Lande--
Herz, mein Herz--was willst du mehr?'

After my father's death we moved to Moscow for good. I was twelve years old. My father died in the night from a stroke. I shall never forget that night. I was sleeping soundly, as children generally do; but I remember, even in my sleep, I was aware of a heavy gasping noise at regular intervals. Suddenly I felt some one taking hold of my shoulder and poking me. I opened my eyes and saw my nurse. 'What is it?' 'Come along, come along, Alexey Mihalitch is dying.' ... I was out of bed and away like a mad thing into his bedroom. I looked: my father was lying with his head thrown back, all red, and gasping fearfully. The servants were crowding round the door with terrified faces; in the hall some one was asking in a thick voice: 'Have they sent for the doctor?' In the yard outside, a horse was being led from the stable, the gates were creaking, a tallow candle was burning in the room on the floor, my mother was there, terribly upset, but not oblivious of the proprieties, nor of her own dignity. I flung myself on my father's bosom, and hugged him, faltering: 'Papa, papa...' He lay motionless, screwing up his eyes in a strange way. I looked into his face--an unendurable horror caught my breath; I shrieked with terror, like a roughly captured bird--they picked me up and carried me away. Only the day before, as though aware his death was at hand, he had caressed me so passionately and despondently.

A sleepy, unkempt doctor, smelling strongly of spirits, was brought. My father died under his lancet, and the next day, utterly stupefied by grief, I stood with a candle in my hands before a table, on which lay the dead man, and listened senselessly to the bass sing-song of the deacon, interrupted from time to time by the weak voice of the priest. The tears kept streaming over my cheeks, my lips, my collar, my shirt-front. I was dissolved in tears; I watched persistently, I watched intently, my father's rigid face, as though I expected something of him; while my mother slowly bowed down to the ground, slowly rose again, and pressed her fingers firmly to her forehead, her shoulders, and her chest, as she crossed herself. I had not a single idea in my head; I was utterly numb, but I felt something terrible was happening to me.... Death looked me in the face that day and took note of me.

We moved to Moscow after my father's death for a very simple cause: all our estate was sold up by auction for debts--that is, absolutely all, except one little village, the one in which I am at this moment living out my magnificent existence. I must admit that, in spite of my youth at the time, I grieved over the sale of our home, or rather, in reality, I grieved over our garden. Almost my only bright memories are associated with our garden. It was there that one mild spring evening I buried my best friend, an old bob-tailed, crook-pawed dog, Trix. It was there that, hidden in the long grass, I used to eat stolen apples--sweet, red, Novgorod apples they were. There, too, I saw for the first time, among the ripe raspberry bushes, the housemaid Klavdia, who, in spite of her turned-up nose and habit of giggling in her kerchief, aroused such a tender passion in me that I could hardly breathe, and stood faint and tongue-tied in her presence; and once at Easter, when it came to her turn to kiss my seignorial hand, I almost flung myself at her feet to kiss her down-trodden goat-skin slippers. My God! Can all that be twenty years ago? It seems not long ago that I used to ride on my shaggy chestnut pony along the old fence of our garden, and, standing up in the stirrups, used to pick the two-coloured poplar leaves. While a man is living he is not conscious of his own life; it becomes audible to him, like a sound, after the lapse of time.

Oh, my garden, oh, the tangled paths by the tiny pond! Oh, the little sandy spot below the tumbledown dike, where I used to catch gudgeons! And you tall birch-trees, with long hanging branches, from beyond which came floating a peas-ant's mournful song, broken by the uneven jolting of the cart, I send you my last farewell!... On parting with life, to you alone I stretch out my hands. Would I might once more inhale the fresh, bitter fragrance of the wormwood, the sweet scent of the mown buckwheat in the fields of my native place! Would I might once more hear far away the modest tinkle of the cracked bell of our parish church; once more lie in the cool shade under the oak sapling on the slope of the familiar ravine; once more watch the moving track of the wind, flitting, a dark wave over the golden grass of our meadow!... Ah, what's the good of all this? But I can't go on to-day. Enough till to-morrow.

March 22.

To-day it's cold and overcast again. Such weather is a great deal more suitable. It's more in harmony with my task. Yesterday, quite inappropriately, stirred up a multitude of useless emotions and memories within me. This shall not occur again. Sentimental out-breaks are like liquorice; when first you suck it, it's not bad, but afterwards it leaves a very nasty taste in the mouth. I will set to work simply and serenely to tell the story of my life. And so, we moved to Moscow....

But it occurs to me, is it really worth while to tell the story of my life?

No, it certainly is not.... My life has not been different in any respect from the lives of numbers of other people. The parental home, the university, the government service in the lower grades, retirement, a little circle of friends, decent poverty, modest pleasures, unambitious pursuits, moderate desires--kindly tell me, is that new to any one? And so I will not tell the story of my life, especially as I am writing for my own pleasure; and if my past does not afford even me any sensation of great pleasure or great pain, it must be that there is nothing in it deserving of attention. I had better try to describe my own character to myself. What manner of man am I?... It may be observed that no one asks me that question--admitted. But there, I'm dying, by Jove!--I'm dying, and at the point of death I really think one may be excused a desire to find out what sort of a queer fish one really was after all.

Thinking over this important question, and having, moreover, no need whatever to be too bitter in my expressions in regard to myself, as people are apt to be who have a strong conviction of their valuable qualities, I must admit one thing. I was a man, or perhaps I should say a fish, utterly superfluous in this world. And that I propose to show to-morrow, as I keep coughing to-day like an old sheep, and my nurse, Terentyevna, gives me no peace: 'Lie down, my good sir,' she says, 'and drink a little tea.'... I know why she keeps on at me: she wants some tea herself. Well! she's welcome! Why not let the poor old woman extract the utmost benefit she can from her master at the last ... as long as there is still the chance?

March 23.

Winter again. The snow is falling in flakes. Superfluous, superfluous.... That's a capital word I have hit on. The more deeply I probe into myself, the more intently I review all my past life, the more I am convinced of the strict truth of this expression. Superfluous--that's just it. To other people that term is not applicable.... People are bad, or good, clever, stupid, pleasant, and disagreeable; but superfluous ... no. Understand me, though: the universe could get on without those people too... no doubt; but uselessness is not their prime characteristic, their most distinctive attribute, and when you speak of them, the word 'superfluous' is not the first to rise to your lips. But I ... there's nothing else one can say about me; I'm superfluous and nothing more. A supernumerary, and that's all. Nature, apparently, did not reckon on my appearance, and consequently treated me as an unexpected and uninvited guest. A facetious gentleman, a great devotee of preference, said very happily about me that I was the forfeit my mother had paid at the game of life. I am speaking about myself calmly now, without any bitterness.... It's all over and done with! Throughout my whole life I was constantly finding my place taken, perhaps because I did not look for my place where I should have done. I was apprehensive, reserved, and irritable, like all sickly people. Moreover, probably owing to excessive self-consciousness, perhaps as the result of the generally unfortunate cast of my personality, there existed between my thoughts and feelings, and the expression of those feelings and thoughts, a sort of inexplicable, irrational, and utterly insuperable barrier; and whenever I made up my mind to overcome this obstacle by force, to break down this barrier, my gestures, the expression of my face, my whole being, took on an appearance of painful constraint. I not only seemed, I positively became unnatural and affected. I was conscious of this myself, and hastened to shrink back into myself. Then a terrible commotion was set up within me. I analysed myself to the last thread, compared myself with others, recalled the slightest glances, smiles, words of the people to whom I had tried to open myself out, put the worst construction on everything, laughed vindictively at my own pretensions to 'be like every one else,'--and suddenly, in the midst of my laughter, collapsed utterly into gloom, sank into absurd dejection, and then began again as before--went round and round, in fact, like a squirrel on its wheel. Whole days were spent in this harassing, fruitless exercise. Well now, tell me, if you please, to whom and for what is such a man of use? Why did this happen to me? what was the reason of this trivial fretting at myself?--who knows? who can tell?

I remember I was driving once from Moscow in the diligence. It was a good road, but the driver, though he had four horses harnessed abreast, hitched on another, alongside of them. Such an unfortunate, utterly useless, fifth horse--fastened somehow on to the front of the shaft by a short stout cord, which mercilessly cuts his shoulder, forces him to go with the most unnatural action, and gives his whole body the shape of a comma--always arouses my deepest pity. I remarked to the driver that I thought we might on this occasion have got on without the fifth horse.... He was silent a moment, shook his head, lashed the horse a dozen times across his thin back and under his distended belly, and with a grin responded: 'Ay, to be sure; why do we drag him along with us? What the devil's he for?' And here am I too dragged along. But, thank goodness, the station is not far off.

Superfluous.... I promised to show the justice of my opinion, and I will carry out my promise. I don't think it necessary to mention the thousand trifles, everyday incidents and events, which would, however, in the eyes of any thinking man, serve as irrefutable evidence in my support--I mean, in support of my contention. I had better begin straight away with one rather important incident, after which probably there will be no doubt left of the accuracy of the term superfluous. I repeat: I do not intend to indulge in minute details, but I cannot pass over in silence one rather serious and significant fact, that is, the strange behaviour of my friends (I too used to have friends) whenever I met them, or even called on them. They used to seem ill at ease; as they came to meet me, they would give a not quite natural smile, look, not into my eyes nor at my feet, as some people do, but rather at my cheeks, articulate hurriedly, 'Ah! how are you, Tchulkaturin!' (such is the surname fate has burdened me with) or 'Ah! here's Tchulkaturin!' turn away at once and positively remain stockstill for a little while after, as though trying to recollect something. I used to notice all this, as I am not devoid of penetration and the faculty of observation; on the whole I am not a fool; I sometimes even have ideas come into my head that are amusing, not absolutely commonplace. But as I am a superfluous man with a padlock on my inner self, it is very painful for me to express my idea, the more so as I know beforehand that I shall express it badly. It positively sometimes strikes me as extraordinary the way people manage to talk, and so simply and freely.... It's marvellous, really, when you think of it. Though, to tell the truth, I too, in spite of my padlock, sometimes have an itch to talk. But I did actually utter words only in my youth; in riper years I almost always pulled myself up. I would murmur to myself: 'Come, we'd better hold our tongue.' And I was still. We are all good hands at being silent; our women especially are great in that line. Many an exalted Russian young lady keeps silent so strenuously that the spectacle is calculated to produce a faint shudder and cold sweat even in any one prepared to face it. But that's not the point, and it's not for me to criticise others. I proceed to my promised narrative.

A few years back, owing to a combination of circumstances, very insignificant in themselves, but very important for me, it was my lot to spend six months in the district town O----. This town is all built on a slope, and very uncomfortably built, too. There are reckoned to be about eight hundred inhabitants in it, of exceptional poverty; the houses are hardly worthy of the name; in the chief street, by way of an apology for a pavement, there are here and there some huge white slabs of rough-hewn limestone, in consequence of which even carts drive round it instead of through it. In the very middle of an astoundingly dirty square rises a diminutive yellowish edifice with black holes in it, and in these holes sit men in big caps making a pretence of buying and selling. In this place there is an extraordinarily high striped post sticking up into the air, and near the post, in the interests of public order, by command of the authorities, there is kept a cartload of yellow hay, and one government hen struts to and fro. In short, existence in the town of O---- is truly delightful. During the first days of my stay in this town, I almost went out of my mind with boredom. I ought to say of myself that, though I am, no doubt, a superfluous man, I am not so of my own seeking; I'm morbid myself, but I can't bear anything morbid.... I'm not even averse to happiness-- indeed, I've tried to approach it right and left.... And so it is no wonder that I too can be bored like any other mortal. I was staying in the town of O---- on official business.

Terentyevna has certainly sworn to make an end of me. Here's a specimen of our conversation:--

TERENTYEVNA. Oh--oh, my good sir! what are you for ever writing for? it's bad for you, keeping all on writing.

I. But I'm dull, Terentyevna.

SHE. Oh, you take a cup of tea now and lie down. By God's mercy you'll get in a sweat and maybe doze a bit.

I. But I'm not sleepy.

SHE. Ah, sir! why do you talk so? Lord have mercy on you! Come, lie down, lie down; it's better for you.

I. I shall die any way, Terentyevna!

SHE. Lord bless us and save us!... Well, do you want a little tea?

I. I shan't live through the week, Terentyevna!

SHE. Eh, eh! good sir, why do you talk so?... Well, I'll go and heat the samovar.

Oh, decrepit, yellow, toothless creature! Am I really, even in your eyes, not a man?

March 24. Sharp frost.

On the very day of my arrival in the town of O----, the official business, above referred to, brought me into contact with a certain Kirilla Matveitch Ozhogin, one of the chief functionaries of the district; but I became intimate, or, as it is called, 'friends' with him a fortnight later. His house was in the principal street, and was distinguished from all the others by its size, its painted roof, and the lions on its gates, lions of that species extraordinarily resembling unsuccessful dogs, whose natural home is Moscow. From those lions alone, one might safely conclude that Ozhogin was a man of property. And so it was; he was the owner of four hundred peasants; he entertained in his house all the best society of the town of O----, and had a reputation for hospitality. At his door was seen the mayor with his wide chestnut-coloured droshky and pair--an exceptionally bulky man, who seemed as though cut out of material that had been laid by for a long time. The other officials, too, used to drive to his receptions: the attorney, a yellowish, spiteful creature; the land surveyor, a wit--of German extraction, with a Tartar face; the inspector of means of communication--a soft soul, who sang songs, but a scandalmonger; a former marshal of the district--a gentleman with dyed hair, crumpled shirt front, and tight trousers, and that lofty expression of face so characteristic of men who have stood on trial. There used to come also two landowners, inseparable friends, both no longer young and indeed a little the worse for wear, of whom the younger was continually crushing the elder and putting him to silence with one and the same reproach. 'Don't you talk, Sergei Sergeitch! What have you to say? Why, you spell the word cork with two *k*'s in it.... Yes, gentlemen,' he would go on, with all the fire of conviction, turning to the bystanders, 'Sergei Sergeitch spells it not cork, but kork.' And every one present would laugh, though probably not one of them was conspicuous for special accuracy in orthography, while the luckless Sergei Sergeitch held his tongue, and with a faint smile bowed his head. But I am forgetting that my hours are numbered, and am letting myself go into too minute descriptions. And so, without further beating about the bush,--Ozhogin was married, he had a daughter, Elizaveta Kirillovna, and I fell in love with this daughter.

Ozhogin himself was a commonplace person, neither good-looking nor bad-looking; his wife resembled an aged chicken; but their daughter had not taken after her parents. She was very pretty and of a bright and gentle disposition. Her clear grey eyes looked out kindly and directly from under childishly arched brows; she was almost always smiling, and she laughed too, pretty often. Her fresh voice had a very pleasant ring; she moved freely, rapidly, and blushed gaily. She did not dress very stylishly, only plain dresses suited her. I did not make friends quickly as a rule, and if I were at ease with any one from the first--which, however, scarcely ever occurred--it said, I must own, a great deal for my new acquaintance. I did not know at all how to behave with women, and in their presence I either scowled and put on a morose air, or grinned in the most idiotic way, and in my embarrassment turned my tongue round and round in my mouth. With Elizaveta Kirillovna, on the contrary, I felt at home from the first moment. It happened in this way.

I called one day at Ozhogin's before dinner, asked, 'At home?' was told, 'The master's at home, dressing; please to walk into the drawing-room.' I went into the drawing-room; I beheld standing at the window, with her back to me, a girl in a white gown, with a cage in her hands. I was, as my way was, somewhat taken aback; however, I showed no sign of it, but merely coughed, for good manners. The girl turned round quickly, so quickly that her curls gave her a slap in the face, saw me, bowed, and with a smile showed me a little box half full of seeds. 'You don't mind?' I, of course, as is the usual practice in such cases, first bowed my head, and at the same time rapidly crooked my knees, and straightened them out again (as though some one had given me a blow from behind in the legs, a sure sign of good breeding and pleasant, easy manners), and then smiled, raised my hand, and softly and carefully brandished it twice in the air. The girl at once turned away from me, took a little piece of board out of the cage, began vigorously scraping it with a knife, and suddenly, without changing her attitude, uttered the following words: 'This is papa's parrot.... Are you fond of parrots?' 'I prefer siskins,' I answered, not without some effort. 'I like siskins, too; but look at him, isn't he pretty? Look, he's not afraid.' (What surprised me was that I was not afraid.) 'Come closer. His name's Popka.' I went up, and bent down. 'Isn't he really sweet?' She turned her face to me; but we were standing so close together, that she had to throw her head back to get a look at me with her clear eyes. I gazed at her; her rosy young face was smiling all over in such a friendly way that I smiled too, and almost laughed aloud with delight. The door opened; Mr. Ozhogin came in. I promptly went up to him, and began talking to him very unconstrainedly. I don't know how it was, but I stayed to dinner, and spent the whole evening with them; and next day the Ozhogins' footman, an elongated, dull-eyed person, smiled upon me as a friend of the family when he helped me off with my overcoat.

To find a haven of refuge, to build oneself even a temporary nest, to feel the comfort of daily intercourse and habits, was a happiness I, a superfluous man, with no family associations, had never before experienced. If anything about me had had any resemblance to a flower, and if the comparison were not so hackneyed, I would venture to say that my soul blossomed from that day. Everything within me and about me was suddenly transformed! My whole life was lighted up by love, the whole of it, down to the paltriest details, like a dark, deserted room when a light has been brought into it. I went to bed, and got up, dressed, ate my breakfast, and smoked my pipe--differently from before. I positively skipped along as I walked, as though wings were suddenly sprouting from my shoulders. I was not for an instant, I remember, in uncertainty with regard to the feeling Elizaveta Kirillovna inspired in me. I fell passionately in love with her from the first day, and from the first day I knew I was in love. During the course of three weeks I saw her every day. Those three weeks were the happiest time in my life; but the recollection of them is painful to me. I can't think of them alone; I cannot help dwelling on what followed after them, and the intensest bitterness slowly takes possession of my softened heart.

When a man is very happy, his brain, as is well known, is not very active. A calm and delicious sensation, the sensation of satisfaction, pervades his whole being; he is swallowed up by it; the consciousness of personal life vanishes in him--he is in beatitude, as badly educated poets say. But when, at last, this 'enchantment' is over, a man is sometimes vexed and sorry that, in the midst of his bliss, he observed himself so little; that he did not, by reflection, by recollection, redouble and prolong his feelings ... as though the 'beatific' man had time, and it were worth his while to reflect on his sensations! The happy man is what the fly is in the sunshine. And so it is that, when I recall those three weeks, it is almost impossible for me to retain in my mind any exact and definite impression, all the more so as during that time nothing very remarkable took place between us.... Those twenty days are present to my imagination as something warm, and young, and fragrant, a sort of streak of light in my dingy, greyish life. My memory becomes all at once remorselessly clear and trustworthy, only from the instant when, to use the phrase of badly-educated writers, the blows of destiny began to fall upon me.

Yes, those three weeks.... Not but what they have left some images in my mind. Sometimes when it happens to me to brood a long while on that time, some memories suddenly float up out of the darkness of the past--like stars which suddenly come out against the evening sky to meet the eyes straining to catch sight of them. One country walk in a wood has remained particularly distinct in my memory. There were four of us, old Madame Ozhogin, Liza, I, and a certain Bizmyonkov, a petty official of the town of O----, a light-haired, good-natured, and harmless person. I shall have more to say of him later. Mr. Ozhogin had stayed at home; he had a headache, from sleeping too long. The day was exquisite; warm and soft. I must observe that pleasure-gardens and picnic-parties are not to the taste of the average Russian. In district towns, in the so-called public gardens, you never meet a living soul at any time of the year; at the most, some old woman sits sighing and moaning on a green garden seat, broiling in the sun, not far from a sickly tree--and that, only if there is no greasy little bench in the gateway near. But if there happens to be a scraggy birchwood in the neighbourhood of the town, tradespeople and even officials gladly make excursions thither on Sundays and holidays, with samovars, pies, and melons; set all this abundance on the dusty grass, close by the road, sit round, and eat and drink tea in the sweat of their brows till evening. Just such a wood there was at that time a mile and a half from the town of O---. We repaired there after dinner, duly drank our fill of tea, and then all four began to wander about the wood. Bizmyonkov walked with Madame Ozhogin on his arm, I with Liza on mine. The day was already drawing to evening. I was at that time in the very fire of first love (not more than a fortnight had passed since our first meeting), in that condition of passionate and concentrated adoration, when your whole soul innocently and unconsciously follows every movement of the beloved being, when you can never have enough of her presence, listen enough to her voice, when you smile with the look of a child convalescent after sickness, and a man of the smallest experience cannot fail at the first glance to recognise a hundred yards off what is the matter with you. Till that day I had never happened to have Liza on my arm. We walked side by side, stepping slowly over the green grass. A light breeze, as it were, flitted about us between the white stems of the birches, every now and then flapping the ribbon of her hat into my face. I incessantly followed her eyes, until at last she turned gaily to me and we both smiled at each other. The birds were chirping approvingly above us, the blue sky peeped caressingly at us through the delicate foliage. My head was going round with excess of bliss. I hasten to remark, Liza was not a bit in love with me. She liked me; she was never shy with any one, but it was not reserved for me to trouble her childlike peace of mind. She walked arm in arm with me, as she would with a brother. She was seventeen then.... And meanwhile, that very evening, before my eyes, there began that soft inward ferment which precedes the metamorphosis of the child into the woman.... I was witness of that transformation of the whole being, that guileless bewilderment, that agitated dreaminess; I was the first to detect the sudden softness of the glance, the sudden ring in the voice--and oh, fool! oh, superfluous man! For a whole week I had the face to imagine that I, I was the cause of this transformation!

This was how it happened.

We walked rather a long while, till evening, and talked little. I was silent, like all inexperienced lovers, and she, probably, had nothing to say to me. But she seemed to be pondering over something, and shook her head in a peculiar way, as she pensively nibbled a leaf she had picked. Sometimes she started walking ahead, so resolutely...then all at once stopped, waited for me, and looked round with lifted eyebrows and a vague smile. On the previous evening we had read together. The Prisoner of the Caucasus. With what eagerness she had listened to me, her face propped in both hands, and her bosom pressed against the table! I began to speak of our yesterday's reading; she flushed, asked me whether I had given the parrot any hemp-seed before starting, began humming some little song aloud, and all at once was silent again. The copse ended on one side in a rather high and abrupt precipice; below coursed a winding stream, and beyond it, over an immense expanse, stretched the boundless prairies, rising like waves, spreading wide like a table-cloth, and broken here and there by ravines. Liza and I were the first to come out at the edge of the wood; Bizmyonkov and the elder lady were behind. We came out, stood still, and involuntarily we both half shut our eyes; directly facing us, across a lurid mist, the vast, purple sun was setting. Half the sky was flushed and glowing; red rays fell slanting on the meadows, casting a crimson reflection even on the side of the ravines in shadow, lying in gleams of fire on the stream, where it was not hidden under the overhanging bushes, and, as it were, leaning on the bosom of the precipice and the copse. We stood, bathed in the blazing brilliance. I am not capable of describing all the impassioned solemnity of this scene. They say that by a blind man the colour red is imagined as the sound of a trumpet. I don't know how far this comparison is correct, but really there was something of a challenge in this glowing gold of the evening air, in the crimson flush on sky and earth. I uttered a cry of rapture and at once turned to Liza. She was looking straight at the sun. I remember the sunset glow was reflected in little points of fire in her eyes. She was overwhelmed, deeply moved. She made no response to my exclamation; for a long while she stood, not stirring, with drooping head.... I held out my hand to her; she turned away from me, and suddenly burst into tears. I looked at her with secret, almost delighted amazement.... The voice of Bizmyonkov was heard a couple of yards off. Liza quickly wiped her tears and looked with a faltering smile at me. The elder lady came out of the copse leaning on the arm of her flaxen-headed escort; they, in their turn, admired the view. The old lady addressed some question to Liza, and I could not help shuddering, I remember, when her daughter's broken voice, like cracked glass, sounded in reply. Meanwhile the sun had set, and the afterglow began to fade. We turned back. Again I took Liza's arm in mine. It was still light in the wood, and I could clearly distinguish her features. She was confused, and did not raise her eyes. The flush that overspread her face did not vanish; it was as though she were still standing in the rays of the setting sun.... Her hand scarcely touched my arm. For a long while I could not frame a sentence; my heart was beating so violently. Through the trees there was a glimpse of the carriage in the distance; the coachman was coming at a walking pace to meet us over the soft sand of the road.

'Lizaveta Kirillovna,' I brought out at last, 'what did you cry for?'

'I don't know,' she answered, after a short silence. She looked at me with her soft eyes still wet with tears--her look struck me as changed, and she was silent again.

'You are very fond, I see, of nature,' I pursued. That was not at all what I meant to say, and the last words my tongue scarcely faltered out to the end. She shook her head. I could not utter another word.... I was waiting for something ... not an avowal--how was that possible? I waited for a confiding glance, a question.... But Liza looked at the ground, and kept silent. I repeated once more in a whisper: 'Why was it?' and received no reply. She had grown, I saw that, ill at ease, almost ashamed.

A quarter of an hour later we were sitting in the carriage driving to the town.

The horses flew along at an even trot; we were rapidly whirled along through the darkening, damp air. I suddenly began talking, more than once addressing first Bizmyonkov, and then Madame Ozhogin. I did not look at Liza, but I could see that from her corner in the carriage her eyes did not once rest on me. At home she roused herself, but would not read with me, and soon went off to bed. A turning-point, that turning-point I have spoken of, had been reached by her. She had ceased to be a little girl, she too had begun ... like me ... to wait for something. She had not long to wait.

But that night I went home to my lodgings in a state of perfect ecstasy. The vague half presentiment, half suspicion, which had been arising within me, had vanished. The sudden constraint in Liza's manner towards me I ascribed to maidenly bashfulness, timidity.... Hadn't I read a thousand times over in many books that the first appearance of love always agitates and alarms a young girl? I felt supremely happy, and was already making all sorts of plans in my head.

If some one had whispered in my ear then: 'You're raving, my dear chap! that's not a bit what's in store for you. What's in store for you is to die all alone, in a wretched little cottage, amid the insufferable grumbling of an old hag who will await your death with impatience to sell your boots for a few coppers...'!

Yes, one can't help saying with the Russian philosopher--'How's one to know what one doesn't know?'

Enough for to-day.

March 25. *A white winter day.*

I have read over what I wrote yesterday, and was all but tearing up the whole manuscript. I think my story's too spun out and too sentimental. However, as the rest of my recollections of that time presents nothing of a pleasurable character, except that peculiar sort of consolation which Lermontov had in view when he said there is pleasure and pain in irritating the sores of old wounds, why not indulge oneself? But one must know where to draw the line. And so I will continue without any sort of sentimentality.

During the whole of the week after the country excursion, my position was in reality in no way improved, though the change in Liza became more noticeable every day. I interpreted this change, as I have said before, in the most favourable way for me.... The misfortune of solitary and timid people--who are timid from self-consciousness--is just that, though they have eyes and indeed open them wide, they see nothing, or see everything in a false light, as though through coloured spectacles. Their own ideas and speculations trip them up at every step. At the commencement of our acquaintance, Liza behaved confidingly and freely with me, like a child; perhaps there may even have been in her attitude to me something more than mere childish liking.... But after this strange, almost instantaneous change had taken place in her, after a period of brief perplexity, she felt constrained in my presence; she unconsciously turned away from me, and was at the same time melancholy and dreamy.... She was waiting ... for what? She did not know ... while I ... I, as I have said above, was delighted at this change.... Yes, by God, I was ready to expire, as they say, with rapture. Though I am prepared to allow that any one else in my place might have been deceived.... Who is free from vanity? I need not say that all this was only clear to me in the course of time, when I had to lower my clipped and at no time over-powerful wings.

The misunderstanding that had arisen between Liza and me lasted a whole week--and there is nothing surprising in that: it has been my lot to be a witness of misunderstandings that have lasted for years and years. Who was it said, by the way, that truth alone is powerful? Falsehood is just as living as truth, if not more so. To be sure, I recollect that even during that week I felt from time to time an uneasy gnawing astir within me ... but solitary people like me, I say again, are as incapable of understanding what is going on within them as what is taking place before their eyes. And, besides, is love a natural feeling? Is it natural for man to love? Love is a sickness; and for sickness there is no law. Granting that there was at times an unpleasant pang in my heart; well, everything inside me was turned upside down. And how is one to know in such circumstances, what is all right and what is all wrong? and what is the cause, and what the significance, of each separate symptom? But, be that as it may, all these misconceptions, presentiments, and hopes were shattered in the following manner.

One day--it was in the morning about twelve o'clock--I had hardly entered Mr. Ozhogin's hall, when I heard an unfamiliar, mellow voice in the drawing-room, the door opened, and a tall and slim man of five-and-twenty appeared in the doorway, escorted by the master of the house. He rapidly put on a military overcoat which lay on the slab, and took cordial leave of Kirilla Matveitch. As he brushed past me, he carelessly touched his foraging cap, and vanished with a clink of his spurs.

'Who is that?' I asked Ozhogin.

'Prince N.,' the latter responded, with a preoccupied face; 'sent from Petersburg to collect recruits. But where are the servants?' he went on in a tone of annoyance; 'no one handed him his coat.'

We went into the drawing-room.

'Has he been here long?' I inquired.

'Arrived yesterday evening, I'm told. I offered him a room here, but he refused. He seems a very nice fellow, though.'

'Has he been long with you?'

'About an hour. He asked me to introduce him to Olimpiada Nikitishna.'

'And did you introduce him?'

'Of course.'

'And Lizaveta Kirillovna, too, did he ...'

'He made her acquaintance, too, of course.'

I was silent for a space.

'Has he come here for long, do you know?'

'Yes, I believe he has to be here for a fortnight.'

And Kirilla Matveitch hurried away to dress. I walked several times up and down the drawing-room. I don't recollect that Prince N.'s arrival made any special impression on me at the time, except that feeling of hostility which usually possesses us on the appearance of any new person in our domestic circle. Possibly there was mingled with this feeling something too of the nature of envy--of a shy and obscure person from Moscow towards a brilliant officer from Petersburg. 'The prince,' I mused, 'is an upstart from the capital; he'll look down upon us....' I had not seen him for more than an instant, but I had had time to perceive that he was good-looking, clever, and at his ease. After pacing the room for some time, I stopped at last before a looking-glass, pulled a comb out of my pocket, gave a picturesque carelessness to my hair, and, as sometimes happens, became suddenly absorbed in the contemplation of my own face. I remember my attention centred anxiously about my nose; the soft and undefined outlines of that feature afforded me no great satisfaction, when suddenly in the dark depths of the sloping mirror, which reflected almost the whole room, the door opened, and the slender figure of Liza appeared. I don't know why I did not stir, and kept the same expression on my face. Liza craned her head forward, looked intently at me, and raising her eyebrows, biting her lips, and holding her breath as any one does who is glad at not being noticed, she cautiously drew back and stealthily drew the door to after her. The door creaked slightly. Liza started and stood rooted to the spot... I still kept from stirring ... she pulled the handle again and vanished. There was no possibility of doubt: the expression of Liza's face at the sight of my figure, that expression in which nothing could be detected except a desire to get away again successfully, to escape a disagreeable interview, the quick flash of delight I had time to catch in her eyes when she fancied she really had managed to creep away unnoticed--it all spoke too clearly; that girl did not love me. For a long, long while I could not take my eyes off that motionless, dumb door, which was once more a patch of white in the looking-glass. I tried to smile at my own long face--dropped my head, went home again, and flung myself on the sofa. I felt extraordinarily heavy at heart, so much so that I could not cry ... and, besides, what was there to cry about...? 'Is it possible?' I repeated incessantly, lying, as though I were murdered, on my back with my hands folded on my breast--'is it possible?'...Don't you think that's rather good, that 'is it possible?'

March 26. Thaw.

When, next day, after long hesitation and with a low sinking at my heart, I went into the Ozhogins' familiar drawing-room, I was no longer the same man as they had known during the last three weeks. All my old peculiarities, which I had begun to get over, under the influence of a new feeling, reappeared and took possession of me, like proprietors returning to their house. People of my sort are usually guided, not so much by positive facts, as by their own impressions: I, who no longer ago than the day before had been dreaming of the 'raptures of love returned,' was that day no less convinced of my 'unhappiness,' and was absolutely despairing, though I was not myself able to find any rational ground for my despair. I could not as yet be jealous of Prince N., and whatever his qualities might be, his mere arrival was not sufficient to extinguish Liza's good-will towards me at once.... But stay, was there any good-will on her part? I recalled the past. 'What of the walk in the wood?' I asked myself. 'What of the expression of her face in the glass?' 'But,' I went on, 'the walk in the wood, I think ... Fie on me! my God, what a wretched creature I am!' I said at last, out loud. Of such sort were the unphrased, incomplete thoughts that went round and round a thousand times over in a monotonous whirl in my head. I repeat, I went back to the Ozhogins' the same hypersensitive, suspicious, constrained creature I had been from my childhood up....

I found the whole family in the drawing-room; Bizmyonkov was sitting there, too, in a corner. Every one seemed in high good-humour; Ozhogin, in particular, positively beamed, and his first word was to tell me that Prince N. had spent the whole of the previous evening with them. Liza gave me a tranquil greeting. 'Oh,' said I to myself; 'now I understand why you're in such spirits.' I must own the prince's second visit puzzled me. I had not anticipated it. As a rule fellows like me anticipate everything in the world, except what is bound to occur in the natural order of things; I sulked and put on the air of an injured but magnanimous person; I tried to punish Liza by showing my displeasure, from which one must conclude I was not yet completely desperate after all. They do say that in some cases when one is really loved, it's positively of use to torment the adored one; but in my position it was indescribably stupid. Liza, in the most innocent way, paid no attention to me. No one but Madame Ozhogin observed my solemn taciturnity, and she inquired anxiously after my health. I replied, of course, with a bitter smile, that I was thankful to say I was perfectly well. Ozhogin continued to expatiate on the subject of their visitor; but noticing that I responded reluctantly, he addressed himself principally to Bizmyonkov, who was listening to him with great attention, when a servant suddenly came in, announcing the arrival of Prince N. Our host jumped up and ran to meet him; Liza, upon whom I at once turned an eagle eye, flushed with delight, and made as though she would move from her seat. The prince came in, all agreeable perfume, gaiety, cordiality....

As I am not composing a romance for a gentle reader, but simply writing for my own amusement, it stands to reason I need not make use of the usual dodges of our respected authors. I will say straight out without further delay that Liza fell passionately in love with the prince from the first day she saw him, and the prince fell in love with her too--partly from having nothing to do, and partly from a propensity for turning women's heads, and also owing to the fact that Liza really was a very charming creature. There was nothing to be wondered at in their falling in love with each other. He had certainly never expected to find such a pearl in such a wretched shell (I am alluding to the God-forsaken town of O----), and she had never in her wildest dreams seen anything in the least like this brilliant, clever, fascinating aristocrat.

After the first courtesies, Ozhogin introduced me to the prince, who was very affable in his behaviour to me. He was as a rule very affable with every one; and in spite of the immeasurable distance between him and our obscure provincial circle, he was clever enough to avoid being a source of constraint to any one, and even to make a show of being on our level, and only living at Petersburg, as it were, by accident.

That first evening.... Oh, that first evening! In our happy days of childhood our teachers used to describe and set up before us as an example the manly fortitude of the young Spartan, who, having stolen a fox and hidden it under his tunic, without uttering one shriek let it devour all his entrails, and so preferred death itself to disgrace.... I can find no better comparison for my indescribable sufferings during the evening on which I first saw the prince by Liza's side. My continual forced smile and painful vigilance, my idiotic silence, my miserable and ineffectual desire to get away--all that was doubtless something truly remarkable in its own way. It was not one wild beast alone gnawing at my vitals; jealousy, envy, the sense of my own insignificance, and helpless hatred were torturing me. I could not but admit that the prince really was a very agreeable young man.... I devoured him with my eyes; I really believe I forgot to blink as usual, as I stared at him. He talked not to Liza alone, but all he said was of course really for her. He must have felt me a great bore. He most likely guessed directly that it was a discarded lover he had to deal with, but from sympathy for me, and also a profound sense of my absolute armlessness, he treated me with extraordinary gentleness. You can fancy how this wounded me! In the course of the evening I tried, I remember, to smooth over my mistake. I positively (don't laugh at me, whoever you may be, who chance to look through these lines--especially as it was my last illusion...) ... I, positively, in the midst of my different sufferings, imagined all of a sudden that Liza wanted to punish me for my haughty coldness at the beginning of my visit, that she was angry with me and only flirting with the prince from pique.... I seized my opportunity and with a meek but gracious smile, I went up to her, and muttered--'Enough, forgive me, not that I'm afraid ...' and suddenly, without awaiting her reply, I gave my features an extraordinarily cheerful and free-and-easy expression, with a set grin, passed my hand above my head in the direction of the ceiling (I wanted, I remember, to set my cravat straight), and was even on the point of pirouetting round on one foot, as though to say, 'All is over, I am happy, let's all be happy,'--I did not, however, execute this manoeuvre, as I was afraid of losing my balance, owing to an unnatural stiffness in my knees.... Liza failed absolutely to understand me; she looked in my face with amazement, gave a hasty smile, as though she wanted to get rid of me as quickly as possible, and again approached the prince. Blind and deaf as I was, I could not but be inwardly aware that she was not in the least angry, and was not annoyed with me at that instant: she simply never gave me a thought. The blow was a final one. My last hopes were shattered with a crash, just as a block of ice, thawed by the sunshine of spring, suddenly falls into tiny morsels. I was utterly defeated at the first skirmish, and, like the Prussians at Jena, lost everything at once in one day. No, she was not angry with me!...

Alas, it was quite the contrary! She too--I saw that--was being swept off her feet by the torrent. Like a young tree, already half torn from the bank, she bent eagerly over the stream, ready to abandon to it for ever the first blossom of her spring and her whole life. A man whose fate it has been to be the witness of such a passion, has lived through bitter moments if he has loved himself and not been loved. I shall for ever remember that devouring attention, that tender gaiety, that innocent self-oblivion, that glance, still a child's and already a woman's, that happy, as it were flowering smile that never left the half-parted lips and glowing cheeks.... All that Liza had vaguely foreshadowed during our walk in the wood had come to pass now--and she, as she gave herself up utterly to love, was at once stiller and brighter, like new wine, which ceases to ferment because its full maturity has come....

I had the fortitude to sit through that first evening and the subsequent evenings ... all to the end! I could have no hope of anything. Liza and the prince became every day more devoted to each other ... But I had absolutely lost all sense of personal dignity, and could not tear myself away from the spectacle of my own misery. I remember one day I tried not to go, swore to myself in the morning that I would stay at home, and at eight o'clock in the evening (I usually set off at seven) leaped up like a madman, put on my hat, and ran breathless into Kirilla Matveitch's drawing-room. My position was excessively absurd. I was obstinately silent; sometimes for whole days together I did not utter a sound. I was, as I have said already, never distinguished for eloquence; but now everything I had in my mind took flight, as it were, in the presence of the prince, and I was left bare and bereft. Besides, when I was alone, I set my wretched brain working so hard, slowly going over everything I had noticed or surmised during the preceding day, that when I went back to the Ozhogins' I scarcely had energy left to observe again. They treated me considerately, as a sick person; I saw that. Every morning I adopted some new, final resolution, for the most part painfully hatched in the course of a sleepless night. At one time I made up my mind to have it out with Liza, to give her friendly advice ... but when I chanced to be alone with her, my tongue suddenly ceased to work, froze as it were, and we both, in great discomfort, waited for the entrance of some third person. Another time I meant to run away, of course for ever, leaving my beloved a letter full of reproaches, and I even one day began this letter; but the sense of justice had not yet quite vanished in me. I realised that I had no right to reproach any one for anything, and I flung what I had written in the fire. Then I suddenly offered myself up wholly as a sacrifice, gave Liza my benediction, praying for her happiness, and smiled in meek and friendly fashion from my corner at the prince. But the cruel-hearted lovers not only never thanked me for my self-sacrifice, they never even noticed me, and were, apparently, quite ready to dispense with my smiles and my blessings....

Then, in wrath, I suddenly flew into quite the opposite mood. I swore to myself, wrapping my cloak about me like a Spaniard, to rush out from some dark corner and stab my lucky rival, and with brutal glee I imagined Liza's despair.... But, in the first place, such corners were few in the town of O----; and, secondly--the wooden fence, the street lamp, the policeman in the distance.... No! in such corners it was somehow far more suitable to sell buns and oranges than to shed human blood. I must own that, among other means of deliverance, as I very vaguely expressed it in my colloquies with myself, I did entertain the idea of having recourse to Ozhogin himself ... of calling the attention of that nobleman to the perilous situation of his daughter, and the mournful consequences of her indiscretion....

I even once began speaking to him on a certain delicate subject; but my remarks were so indirect and misty, that after listening and listening to me, he suddenly, as it were, waking up, rubbed his hand rapidly and vigorously all over his face, not sparing his nose, gave a snort, and walked away from me. It is needless to say that in resolving on this step I persuaded myself that I was acting from the most disinterested motives, was desirous of the general welfare, and was doing my duty as a friend of the house.... But I venture to think that even had Kirilla Matveitch not cut short my outpourings, I should in any case not have had courage to finish my monologue. At times I set to work with all the solemnity of some sage of antiquity, weighing the qualities of the prince; at times I comforted myself with the hope that it was all of no consequence, that Liza would recover her senses, that her love was not real love ... oh, no! In short, I know no idea that I did not worry myself with at that time. There was only one resource which never, I candidly admit, entered my head: I never once thought of taking my life. Why it did not occur to me I don't know.... Possibly, even then, I had a presentiment I should not have long to live in any case.

It will be readily understood that in such unfavourable circumstances my manner, my behaviour with people, was more than ever marked by unnaturalness and constraint. Even Madame Ozhogin--that creature dull-witted from her birth up--began to shun me, and at times did not know in what way to approach me. Bizmyonkov, always polite and ready to do services, avoided me. I fancied even at that time that I had in him a companion in misfortune--that he too loved Liza. But he never responded to my hints, and altogether showed a reluctance to converse with me. The prince behaved in a very friendly way to him; the prince, one might say, respected him. Neither Bizmyonkov nor I was any obstacle to the prince and Liza; but he did not shun them as I did, nor look savage nor injured--and readily joined them when they desired it. It is true that on such occasions he was not conspicuous for any special mirthfulness; but his good-humour had always been somewhat subdued in character.

In this fashion about a fortnight passed by. The prince was not only handsome and clever: he played the piano, sang, sketched fairly well, and was a good hand at telling stories. His anecdotes, drawn from the highest circles of Petersburg society, always made a great impression on his audience, all the more so from the fact that he seemed to attach no importance to them....

The consequence of this, if you like, simple accomplishment of the prince's was that in the course of his not very protracted stay in the town of O---- he completely fascinated all the neighbourhood. To fascinate us poor dwellers in the steppes is at all times a very easy task for any one coming from higher spheres. The prince's frequent visits to the Ozhogins (he used to spend his evenings there) of course aroused the jealousy of the other worthy gentry and officials of the town. But the prince, like a clever person and a man of the world, never neglected a single one of them; he called on all of them; to every married lady and every unmarried miss he addressed at least one flattering phrase, allowed them to feed him on elaborately solid edibles, and to make him drink wretched wines with magnificent names; and conducted himself, in short, like a model of caution and tact. Prince N---- was in general a man of lively manners, sociable and genial by inclination, and in this case incidentally from prudential motives also; he could not fail to be a complete success in everything.

Ever since his arrival, all in the house had felt that the time had flown by with unusual rapidity; everything had gone off beautifully. Papa Ozhogin, though he pretended that he noticed nothing, was doubtless rubbing his hands in private at the idea of such a son-in-law. The prince, for his part, managed matters with the utmost sobriety and discretion, when, all of a sudden, an unexpected incident....

Till to-morrow. To-day I'm tired. These recollections irritate me even at the edge of the grave. Terentyevna noticed to-day that my nose has already begun to grow sharp; and that, they say, is a bad sign.

March 27. Thaw continuing.

Things were in the position described above: the prince and Liza were in love with each other; the old Ozhogins were waiting to see what would come of it; Bizmyonkov was present at the proceedings--there was nothing else to be said of him. I was struggling like a fish on the ice, and watching with all my might,--I remember that at that time I set myself the task of preventing Liza at least from falling into the snares of a seducer, and consequently began paying particular attention to the maidservants and the fateful 'back stairs'--though, on the other hand, I often spent whole nights in dreaming with what touching magnanimity I would one day hold out a hand to the betrayed victim and say to her, 'The traitor has deceived thee; but I am thy true friend ... let us forget the past and be happy!'--when sudden and glad tidings overspread the whole town. The marshal of the district proposed to give a great ball in honour of their respected guest, on his private estate Gornostaevka. All the official world, big and little, of the town of O---- received invitations, from the mayor down to the apothecary, an excessively emaciated German, with ferocious pretensions to a good Russian accent, which led him into continually and quite inappropriately employing racy colloquialisms.... Tremendous preparations were, of course, put in hand. One purveyor of cosmetics sold sixteen dark-blue jars of pomatum, which bore the inscription *a la jesmin*. The young ladies provided themselves with tight dresses, agonising in the waist and jutting out sharply over the stomach; the mammas put formidable erections on their heads by way of caps; the busy papas were half dead with the bustle. The longed-for day arrived at last. I was among those invited. From the town to Gornostaevka was reckoned between seven and eight miles. Kirilla Matveitch offered me a seat in his coach; but I refused.... In the same way children, who have been punished, wishing to pay their parents out, refuse their favourite dainties at table. Besides, I felt that my presence would be felt as a constraint by Liza. Bizmyonkov took my place. The prince drove in his own carriage, and I in a wretched little droshky, hired for an immense sum for this solemn occasion. I am not going to describe that ball. Everything about it was just as it always is. There was a band, with trumpets extraordinarily out of tune, in the gallery; there were country gentlemen, greatly flustered, with their inevitable families, mauve ices, viscous lemonade; servants in boots trodden down at heel and knitted cotton gloves; provincial lions with spasmodically contorted faces, and so on and so on. And all this little world was revolving round its sun--round the prince. Lost in the crowd, unnoticed even by the young ladies of eight-and-forty, with red pimples on their brows and blue flowers on the top of their heads, I stared incessantly, first at the prince, then at Liza. She was very charmingly dressed and very pretty that evening. They only twice danced together (it is true, he danced the mazurka with her); but it seemed, to me at least, that there was a sort of secret, continuous communication between them. Even while not looking at her, while not speaking to her, he was still, as it were, addressing her, and her alone. He was handsome and brilliant and charming with other people--for her sake only. She was apparently conscious that she was the queen of the ball, and that she was loved. Her face at once beamed with childlike delight and innocent pride, and was suddenly illuminated by another, deeper feeling. Happiness radiated from her. I observed all this.... It was not the first time I had watched them.... At first this wounded me intensely; afterwards it, as it were, touched me; but, finally, it infuriated me. I suddenly felt extraordinarily wrathful, and, I remember, was extraordinarily delighted at this new sensation, and even conceived a certain respect for myself. 'We'll show them we're not crushed yet,' I said to myself. When the first inviting notes of the mazurka sounded, I looked about me with composure, and with a cool and easy air approached a long-faced young lady with a red and shiny nose, a mouth that stood awkwardly open, as though it had come unbuttoned, and a scraggy neck that re-called the handle of a bass-viol. I went up to her, and, with a perfunctory scrape of my heels, invited her to the dance. She was wearing a dress of faded rosebud pink, not full-blown rose colour; on her head quivered a striped and dejected beetle of some sort on a thick bronze pin; and altogether this lady was, if one may so express it, soaked through and through with a sort of sour ennui and inveterate lack of suc-cess. From the very commencement of the evening she had not once stirred from her seat; no one had thought of asking her to dance. One flaxen-headed youth of sixteen had, through lack of a partner, been on the point of addressing this lady, and had taken a step in her direction, but had thought better of it, stared at her, and hurriedly dived into the crowd. You can fancy with what joyful amazement she agreed to my proposal! I led her in triumph right across the ballroom, picked out two chairs, and sat down with her in the ring of the mazurka, among ten couples, almost opposite the prince, who had, of course, been offered the first place. The prince, as I have said already, was dancing with Liza. Neither I nor my partner was disturbed by invitations; consequently, we had plenty of time for conversation. To tell the truth, my partner was not conspicuous for her capacity for the utterance of words in consecutive speech; she used her mouth principally for the achievement of a strange downward smile such as I had never till then beheld; while she raised her eyes upward, as though some unseen force were pulling her face in two. But I did not feel her lack of eloquence. Happily I felt full of wrath, and my partner did not make me shy. I fell to finding fault with everything and every one in the world, with especial emphasis on town-bred youngsters and Petersburg dandies; and went to such lengths at last, that my partner gradually ceased smiling, and instead of turn-ing her eyes upward, began suddenly--from astonishment, I suppose--to squint, and that so strangely, as though she had for the first time observed the fact that she had a nose on her face. And one of the lions, referred to above, who was sitting next me, did not once take his eyes off me; he positively turned to me with the expression of an actor on the stage, who has waked up in an unfamiliar place, as though he would say, 'Is it really you!' While I poured forth this tirade, I still, however, kept watch on the prince and Liza. They were continually invited; but I suffered less when they were both dancing; and even when they were sitting side by side, and smiling as they talked to each other that sweet smile which hardly leaves the faces of happy lovers, even then I was not in such torture; but when Liza flitted across the room with some desperate dandy of an hussar, while the prince with her blue gauze scarf on his knees followed her dreamily with his eyes, as though delighting in his conquest;--then, oh! then, I went through intolerable agonies, and in my anger gave vent to such spiteful observations, that the pupils of my partner's eyes simply fastened on her nose!

Meanwhile the mazurka was drawing to a close. They were beginning the figure called *la confidente*. In this figure the lady sits in the middle of a circle, chooses another lady as her confidant, and whispers in her ear the name of the gentleman with whom she wishes to dance.

Her partner conducts one after another of the dancers to her; but the lady, who is in the secret, refuses them, till at last the happy man fixed on beforehand arrives. Liza sat in the middle of the circle and chose the daughter of the host, one of those young ladies of whom one says, 'God help them!'... The prince proceeded to discover her choice. After presenting about a dozen young men to her in vain (the daughter of the house refused them all with the most amiable of smiles), he at last turned to me.

Something extraordinary took place within me at that instant; I, as it were, twitched all over, and would have refused, but got up and went along. The prince conducted me to Liza.... She did not even look at me; the daughter of the house shook her head in refusal, the prince turned to me, and, probably incited by the goose-like expression of my face, made me a deep bow. This sarcastic bow, this refusal, transmitted to me through my triumphant rival, his careless smile, Liza's indifferent inattention, all this lashed me to frenzy.... I moved up to the prince and whispered furiously, 'You think fit to laugh at me, it seems?'

The prince looked at me with contemptuous surprise, took my arm again, and making a show of re-conducting me to my seat, answered coldly, 'I?'

'Yes, you!' I went on in a whisper, obeying, however--that is to say, following him to my place; 'you; but I do not intend to permit any empty-headed Petersburg up-start----'

The prince smiled tranquilly, almost condescendingly, pressed my arm, whispered, 'I understand you; but this is not the place; we will have a word later,' turned away from me, went up to Bizmyonkov, and led him up to Liza. The pale little official turned out to be the chosen partner. Liza got up to meet him.

Sitting beside my partner with the dejected beetle on her head, I felt almost a hero. My heart beat violently, my breast heaved gallantly under my starched shirt front, I drew deep and hurried breaths, and suddenly gave the local lion near me such a magnificent glare that there was an involuntary quiver of his foot in my direction. Having disposed of this person, I scanned the whole circle of dancers.... I fancied two or three gentlemen were staring at me with some perplexity; but, in general, my conversation with the prince had passed unnoticed.... My rival was already back in his chair, perfectly composed, and with the same smile on his face. Bizmyonkov led Liza back to her place. She gave him a friendly bow, and at once turned to the prince, as I fancied, with some alarm. But he laughed in response, with a graceful wave of his hand, and must have said something very agreeable to her, for she flushed with delight, dropped her eyes, and then bent them with affectionate reproach upon him.

The heroic frame of mind, which had suddenly developed in me, had not disappeared by the end of the mazurka; but I did not indulge in any more epigrams or 'quizzing.' I contented myself with glancing occasionally with gloomy severity at my partner, who was obviously beginning to be afraid of me, and was utterly tongue-tied and continuously blinking by the time I placed her under the protection of her mother, a very fat woman with a red cap on her head. Having consigned the scared maiden lady to her natural belongings, I turned away to a window, folded my arms, and began to await what would happen. I had rather long to wait. The prince was the whole time surrounded by his host--surrounded, simply, as England is surrounded by the sea,--to say nothing of the other members of the marshal's family and the rest of the guests. And besides, he could hardly go up to such an insignificant person as me and begin to talk without arousing a general feeling of surprise. This insignificance, I remember, was positively a joy to me at the time. 'All right,' I thought, as I watched him courteously addressing first one and then another highly respected personage, honoured by his notice, if only for an 'instant's flash,' as the poets say;--'all right, my dear ... you'll come to me soon--I've insulted you, anyway.' At last the prince, adroitly escaping from the throng of his adorers, passed close by me, looked somewhere between the window and my hair, was turning away, and suddenly stood still, as though he had recollected something. 'Ah, yes!' he said, turning to me with a smile, 'by the way, I have a little matter to talk to you about.'

Two country gentlemen, of the most persistent, who were obstinately pursuing the prince, probably imagined the 'little matter' to relate to official business, and respectfully fell back. The prince took my arm and led me apart. My heart was thumping at my ribs.

'You, I believe,' he began, emphasising the word *you,* and looking at my chin with a contemptuous expression, which, strange to say, was supremely becoming to his fresh and handsome face, 'you said something abusive to me?'

'I said what I thought,' I replied, raising my voice.

'Sh ... quietly,' he observed; 'decent people don't bawl. You would like, perhaps, to fight me?'

'That's your affair,' I answered, drawing myself up.

'I shall be obliged to challenge you,' he remarked carelessly, 'if you don't withdraw your expressions....'

'I do not intend to withdraw from anything,' I rejoined with pride.

'Really?' he observed, with an ironical smile.

'In that case,' he continued, after a brief pause, 'I shall have the honour of sending my second to you to-morrow.'

'Very good, 'I said in a voice, if possible, even more indifferent.

The prince gave a slight bow.

'I cannot prevent you from considering me empty-headed,' he added, with a haughty droop of his eyelids; 'but the Princes' N---- cannot be upstarts. Good-bye till we meet, Mr.... Mr. Shtukaturin.'

He quickly turned his back on me, and again approached his host, who was already beginning to get excited.

Mr. Shtukaturin!... My name is Tchulkaturin.... I could think of nothing to say to him in reply to this last insult, and could only gaze after him with fury. 'Till to-morrow,' I muttered, clenching my teeth, and I at once looked for an officer of my acquaintance, a cavalry captain in the Uhlans, called Koloberdyaev, a desperate rake, and a very good fellow. To him I related, in few words, my quarrel with the prince, and asked him to be my second. He, of course, promptly consented, and I went home.

I could not sleep all night--from excitement, not from cowardice. I am not a coward. I positively thought very little of the possibility confronting me of losing my life--that, as the Germans assure us, highest good on earth. I could think only of Liza, of my ruined hopes, of what I ought to do. 'Ought I to try to kill the prince?' I asked myself; and, of course, I wanted to kill him--not from revenge, but from a desire for Liza's good. 'But she will not survive such a blow,' I went on. 'No, better let him kill me!' I must own it was an agreeable reflection, too, that I, an obscure provincial person, had forced a man of such consequence to fight a duel with me.

The morning light found me still absorbed in these reflections; and, not long after it, appeared Koloberdyaev.

'Well,' he asked me, entering my room with a clatter, 'where's the prince's second?' 'Upon my word,' I answered with annoyance, 'it's seven o'clock at the most; the prince is still asleep, I should imagine.' 'In that case,' replied the cavalry officer, in nowise daunted, 'order some tea for me. My head aches from yesterday evening.... I've not taken my clothes off all night. Though, indeed,' he added with a yawn, 'I don't as a rule often take my clothes off.'

Some tea was given him. He drank off six glasses of tea and rum, smoked four pipes, told me he had on the previous day bought, for next to nothing, a horse the coachman refused to drive, and that he was meaning to drive her out with one of her fore legs tied up, and fell asleep, without undressing, on the sofa, with a pipe in his mouth. I got up and put my papers to rights. One note of invitation from Liza, the one note I had received from her, I was on the point of putting in my bosom, but on second thoughts I flung it in a drawer. Koloberdyaev was snoring feebly, with his head hanging from the leather pillow.... For a long while, I remember, I scrutinised his unkempt, daring, careless, and good-natured face. At ten o'clock the man announced the arrival of Bizmyonkov. The prince had chosen him as second.

We both together roused the soundly sleeping cavalry officer. He sat up, stared at us with dim eyes, in a hoarse voice demanded vodka. He recovered himself, and exchanging greetings with Bizmyonkov, he went with him into the next room to arrange matters. The consultation of the worthy seconds did not last long. A quarter of an hour later, they both came into my bedroom. Koloberdyaev announced to me that 'we're going to fight to-day at three o'clock with pistols.' In silence I bent my head, in token of my agreement. Bizmyonkov at once took leave of us, and departed. He was rather pale and inwardly agitated, like a man unused to such jobs, but he was, nevertheless, very polite and chilly. I felt, as it were, conscience-stricken in his presence, and did not dare look him in the face. Koloberdyaev began telling me about his horse. This conversation was very welcome to me. I was afraid he would mention Liza. But the good-natured cavalry officer was not a gossip, and, moreover, he despised all women, calling them, God knows why, green stuff. At two o'clock we had lunch, and at three we were at the place fixed upon--the very birch copse in which I had once walked with Liza, a couple of yards from the precipice.

We arrived first; but the prince and Bizmyonkov did not keep us long waiting. The prince was, without exaggeration, as fresh as a rose; his brown eyes looked out with excessive cordiality from under the peak of his cap. He was smoking a cigar, and on seeing Koloberdyaev shook his hand in a friendly way.

Even to me he bowed very genially. I was conscious, on the contrary, of being pale, and my hands, to my terrible vexation, were slightly trembling ... my throat was parched.... I had never fought a duel before. 'O God!' I thought; 'if only that ironical gentleman doesn't take my agitation for timidity!' I was inwardly cursing my nerves; but glancing, at last, straight in the prince's face, and catching on his lips an almost imperceptible smile, I suddenly felt furious again, and was at once at my ease. Meanwhile, our seconds were fixing the barrier, measuring out the paces, loading the pistols. Koloberdyaev did most; Bizmyonkov rather watched him. It was a magnificent day--as fine as the day of that ever-memorable walk. The thick blue of the sky peeped, as then, through the golden green of the leaves. Their lisping seemed to mock me. The prince went on smoking his cigar, leaning with his shoulder against the trunk of a young lime-tree....

'Kindly take your places, gentlemen; ready,' Koloberdyaev pronounced at last, handing us pistols.

The prince walked a few steps away, stood still, and, turning his head, asked me over his shoulder, 'You still refuse to take back your words, then?'

I tried to answer him; but my voice failed me, and I had to content myself with a contemptuous wave of the hand. The prince smiled again, and took up his position in his place. We began to approach one another. I raised my pistol, was about to aim at my enemy's chest--but suddenly tilted it up, as though some one had given my elbow a shove, and fired. The prince tottered, and put his left hand to his left temple--a thread of blood was flowing down his cheek from under the white leather glove, Bizmyonkov rushed up to him.

'It's all right,' he said, taking off his cap, which the bullet had pierced; 'since it's in the head, and I've not fallen, it must be a mere scratch.'

He calmly pulled a cambric handkerchief out of his pocket, and put it to his blood-stained curls.

I stared at him, as though I were turned to stone, and did not stir.

'Go up to the barrier, if you please!' Koloberdyaev observed severely.

I obeyed.

'Is the duel to go on?' he added, addressing Bizmyonkov.

Bizmyonkov made him no answer. But the prince, without taking the handkerchief from the wound, without even giving himself the satisfaction of tormenting me at the barrier, replied with a smile. 'The duel is at an end,' and fired into the air. I was almost crying with rage and vexation. This man by his magnanimity had utterly trampled me in the mud; he had completely crushed me. I was on the point of making objections, on the point of demanding that he should fire at me. But he came up to me, and held out his hand.

'It's all forgotten between us, isn't it?' he said in a friendly voice.

I looked at his blanched face, at the blood-stained handkerchief, and utterly confounded, put to shame, and annihilated, I pressed his hand.

'Gentlemen!' he added, turning to the seconds, 'everything, I hope, will be kept secret?'

'Of course!' cried Koloberdyaev; 'but, prince, allow me ...'

And he himself bound up his head.

The prince, as he went away, bowed to me once more. But Bizmyonkov did not even glance at me. Shattered--morally shattered--went homewards with Koloberdyaev.

'Why, what's the matter with you?' the cavalry captain asked me. 'Set your mind at rest; the wound's not serious. He'll be able to dance by to-morrow, if you like. Or are you sorry you didn't kill him? You're wrong, if you are; he's a first-rate fellow.'

'What business had he to spare me!' I muttered at last.

'Oh, so that's it!' the cavalry captain rejoined tranquilly... 'Ugh, you writing fellows are too much for me!'

I don't know what put it into his head to consider me an author.

I absolutely decline to describe my torments during the evening following upon that luckless duel. My vanity suffered indescribably. It was not my conscience that tortured me; the consciousness of my imbecility crushed me. 'I have given myself the last decisive blow by my own act!' I kept repeating, as I strode up and down my room. 'The prince, wounded by me, and forgiving me... Yes, Liza is now his. Now nothing can save her, nothing can hold her back on the edge of the abyss.' I knew very well that our duel could not be kept secret, in spite of the prince's words; in any case, it could not remain a secret for Liza.

'The prince is not such a fool,' I murmured in a frenzy of rage, 'as not to profit by it.'... But, meanwhile, I was mistaken. The whole town knew of the duel and of its real cause next day, of course. But the prince had not blabbed of it; on the contrary, when, with his head bandaged and an explanation ready, he made his appearance before Liza, she had already heard everything.... Whether Bizmyonkov had betrayed me, or the news had reached her by other channels, I cannot say. Though, indeed, can anything ever be concealed in a little town? You can fancy how Liza received him, how all the family of the Ozhogins received him! As for me, I suddenly became an object of universal indignation and loathing, a monster, a jealous bloodthirsty madman. My few acquaintances shunned me as if I were a leper. The authorities of the town promptly addressed the prince, with a proposal to punish me in a severe and befitting manner. Nothing but the persistent and urgent entreaties of the prince himself averted the calamity that menaced me. That man was fated to annihilate me in every way. By his generosity he had shut, as it were, a coffin-lid down upon me. It's needless to say that the Ozhogins' doors were at once closed against me. Kirilla Matveitch even sent me back a bit of pencil I had left in his house. In reality, he, of all people, had no reason to be angry with me. My 'insane' (that was the expression current in the town) jealousy had pointed out, defined, so to speak, the relations of the prince to Liza. Both the old Ozhogins themselves and their fellow-citizens began to look on him almost as betrothed to her. This could not, as a fact, have been quite to his liking. But he was greatly attracted by Liza; and meanwhile, he had not at that time attained his aims. With all the adroitness of a clever man of the world, he took advantage of his new position, and promptly entered, as they say, into the spirit of his new part....

But I!... For myself, for my future, I renounced all hopes, at that time. When suffering reaches the point of making our whole being creak and groan, like an overloaded cart, it ought to cease to be ridiculous ... but no! laughter not only ac-companies tears to the end, to exhaustion, to the impossibility of shedding more--it even rings and echoes, where the tongue is dumb, and complaint itself is dead.... And so, as in the first place I don't intend to expose myself as ridiculous, even to myself, and secondly as I am fearfully tired, I will put off the continuation, and please God the conclusion, of my story till tomorrow....

March 29.

A slight frost; yesterday it was thawing.

Yesterday I had not the strength to go on with my diary; like Poprishtchin, I lay, for the most part, on my bed, and talked to Terentyevna. What a woman! Sixty years ago she lost her first betrothed from the plague, she has outlived all her chil-dren, she is inexcusably old, drinks tea to her heart's desire, is well fed, and warmly clothed; and what do you suppose she was talking to me about, all day yesterday? I had sent another utterly destitute old woman the collar of an old livery, half moth-eaten, to put on her vest (she wears strips over the chest by way of vest) ... and why wasn't it given to her? 'But I'm your nurse; I should think... Oh ... oh, my good sir, it's too bad of you ... after I've looked after you as I have!' ... and so on. The merci-less old woman utterly wore me out with her reproaches.... But to get back to my story.

And so, I suffered like a dog, whose hindquarters have been run over by a wheel. It was only then, only after my banishment from the Ozhogins' house, that I fully realised how much happiness a man can extract from the contemplation of his own unhappiness. O men! pitiful race, indeed!

... But, away with philosophical reflections.... I spent my days in complete soli-tude, and could only by the most roundabout and even humiliating methods find out what was passing in the Ozhogins' household, and what the prince was doing. My man had made friends with the cousin of the latter's coachman's wife. This acquaintance afforded me some slight relief, and my man soon guessed, from my hints and little presents, what he was to talk about to his master when he pulled his boots off every evening. Sometimes I chanced to meet some one of the Ozhogins' family, Bizmyonkov, or the prince in the street.... To the prince and to Bizmyonkov I bowed, but I did not enter into conversation with them. Liza I only saw three times: once, with her mamma, in a fashionable shop; once, in an open carriage with her father and mother and the prince; and once, in church. Of course, I was not impudent enough to approach her, and only watched her from a distance. In the shop she was very much preoccupied, but cheerful.... She was ordering something for herself, and busily matching ribbons. Her mother was gazing at her, with her hands folded on her lap, and her nose in the air, smiling with that foolish and devoted smile which is only permissible in adoring mothers. In the carriage with the prince, Liza was ... I shall never forget that meeting! The old people were sitting in the back seats of the carriage, the prince and Liza in the front. She was paler than usual; on her cheek two patches of pink could just be seen. She was half facing the prince; leaning on her straight right arm (in the left hand she was holding a sunshade), with her little head drooping languidly, she was looking straight into his face with her expressive eyes. At that instant she surrendered herself utterly to him, intrusted herself to him for ever. I had not time to get a good look at his face--the carriage galloped by too quickly,--but I fancied that he too was deeply touched.

The third time I saw her in church. Not more than ten days had passed since the day when I met her in the carriage with the prince, not more than three weeks since the day of my duel. The business upon which the prince had come to O---- was by now completed. But he still kept putting off his departure. At Petersburg, he was reported to be ill. In the town, it was expected every day that he would make a proposal in form to Kirilla Matveitch. I was myself only awaiting this final blow to go away for ever. The town of O---- had grown hateful to me. I could not stay indoors, and wandered from morning to night about the suburbs. One grey, gloomy day, as I was coming back from a walk, which had been cut short by the rain, I went into a church. The evening service had only just begun, there were very few people; I looked round me, and suddenly, near a window, caught sight of a familiar profile.

For the first instant, I did not recognise it: that pale face, that spiritless glance, those sunken cheeks--could it be the same Liza I had seen a fortnight before? Wrapped in a cloak, without a hat on, with the cold light from the broad white window falling on her from one side, she was gazing fixedly at the holy image, and seemed striving to pray, striving to awake from a sort of listless stupor. A red-cheeked, fat little page with yellow trimmings on his chest was standing behind her, and, with his hands clasped behind his back, stared in sleepy bewilderment at his mistress. I trembled all over, was about to go up to her, but stopped short. I felt choked by a torturing presentiment. Till the very end of the evening service, Liza did not stir. All the people went out, a beadle began sweeping out the church, but still she did not move from her place. The page went up to her, said something to her, touched her dress; she looked round, passed her hand over her face, and went away. I followed her home at a little distance, and then returned to my lodging.

'She is lost!' I cried, when I had got into my room.

As a man, I don't know to this day what my sensations were at that moment. I flung myself, I remember, with clasped hands, on the sofa and fixed my eyes on the floor. But I don't know--in the midst of my woe I was, as it were, pleased at something.... I would not admit this for anything in the world, if I were not writing only for myself.... I had been tormented, certainly, by terrible, harassing suspicions ... and who knows, I should, perhaps, have been greatly disconcerted if they had not been fulfilled. 'Such is the heart of man!' some middle-aged Russian teacher would exclaim at this point in an expressive voice, while he raises a fat forefinger, adorned with a cornelian ring. But what have we to do with the opinion of a Russian teacher, with an expressive voice and a cornelian on his finger?

Be that as it may, my presentiment turned out to be well founded. Suddenly the news was all over the town that the prince had gone away, presumably in consequence of a summons from Petersburg; that he had gone away without making any proposal to Kirilla Matveitch or his wife, and that Liza would have to deplore his treachery till the end of her days. The prince's departure was utterly unexpected, for only the evening before his coachman, so my man assured me, had not the slightest suspicion of his master's intentions. This piece of news threw me into a perfect fever. I at once dressed, and was on the point of hastening to the Ozhogins', but on thinking the matter over I considered it more seemly to wait till the next day. I lost nothing, however, by remaining at home. The same evening, there came to see me in all haste a certain Pandopipopulo, a wandering Greek, stranded by some chance in the town of O----, a scandalmonger of the first magnitude, who had been more indignant with me than any one for my duel with the prince. He did not even give my man time to announce him; he fairly burst into my room, warmly pressed my hand, begged my pardon a thousand times, called me a paragon of magnanimity and courage, painted the prince in the darkest colours, censured the old Ozhogins, who, in his opinion, had been punished as they deserved, made a slighting reference to Liza in passing, and hurried off again, kissing me on my shoulder. Among other things, I learned from him that the prince, *en vrai grand seigneur*, on the eve of his departure, in response to a delicate hint from Kirilla Matveitch, had answered coldly that he had no intention of deceiving any one, and no idea of marrying, had risen, made his bow, and that was all.... Next day I set off to the Ozhogins'. The shortsighted footman leaped up from his bench on my appearance, with the rapidity of lightning. I bade him announce me; the footman hurried away and returned at once. 'Walk in,' he said; 'you are begged to go in.' I went into Kirilla Matveitch's study.... The rest to-morrow.

March 30. Frost.

And so I went into Kirilla Matveitch's study. I would pay any one handsomely, who could show me now my own face at the moment when that highly respected official, hurriedly flinging together his dressing-gown, approached me with outstretched arms. I must have been a perfect picture of modest triumph, indulgent sympathy, and boundless magnanimity.... I felt myself something in the style of Scipio Africanus. Ozhogin was visibly confused and cast down, he avoided my eyes, and kept fidgeting about. I noticed, too, that he spoke unnaturally loudly, and in general expressed himself very vaguely. Vaguely, but with warmth, he begged my forgiveness, vaguely alluded to their departed guest, added a few vague generalities about deception and the instability of earthly blessings, and, suddenly feeling the tears in his eyes, hastened to take a pinch of snuff, probably in order to deceive me as to the cause of his tearfulness.... He used the Russian green snuff, and it's well known that that article forces even old men to shed tears that make the human eye look dull and senseless for several minutes.

I behaved, of course, very cautiously with the old man, inquired after the health of his wife and daughter, and at once artfully turned the conversation on to the interesting subject of the rotation of crops. I was dressed as usual, but the feeling of gentle propriety and soft indulgence which filled me gave me a fresh and festive sensation, as though I had on a white waistcoat and a white cravat. One thing agitated me, the thought of seeing Liza.... Ozhogin, at last, proposed of his own accord to take me up to his wife. The kind-hearted but foolish woman was at first terribly embarrassed on seeing me; but her brain was not capable of retaining the same impression for long, and so she was soon at her ease. At last I saw Liza ... she came into the room....

I had expected to find in her a shamed and penitent sinner, and had assumed beforehand the most affectionate and reassuring expression of face.... Why lie about it? I really loved her and was thirsting for the happiness of forgiving her, of holding out a hand to her; but to my unutterable astonishment, in response to my significant bow, she laughed coldly, observed carelessly, 'Oh, is that you?' and at once turned away from me. It is true that her laugh struck me as forced, and in any case did not accord well with her terribly thin face ... but, all the same, I had not expected such a reception.... I looked at her with amazement ... what a change had taken place in her! Between the child she had been and the woman before me, there was nothing in common. She had, as it were, grown up, straightened out; all the features of her face, especially her lips, seemed defined ... her gaze had grown deeper, harder, and gloomier. I stayed on at the Ozhogins' till dinner-time. She got up, went out of the room, and came back again, answered questions with composure, and designedly took no notice of me. She wanted, I saw, to make me feel that I was not worth her anger, though I had been within an ace of killing her lover. I lost patience at last; a malicious allusion broke from my lips.... She started, glanced swiftly at me, got up, and going to the window, pronounced in a rather shaky voice, 'You can say anything you like, but let me tell you that I love that man, and always shall love him, and do not consider that he has done me any injury, quite the contrary.'... Her voice broke, she stopped ... tried to control herself, but could not, burst into tears, and went out of the room.... The old people were much upset.... I pressed the hands of both, sighed, turned my eyes heavenward, and withdrew.

I am too weak, I have too little time left, I am not capable of describing in the same detail the new range of torturing reflections, firm resolutions, and all the other fruits of what is called inward conflict, that arose within me after the renewal of my acquaintance with the Ozhogins. I did not doubt that Liza still loved, and would long love, the prince ... but as one reconciled to the inevitable, and anxious myself to conciliate, I did not even dream of her love. I desired only her affection, I desired to gain her confidence, her respect, which, we are assured by persons of experience, forms the surest basis for happiness in marriage.... Unluckily, I lost sight of one rather important circumstance, which was that Liza had hated me ever since the day of the duel. I found this out too late. I began, as before, to be a frequent visitor at the house of the Ozhogins. Kirilla Matveitch received me with more effusiveness and affability than he had ever done. I have even ground for believing that he would at that time have cheerfully given me his daughter, though I was certainly not a match to be coveted. Public opinion was very severe upon him and Liza, while, on the other hand, it extolled me to the skies. Liza's attitude to me was unchanged. She was, for the most part, silent; obeyed, when they begged her to eat, showed no outward signs of sorrow, but, for all that, was wasting away like a candle. I must do Kirilla Matveitch the justice to say that he spared her in every way. Old Madame Ozhogin only ruffled up her feathers like a hen, as she looked at her poor nestling. There was only one person Liza did not shun, though she did not talk much even to him, and that was Bizmyonkov. The old people were rather short, not to say rude, in their behaviour to him. They could not forgive him for having been second in the duel. But he went on going to see them, as though he did not notice their una-miability. With me he was very chilly, and--strange to say--I felt, as it were, afraid of him. This state of things went on for a fortnight. At last, after a sleepless night, I resolved to have it out with Liza, to open my heart to her, to tell her that, in spite of the past, in spite of all possible gossip and scandal, I should consider myself only too happy if she would give me her hand, and restore me her confidence. I really did seriously imagine that I was showing what they call in the school reading-books an unparalleled example of magnanimity, and that, from sheer amazement alone, she would consent. In any case, I resolved to have an explanation and to escape, at last, from suspense.

Behind the Ozhogins' house was a rather large garden, which ended in a little grove of lime-trees, neglected and overgrown. In the middle of this thicket stood an old summer-house in the Chinese style: a wooden paling separated the garden from a blind alley. Liza would sometimes walk, for hours together, alone in this garden. Kirilla Matveitch was aware of this, and forbade her being disturbed or followed; let her grief wear itself out, he said. When she could not be found indoors, they had only to ring a bell on the steps at dinner-time and she made her appearance at once, with the same stubborn silence on her lips and in her eyes, and some little leaf crushed up in her hand. So, noticing one day that she was not in the house, I made a show of going away, took leave of Kirilla Matveitch, put on my hat, and went out from the hall into the courtyard, and from the courtyard into the street, but promptly darted in at the gate again with extraordinary rapidity and hurried past the kitchen into the garden. Luckily no one noticed me. Without losing time in deliberation, I went with rapid steps into the grove. In a little path before me was standing Liza. My heart beat violently. I stood still, drew a deep sigh, and was just on the point of going up to her, when suddenly she lifted her hand without turning round, and began listening.... From behind the trees, in the direction of the blind alley, came a distinct sound of two knocks, as though some one were tapping at the paling. Liza clapped her hands together, there was heard the faint creak of the gate, and out of the thicket stepped Bizmyonkov. I hastily hid behind a tree. Liza turned towards him without speaking.... Without speaking, he drew her arm in his, and the two walked slowly along the path together. I looked after them in amazement. They stopped, looked round, disappeared behind the bushes, reappeared again, and finally went into the summer-house. This summer-house was a diminutive round edifice, with a door and one little window. In the middle stood an old one-legged table, overgrown with fine green moss; two discoloured deal benches stood along the sides, some distance from the damp and darkened walls. Here, on exceptionally hot days, in bygone times, perhaps once a year or so, they had drunk tea. The door did not quite shut, the window-frame had long ago come out of the window, and hung disconsolately, only attached at one corner, like a bird's broken wing. I stole up to the summer-house, and peeped cautiously through the chink in the window. Liza was sitting on one of the benches, with her head drooping. Her right hand lay on her knees, the left Bizmyonkov was holding in both his hands. He was looking sympathetically at her.

'How do you feel to-day?' he asked her in a low voice.

'Just the same,' she answered, 'not better, nor worse.--The emptiness, the fearful emptiness!' she added, raising her eyes dejectedly.

Bizmyonkov made her no answer.

'What do you think,' she went on: 'will he write to me once more?'

'I don't think so, Lizaveta Kirillovna!'

She was silent.

'And after all, why should he write? He told me everything in his first letter. I could not be his wife; but I have been happy ... not for long ... I have been happy ...'

Bizmyonkov looked down.

'Ah,' she went on quickly, 'if you knew how I loathe that Tchulkaturin ... I always fancy I see on that man's hands ... his blood.' (I shuddered behind my chink.) 'Though indeed,' she added, dreamily, 'who knows, perhaps, if it had not been for that duel.... Ah, when I saw him wounded I felt at once that I was altogether his.'

'Tchulkaturin loves you,' observed Bizmyonkov.

'What is that to me? I don't want any one's love.'... She stopped and added slowly, 'Except yours. Yes, my friend, your love is necessary to me; except for you, I should be lost. You have helped me to bear terrible moments ...'

She broke off ... Bizmyonkov began with fatherly tenderness stroking her hand.

'There's no help for it! What is one to do! what is one to do, Lizaveta Kirillovna!' he repeated several times.

'And now indeed,' she went on in a lifeless voice, 'I should die, I think, if it were not for you. It's you alone that keep me up; besides, you remind me of him.... You knew all about it, you see. Do you remember how fine he was that day.... But forgive me; it must be hard for you....'

'Go on, go on! Nonsense! Bless you!' Bizmyonkov interrupted her.

She pressed his hand.

'You are very good, Bizmyonkov,' she went on;' you are good as an angel. What can I do! I feel I shall love him to the grave. I have forgiven him, I am grateful to him. God give him happiness! May God give him a wife after his own heart'--and her eyes filled with tears--'if only he does not forget me, if only he will sometimes think of his Liza!--Let us go,' she added, after a brief silence.

Bizmyonkov raised her hand to his lips.

'I know,' she began again hotly, 'every one is blaming me now, every one is throwing stones at me. Let them! I wouldn't, any way, change my misery for their happiness ... no! no!... He did not love me for long, but he loved me! He never deceived me, he never told me I should be his wife; I never dreamed of it myself. It was only poor papa hoped for it. And even now I am not altogether unhappy; the memory remains to me, and however fearful the results ... I'm stifling here ... it was here I saw him the last time.... Let's go into the air.'

They got up. I had only just time to skip on one side and hide behind a thick lime-tree. They came out of the summer-house, and, as far as I could judge by the sound of their steps, went away into the thicket. I don't know how long I went on standing there, without stirring from my place, plunged in a sort of senseless amazement, when suddenly I heard steps again. I started, and peeped cautiously out from my hiding-place. Bizmyonkov and Liza were coming back along the same path. Both were greatly agitated, especially Bizmyonkov.

I fancied he was crying. Liza stopped, looked at him, and distinctly uttered the following words: 'I do consent, Bizmyonkov. I would never have agreed if you were only trying to save me, to rescue me from a terrible position, but you love me, you know everything--and you love me. I shall never find a trustier, truer friend. I will be your wife.'

Bizmyonkov kissed her hand: she smiled at him mournfully and moved away towards the house. Bizmyonkov rushed into the thicket, and I went my way. Seeing that Bizmyonkov had apparently said to Liza precisely what I had intended to say to her, and she had given him precisely the reply I was longing to hear from her, there was no need for me to trouble myself further. Within a fortnight she was married to him. The old Ozhogins were thankful to get any husband for her.

Now, tell me, am I not a superfluous man? Didn't I play throughout the whole story the part of a superfluous person? The prince's part ... of that it's needless to speak; Bizmyonkov's part, too, is comprehensible.... But I--with what object was I mixed up in it?... A senseless fifth wheel to the cart!... Ah, it's bitter, bitter for me!... But there, as the barge-haulers say, 'One more pull, and one more yet,'--one day more, and one more yet, and there will be no more bitter nor sweet for me.

March 31.

I'm in a bad way. I am writing these lines in bed. Since yesterday evening there has been a sudden change in the weather. To-day is hot, almost a summer day. Everything is thawing, breaking up, flowing away. The air is full of the smell of the opened earth, a strong, heavy, stifling smell. Steam is rising on all sides. The sun seems beating, seems smiting everything to pieces. I am very ill, I feel that I am breaking up.

I meant to write my diary, and, instead of that, what have I done? I have related one incident of my life. I gossiped on, slumbering reminiscences were awakened and drew me away. I have written, without haste, in detail, as though I had years before me. And here now, there's no time to go on. Death, death is coming. I can hear her menacing *crescendo*. The time is come ... the time is come!...

And indeed, what does it matter? Isn't it all the same whatever I write? In sight of death the last earthly cares vanish. I feel I have grown calm; I am becoming simpler, clearer. Too late I've gained sense!... It's a strange thing! I have grown calm--certainly, and at the same time ... I'm full of dread. Yes, I'm full of dread. Half hanging over the silent, yawning abyss, I shudder, turn away, with greedy intentness gaze at everything about me. Every object is doubly precious to me. I cannot gaze enough at my poor, cheerless room, saying farewell to each spot on my walls. Take your fill for the last time, my eyes. Life is retreating; slowly and smoothly she is flying away from me, as the shore flies from the eyes of one at sea. The old yellow face of my nurse, tied up in a dark kerchief, the hissing samovar on the table, the pot of geranium in the window, and you, my poor dog, Tresor, the pen I write these lines with, my own hand, I see you now ... here you are, here.... Is it possible ... can it be, to-day ... I shall never see you again! It's hard for a live creature to part with life! Why do you fawn on me, poor dog? why do you come putting your forepaws on the bed, with your stump of a tail wagging so violently, and your kind, mournful eyes fixed on me all the while? Are you sorry for me? or do you feel already that your master will soon be gone? Ah, if I could only keep my thoughts, too, resting on all the objects in my room! I know these reminiscences are dismal and of no importance, but I have no other. 'The emptiness, the fearful emptiness!' as Liza said.

O my God, my God! Here I am dying.... A heart capable of loving and ready to love will soon cease to beat.... And can it be it will be still for ever without having once known happiness, without having once expanded under the sweet burden of bliss? Alas! it's impossible, impossible, I know.... If only now, at least, before death-

-for death after all is a sacred thing, after all it elevates any being--if any kind, sad, friendly voice would sing over me a farewell song of my own sorrow, I could, perhaps, be resigned to it. But to die stupidly, stupidly....

I believe I'm beginning to rave.

Farewell, life! farewell, my garden! and you, my lime-trees! When the summer comes, do not forget to be clothed with flowers from head to foot ... and may it be sweet for people to lie in your fragrant shade, on the fresh grass, among the whispering chatter of your leaves, lightly stirred by the wind. Farewell, farewell! Farewell, everything and for ever!

Farewell, Liza! I wrote those two words, and almost laughed aloud. This exclamation strikes me as taken out of a book. It's as though I were writing a sentimental novel and ending up a despairing letter....

To-morrow is the first of April. Can I be going to die to-morrow? That would be really too unseemly. It's just right for me, though ...

How the doctor did chatter to-day.

April 1.

It is over.... Life is over. I shall certainly die to-day. It's hot outside ... almost suffocating ... or is it that my lungs are already refusing to breathe? My little comedy is played out. The curtain is falling.

Sinking into nothing, I cease to be superfluous ...

Ah, how brilliant that sun is! Those mighty beams breathe of eternity ...

Farewell, Terentyevna!... This morning as she sat at the window she was crying ... perhaps over me ... and perhaps because she too will soon have to die. I have made her promise not to kill Tresor.

It's hard for me to write.... I will put down the pen.... It's high time; death is already approaching with ever-increasing rumble, like a carriage at night over the pavement; it is here, it is flitting about me, like the light breath which made the prophet's hair stand up on end.

I am dying.... Live, you who are living,

    'And about the grave May youthful life rejoice,   And nature heedless Glow with eternal beauty.

Note by the Editor.--Under this last line was a head in profile with a big streak of hair and moustaches, with eyes *en face*, and eyelashes like rays; and under the head some one had written the following words:

'This manuscript was read   And the Contents of it Not Approved   By Peter Zudotyeshin   My My My   My dear Sir,   Peter Zudotyeshin,   Dear Sir.'

But as the handwriting of these lines was not in the least like the handwriting in which the other part of the manuscript was written, the editor considers that he is justified in concluding that the above lines were added subsequently by another person, especially since it has come to his (the editor's) knowledge that Mr. Tchulkaturin actually did die on the night between the 1st and 2nd of April in the year 18--, at his native place, Sheep's Springs.

A TOUR IN THE FOREST

FIRST DAY

The sight of the vast pinewood, embracing the whole horizon, the sight of the 'Forest,' recalls the sight of the ocean. And the sensations it arouses are the same; the same primaeval untouched force lies outstretched in its breadth and majesty before the eyes of the spectator. From the heart of the eternal forest, from the undying bosom of the waters, comes the same voice: 'I have nothing to do with thee,'--nature says to man, 'I reign supreme, while do thou bestir thyself to thy utmost to escape dying.' But the forest is gloomier and more monotonous than the sea, especially the pine forest, which is always alike and almost soundless. The ocean menaces and caresses, it frolics with every colour, speaks with every voice; it reflects the sky, from which too comes the breath of eternity, but an eternity as it were not so remote from us.... The dark, unchanging pine-forest keeps sullen silence or is filled with a dull roar--and at the sight of it sinks into man's heart more deeply, more irresistibly, the sense of his own nothingness. It is hard for man, the creature of a day, born yesterday, and doomed to death on the morrow, it is hard for him to bear the cold gaze of the eternal Isis, fixed without sympathy upon him: not only the daring hopes and dreams of youth are humbled and quenched within him, enfolded by the icy breath of the elements; no--his whole soul sinks down and swoons within him; he feels that the last of his kind may vanish off the face of the earth--and not one needle will quiver on those twigs; he feels his isolation, his feebleness, his fortuitousness;--and in hurried, secret panic, he turns to the petty cares and labours of life; he is more at ease in that world he has himself created; there he is at home, there he dares yet believe in his own importance and in his own power.

Such were the ideas that came into my mind, some years ago, when, standing on the steps of a little inn on the bank of the marshy little river Ressetta, I first gazed upon the forest. The bluish masses of fir-forest lay in long, continuous ridges before me; here and there was the green patch of a small birch-copse; the whole sky-line was hugged by the pine-wood; nowhere was there the white gleam of a church, nor bright stretches of meadow--it was all trees and trees, everywhere the ragged edge of the tree-tops, and a delicate dim mist, the eternal mist of the forest, hung over them in the distance. It was not indolent repose this immobility of life suggested; no--the absence of life, something dead, even in its grandeur, was what came to me from every side of the horizon. I remember big white clouds were swimming by, slowly and very high up, and the hot summer day lay motionless upon the silent earth. The reddish water of the stream glided without a splash among the thick reeds: at its bottom could be dimly discerned round cushions of pointed moss, and its banks sank away in the swampy mud, and sharply reappeared again in white hillocks of fine crumbling sand. Close by the little inn ran the trodden highroad.

On this road, just opposite the steps, stood a cart, loaded with boxes and hampers. Its owner, a thin pedlar with a hawk nose and mouse-like eyes, bent and lame, was putting in it his little nag, lame like himself. He was a gingerbread-seller, who was making his way to the fair at Karatchev. Suddenly several people appeared on the road, others straggled after them ... at last, quite a crowd came trudging into sight; all of them had sticks in their hands and satchels on their shoulders. From their fatigued yet swinging gait, and from their sun-burnt faces, one could see they had come from a long distance. They were leatherworkers and diggers coming back from working for hire.

An old man of seventy, white all over, seemed to be their leader. From time to time he turned round and with a quiet voice urged on those who lagged behind. 'Now, now, now, lads,' he said, 'no--ow.' They all walked in silence, in a sort of solemn hush. Only one of them, a little man with a wrathful air, in a sheepskin coat wide open, and a lambswool cap pulled right over his eyes, on coming up to the gingerbread man, suddenly inquired: 'How much is the gingerbread, you tomfool?'

'What sort of gingerbread will it be, worthy sir?' the disconcerted gingerbread--man responded in a thin, little voice. 'Some are a farthing--and others cost a halfpenny. Have you a halfpenny in your purse?'

'But I guess it will sweeten the belly too much,' retorted the sheepskin, and he retreated from the cart.

'Hurry up, lads, hurry up,' I heard the old man's voice: 'it's far yet to our night's rest.'

'An uneducated folk,' said the gingerbread-man, with a squint at me, directly all the crowd had trudged past: 'is such a dainty for the likes of them?'

And quickly harnessing his horse, he went down to the river, where a little wooden ferry could be seen. A peasant in a white felt 'schlik' (the usual headgear in the forest) came out of a low mud hut to meet him, and ferried him over to the opposite bank. The little cart, with one wheel creaking from time to time, crawled along the trodden and deeply rutted road.

I fed my horses, and I too was ferried over. After struggling for a couple of miles through the boggy prairie, I got at last on to a narrow raised wooden cause-way to a clearing in the forest. The cart jolted unevenly over the round beams of the causeway: I got out and went along on foot. The horses moved in step snorting and shaking their heads from the gnats and flies. The forest took us into its bosom. On the outskirts, nearer to the prairie, grew birches, aspens, limes, maples, and oaks. Then they met us more rarely, the dense firwood moved down on us in an unbroken wall. Further on were the red, bare trunks of pines, and then again a stretch of mixed copse, overgrown with underwood of hazelnut, mountain ash, and bramble, and stout, vigorous weeds. The sun's rays threw a brilliant light on the tree-tops, and, filtering through the branches, here and there reached the ground in pale streaks and patches. Birds I scarcely heard--they do not like great forests. Only from time to time there came the doleful, thrice-repeated call of a hoopoe, and the angry screech of a nuthatch or a jay; a silent, always solitary bird kept flut-tering across the clearing, with a flash of golden azure from its lovely feathers. At times the trees grew further apart, ahead of us the light broke in, the cart came out on a cleared, sandy, open space. Thin rye was growing over it in rows, noiselessly nodding its pale ears. On one side there was a dark, dilapidated little chapel, with a slanting cross over a well. An unseen brook was babbling peaceably with changing, ringing sounds, as though it were flowing into an empty bottle. And then suddenly the road was cut in half by a birch-tree recently fallen, and the forest stood around, so old, lofty, and slumbering, that the air seemed pent in. In places the clearing lay under water. On both sides stretched a forest bog, all green and dark, all covered with reeds and tiny alders. Ducks flew up in pairs--and it was strange to see those water-birds darting rapidly about among the pines. 'Ga, ga, ga, ga,' their drawn-out call kept rising unexpectedly. Then a shepherd drove a flock through the under-wood: a brown cow with short, pointed horns broke noisily through the bushes and stood stockstill at the edge of the clearing, her big, dark eyes fixed on the dog running before me. A slight breeze brought the delicate, pungent smell of burnt wood. A white smoke in the distance crept in eddying rings over the pale, blue forest air, showing that a peasant was charcoal-burning for a glass-factory or for a foundry. The further we went on, the darker and stiller it became all round us. In the pine-forest it is always still; there is only, high overhead, a sort of prolonged murmur and subdued roar in the tree-tops. One goes on and on, and this eternal murmur of the forest never ceases, and the heart gradually begins to sink, and a man longs to come out quickly into the open, into the daylight; he longs to draw a full breath again, and is oppressed by the fragrant damp and decay....

For about twelve miles we drove on at a walking pace, rarely at a trot. I wanted to get by daylight to Svyatoe, a hamlet lying in the very heart of the forest. Twice we met peasants with stripped bark or long logs on carts.

'Is it far to Svyatoe?' I asked one of them.

'No, not far.'

'How far?'

'It'll be a little over two miles.'

Another hour and a half went by. We were still driving on and on. Again we heard the creak of a laden cart. A peasant was walking beside it.

'How far, brother, is it still to Svyatoe?'

'What?'

'How far to Svyatoe?'

'Six miles.'

The sun was already setting when at last I got out of the forest and saw facing me a little village. About twenty homesteads were grouped close about an old wooden church, with a single green cupola, and tiny windows, brilliantly red in the evening glow. This was Svyatoe. I drove into its outskirts. A herd returning homewards overtook my cart, and with lowing, grunting and bleating moved by us. Young girls and bustling peasant women came to meet their beasts. Whiteheaded boys with merry shrieks went in chase of refractory pigs. The dust swirled along the street in light clouds, flushed crimson as they rose higher in the air.

I stopped at the house of the village elder, a crafty and clever 'forester,' one of those foresters of whom they say he can see two yards into the ground. Early next morning, accompanied by the village elder's son, and another peasant called Yegor, I set off in a little cart with a pair of peasant's horses, to shoot woodcocks and moorhens. The forest formed a continuous bluish ring all round the sky-line; there was reckoned to be two hundred acres, no more, of ploughed land round Svyatoe; but one had to go some five miles to find good places for game. The elder's son was called Kondrat. He was a flaxen-haired, rosy-cheeked young fellow, with a good-natured, peaceable expression of face, obliging and talkative. He drove the horses. Yegor sat by my side. I want to say a few words about him.

He was considered the cleverest sportsman in the whole district. Every step of the ground for fifty miles round he had been over again and again. He seldom fired at a bird, for lack of powder and shot; but it was enough for him to decoy a moorhen or to detect the track of a grouse. Yegor had the character of being a straightforward fellow and 'no talker.' He did not care for talking and never exaggerated the number of birds he had taken--a trait rare in a sportsman. He was of medium height, thin, and had a pale, long face, and big, honest eyes. All his features, especially his straight and never-moving lips, were expressive of untroubled serenity. He gave a slight, as it were inward smile, whenever he uttered a word--very sweet was that quiet smile. He never drank spirits, and worked industriously; but nothing prospered with him. His wife was always ailing, his children didn't live; he got poorer and poorer and could never pick up again. And there is no denying that a passion for the chase is no good for a peasant, and any one who 'plays with a gun' is sure to be a poor manager of his land. Either from constantly being in the forest, face to face with the stern and melancholy scenery of that inhuman country, or from the peculiar cast and formation of his character, there was noticeable in every action of Yegor's a sort of modest dignity and stateliness--stateliness it was, and not melancholy--the stateliness of a majestic stag. He had in his time killed seven bears, lying in wait for them in the oats. The last he had only succeeded in killing on the fourth night of his ambush; the bear persisted in not turning sideways to him, and he had only one bullet. Yegor had killed him the day before my arrival. When Kondrat brought me to him, I found him in his back yard; squatting on his heels before the huge beast, he was cutting the fat out with a short, blunt knife.

'What a fine fellow you've knocked over there!' I observed.

Yegor raised his head and looked first at me, then at the dog, who had come with me.

'If it's shooting you've come after, sir, there are woodcocks at Moshnoy--three coveys, and five of moorhens,' he observed, and set to work again.

With Yegor and with Kondrat I went out the next day in search of sport. We drove rapidly over the open ground surrounding Svyatoe, but when we got into the forest we crawled along at a walking pace once more.

'Look, there's a wood-pigeon,' said Kondrat suddenly, turning to me: 'better knock it over!'

Yegor looked in the direction Kondrat pointed, but said nothing. The wood-pigeon was over a hundred paces from us, and one can't kill it at forty paces; there is such strength in its feathers. A few more remarks were made by the conversational Kondrat; but the forest hush had its influence even on him; he became silent. Only rarely exchanging a word or two, looking straight ahead, and listening to the puffing and snorting of the horses, we got at last to 'Moshnoy.' That is the name given to the older pine-forest, overgrown in places by fir saplings. We got out; Kondrat led the cart into the bushes, so that the gnats should not bite the horses. Yegor examined the cock of his gun and crossed himself: he never began anything without the sign of the cross.

The forest into which we had come was exceedingly old. I don't know whether the Tartars had wandered over it, but Russian thieves or Lithuanians, in disturbed times, might certainly have hidden in its recesses. At a respectful distance from one another stood the mighty pines with their slightly curved, massive, pale-yellow trunks. Between them stood in single file others, rather younger. The ground was covered with greenish moss, sprinkled all over with dead pine-needles; blueberries grew in dense bushes; the strong perfume of the berries, like the smell of musk, oppressed the breathing. The sun could not pierce through the high network of the pine-branches; but it was stiflingly hot in the forest all the same, and not dark;

like big drops of sweat the heavy, transparent resin stood out and slowly trickled down the coarse bark of the trees. The still air, with no light or shade in it, stung the face. Everything was silent; even our footsteps were not audible; we walked on the moss as on a carpet. Yegor in particular moved as silently as a shadow; even the brushwood did not crackle under his feet. He walked without haste, from time to time blowing a shrill note on a whistle; a woodcock soon answered back, and before my eyes darted into a thick fir-tree. But in vain Yegor pointed him out to me; however much I strained my eyes, I could not make him out. Yegor had to take a shot at him. We came upon two coveys of moorhens also. The cautious birds rose at a distance with an abrupt, heavy sound. We succeeded, however, in killing three young ones.

At one *meidan*[1] Yegor suddenly stopped and called me up.

'A bear has been trying to get water,' he observed, pointing to a broad, fresh scratch, made in the very middle of a hole covered with fine moss.

'Is that the print of his paw?' I inquired.

'Yes; but the water has dried up. That's the track of him too on that pine; he has been climbing after honey. He has cut into it with his claws as if with a knife.'

We went on making our way into the inner-most depths of the forest. Yegor only rarely looked upwards, and walked on serenely and confidently. I saw a high, round rampart, enclosed by a half-choked-up ditch.

'What's that? a *meidan* too?' I inquired.

'No,' answered Yegor; 'here's where the thieves' town stood.'

'Long ago?'

'Long ago; our grandfathers remember it. Here they buried their treasure. And they took a mighty oath: on human blood.'

We went on another mile and a half; I began to feel thirsty.

'Sit down a little while,' said Yegor: 'I will go for water; there is a well not far from here.'

He went away; I was left alone.

I sat down on a felled stump, leaned my elbows on my knees, and after a long stillness, raised my head and looked around me. Oh, how still and sullenly gloomy was everything around me--no, not gloomy even, but dumb, cold, and menacing

---

1 *Meidan* is the name given to a place where tar has been made.--Author's Note.

at the same time! My heart sank. At that instant, at that spot, I had a sense of death breathing upon me, I felt I almost touched its perpetual closeness. If only one sound had vibrated, one momentary rustle had arisen, in the engulfing stillness of the pine-forest that hemmed me in on all sides! I let my head sink again, almost in terror; it was as though I had looked in, where no man ought to look.... I put my hand over my eyes--and all at once, as though at some mysterious bidding, I began to remember all my life....

There passed in a flash before me my childhood, noisy and peaceful, quarrelsome and good-hearted, with hurried joys and swift sorrows; then my youth rose up, vague, queer, self-conscious, with all its mistakes and beginnings, with disconnected work, and agitated indolence.... There came back, too, to my memory the comrades who shared those early aspirations ... then like lightning in the night there came the gleam of a few bright memories ... then the shadows began to grow and bear down on me, it was darker and darker about me, more dully and quietly the monotonous years ran by--and like a stone, dejection sank upon my heart. I sat without stirring and gazed, gazed with effort and perplexity, as though I saw all my life before me, as though scales had fallen from my eyes. Oh, what have I done! my lips involuntarily murmured in a bitter whisper. O life, life, where, how have you gone without a trace? How have you slipped through my clenched fingers? Have you deceived me, or was it that I knew not how to make use of your gifts? Is it possible? is this fragment, this poor handful of dusty ashes, all that is left of you? Is this cold, stagnant, unnecessary something--I, the I of old days? How? The soul was athirst for happiness so perfect, she rejected with such scorn all that was small, all that was insufficient, she waited: soon happiness would burst on her in a torrent-- and has not one drop moistened the parched lips? Oh, my golden strings, you that once so delicately, so sweetly quivered,--I have never, it seems, heard your music ... you had but just sounded--when you broke. Or, perhaps, happiness, the true happiness of all my life, passed close by me, smiled a resplendent smile upon me--and I failed to recognise its divine countenance. Or did it really visit me, sit at my bedside, and is forgotten by me, like a dream? Like a dream, I repeated disconsolately. Elusive images flitted over my soul, awakening in it something between pity and bewilderment ... you too, I thought, dear, familiar, lost faces, you, thronging about me in this deadly solitude, why are you so profoundly and mournfully silent? From what abyss have you arisen? How am I to interpret your enigmatic glances? Are you greeting me, or bidding me farewell? Oh, can it be there is no hope, no turning back? Why are these heavy, belated drops trickling from my eyes? O heart, why, to what end, grieve more? try to forget if you would have peace, harden yourself to the meek acceptance of the last parting, to the bitter words 'good-bye' and 'for ever.' Do not look back, do not remember, do not strive to reach where it is light, where youth laughs, where hope is wreathed with the flowers of spring, where dovelike delight soars on azure wings, where love, like dew in the sunrise, flashes with tears of ecstasy; look not where is bliss, and faith and power--that is not our place!

'Here is water for you,' I heard Yegor's musical voice behind me: 'drink, with God's blessing.'

I could not help starting; this living speech shook me, sent a delightful tremor all through me. It was as though I had fallen into unknown, dark depths, where all was hushed about me, and nothing could be heard but the soft, persistent moan of some unending grief.... I was faint and could not struggle, and all at once there floated down to me a friendly voice, and some mighty hand with one pull drew me up into the light of day. I looked round, and with unutterable consolation saw the serene and honest face of my guide. He stood easily and gracefully before me, and with his habitual smile held out a wet flask full of clear liquid.... I got up.

'Let's go on; lead the way,' I said eagerly. We set off and wandered a long while, till evening. Directly the noonday heat was over, it became cold and dark so rapidly in the forest that one felt no desire to remain in it.

'Away, restless mortals,' it seemed whispering sullenly from each pine. We came out, but it was some time before we could find Kondrat. We shouted, called to him, but he did not answer. All of a sudden, in the profound stillness of the air, we heard his 'wo, wo,' sound distinctly in a ravine close to us.... The wind, which had suddenly sprung up, and as suddenly dropped again, had prevented him from hearing our calls. Only on the trees which stood some distance apart were traces of its onslaught to be seen; many of the leaves were blown inside out, and remained so, giving a variegated look to the motionless foliage. We got into the cart, and drove home. I sat, swaying to and fro, and slowly breathing in the damp, rather keen air; and all my recent reveries and regrets were drowned in the one sensation of drowsiness and fatigue, in the one desire to get back as soon as possible to the shelter of a warm house, to have a good drink of tea with cream, to nestle into the soft, yielding hay, and to sleep, to sleep, to sleep....

SECOND DAY

The next morning the three of us set off to the 'Charred Wood.' Ten years before, several thousand acres in the 'Forest' had been burnt down, and had not up to that time grown again; here and there, young firs and pines were shooting up, but for the most part there was nothing but moss and ashes. In this 'Charred Wood,' which is reckoned to be about nine miles from Svyatoe, there are all sorts of berries growing in great profusion, and it is a favourite haunt of grouse, who are very fond of strawberries and bilberries.

We were driving along in silence, when suddenly Kondrat raised his head.

'Ah!' he exclaimed: 'why, that's never Efrem standing yonder! 'Morning to you, Alexandritch,' he added, raising his voice, and lifting his cap.

A short peasant in a short, black smock, with a cord round the waist, came out from behind a tree, and approached the cart.

'Why, have they let you off?' inquired Kondrat.

'I should think so!' replied the peasant, and he grinned. 'You don't catch them keeping the likes of me.'

'And what did Piotr Filippitch say to it?'

'Filippov, is it? Oh, he's all right.'

'You don't say so! Why, I thought, Alexandritch--well, brother, thought I, now you 're the goose that must lie down in the frying-pan!'

'On account of Piotr Filippov, hey? Get along! We've seen plenty like him. He tries to pass for a wolf, and then slinks off like a dog.--Going shooting your honour, hey?' the peasant suddenly inquired, turning his little, screwed-up eyes rapidly upon me, and at once dropping them again.

'Yes.'

'And whereabouts, now?'

'To the Charred Wood,' said Kondrat.

'You 're going to the Charred Wood? mind you don't get into the fire.'

'Eh?'

'I've seen a lot of woodcocks,' the peasant went on, seeming all the while to be laughing, and making Kondrat no answer. 'But you'll never get there; as the crow flies it'll be fifteen miles. Why, even Yegor here--not a doubt but he's as at home in the forest as in his own back-yard, but even he won't make his way there. Hullo, Yegor, you honest penny halfpenny soul!' he shouted suddenly.

'Good morning, Efrem,' Yegor responded deliberately.

I looked with curiosity at this Efrem. It was long since I had seen such a queer face. He had a long, sharp nose, thick lips, and a scanty beard. His little blue eyes positively danced, like little imps. He stood in a free-and-easy pose, his arms akimbo, and did not touch his cap.

'Going home for a visit, eh?' Kondrat questioned him.

'Go on! on a visit! It's not the weather for that, my lad; it's set fair. It's all open and free, my dear; one may lie on the stove till winter time, not a dog will stir. When I was in the town, the clerk said: "Give us up," says he, "'Lexandritch; you just get out of the district, we'll let you have a passport, first-class one ..." but there, I'd pity on you Svyatoe fellows: you'd never get another thief like me.'

Kondrat laughed. 'You will have your joke, uncle, you will, upon my word,' he said, and he shook the reins. The horses started off.

'Wo,' said Efrem. The horses stopped. Kondrat did not like this prank.

'Enough of your nonsense, Alexandritch,' he observed in an undertone: 'don't you see we're out with a gentleman? You mind; he'll be angry.'

'Get on with you, sea-drake! What should he be angry about? He's a good-natured gentleman. You see, he'll give me something to drink. Hey, master, give a poor scoundrel a dram! Won't I drink it!' he added, shrugging his shoulder up to his ear, and grating his teeth.

I could not help smiling, gave him a copper, and told Kondrat to drive on.

'Much obliged, your honour,' Efrem shouted after us in soldierly fashion. 'And you'll know, Kondrat, for the future from whom to learn manners. Faint heart never wins; 'tis boldness gains the day. When you come back, come to my place, d'ye hear? There'll be drinking going on three days at home; there'll be some necks broken, I can tell you; my wife's a devil of a woman; our yard's on the side of a precipice.... Ay, magpie, have a good time till your tail gets pinched.' And with a sharp whistle, Efrem plunged into the bushes.

'What sort of man is he?' I questioned Kondrat, who, sitting in the front, kept shaking his head, as though deliberating with himself.

'That fellow?' replied Kondrat, and he looked down. 'That fellow?' he repeated.

'Yes. Is he of your village?'

'Yes, he's a Svyatoe man. He's a fellow.... You wouldn't find the like of him, if you hunted for a hundred miles round. A thief and cheat--good Lord, yes! Another man's property simply, as it were, takes his eye. You may bury a thing underground, and you won't hide it from him; and as to money, you might sit on it, and he'd get it from under you without your noticing it.'

'What a bold fellow he is!'

'Bold? Yes, he's not afraid of any one. But just look at him; he's a beast by his physiognomy; you can see by his nose.' (Kondrat often used to drive with gentlemen, and had been in the chief town of the province, and so liked on occasion to show off his attainments.) 'There's positively no doing anything with him. How many times they've taken him off to put him in the prison!--it's simply trouble thrown away. They start tying him up, and he'll say, "Come, why don't you fasten that leg? fasten that one too, and a little tighter: I'll have a little sleep meanwhile; and I shall get home before your escort." And lo and behold! there he is back again, yes, back again, upon my soul! Well as we all about here know the forest, being used to it from childhood, we're no match for him there. Last summer he came at night straight across from Altuhin to Svyatoe, and no one had ever been known to walk it--it'll be over thirty miles. And he steals honey too; no one can beat him at that; and the bees don't sting him. There's not a hive he hasn't plundered.'

'I expect he doesn't spare the wild bees either?'

'Well, no, I won't lay a false charge against him. That sin's never been observed in him. The wild bees' nest is a holy thing with us. A hive is shut in by fences; there's a watch kept; if you get the honey--it's your luck; but the wild bee is a thing of God's, not guarded; only the bear touches it.'

'Because he is a bear,' remarked Yegor.

'Is he married?'

'To be sure. And he has a son. And won't he be a thief too, the son! He's taken after his father. And he's training him now too. The other day he took a pot with some old coppers in it, stolen somewhere, I've no doubt, went and buried it in a clearing in the forest, and went home and sent his son to the clearing. "Till you find the pot," says he, "I won't give you anything to eat, or let you into the place." The son stayed the whole day in the forest, and spent the night there, but he found the pot. Yes, he's a smart chap, that Efrem. When he's at home, he's a civil fellow, presses every one; you may eat and drink as you will, and there'll be dancing got up at his place and merry-making of all sorts. And when he comes to the meeting-- we have a parish meeting, you know, in our village--well, no one talks better sense than he does; he'll come up behind, listen, say a word as if he chopped it off, and away again; and a weighty word it'll be, too. But when he's about in the forest, ah! that means trouble! We've to look out for mischief. Though, I must say, he doesn't touch his own people unless he's in a fix. If he meets a Svyatoe man: "Go along with you, brother," he'll shout, a long way away; "the forest devil's upon me: I shall kill you!"--it's a bad business!'

'What can you all be thinking about? A whole district can't get even with one man?'

'Well, that's just how it is, any way.'

'Is he a sorcerer, then?'

'Who can say! Here, some days ago, he crept round at night to the deacon's near, after the honey, and the deacon was watching the hive himself. Well, he caught him, and in the dark he gave him a good hiding. When he'd done, Efrem, he says to him: "But d'you know who it is you've been beating?" The deacon, when he knew him by his voice, was fairly dumfoundered.

"Well, my good friend," says Efrem, "you won't get off so easily for this." The deacon fell down at his feet. "Take," says he, "what you please." "No," says he. "I'll take it from you at my own time and as I choose." And what do you think? Since that day the deacon's as though he'd been scalded; he wanders about like a ghost. "It's taken," says he, "all the heart out of me; it was a dreadful, powerful saying, to be sure, the brigand fastened upon me." That's how it is with him, with the deacon.'

'That deacon must be a fool,' I observed.

'A fool? Well, but what do you say to this? There was once an order issued to seize this fellow, Efrem. We had a police commissary then, a sharp man. And so a dozen chaps went off into the forest to take Efrem. They look, and there he is coming to meet them.... One of them shouts, "Here he is, hold him, tie him!" But Efrem stepped into the forest and cut himself a branch, two fingers' thickness, like this, and then out he skips into the road again, looking so frightful, so terrible, and gives the command like a general at a review: "On your knees!" All of them fairly fell down. "But who," says he, "shouted hold him, tie him? You, Seryoga?" The fellow simply jumped up and ran ... and Efrem after him, and kept swinging his branch at his heels.... For nearly a mile he stroked him down. And afterwards he never ceased to regret: "Ah," he'd say, "it is annoying I didn't lay him up for the confession." For it was just before St. Philip's day. Well, they changed the police commissary soon after, but it all ended the same way.'

'Why did they all give in to him?'

'Why! well, it is so....'

'He has frightened you all, and now he does as he likes with you.'

'Frightened, yes.... He'd frighten any one. And he's a wonderful hand at contrivances, my goodness, yes! I once came upon him in the forest; there was a heavy rain falling; I was for edging away.... But he looked at me, and beckoned to me with his hand like this. "Come along," says he, "Kondrat, don't be afraid. Let me show you how to live in the forest, and to keep dry in the rain." I went up to him, and he was sitting under a fir-tree, and he'd made a fire of damp twigs: the smoke hung about in the fir-tree, and kept the rain from dripping through. I was astonished at him then. And I'll tell you what he contrived one time' (and Kondrat laughed); 'he really did do a funny thing. They'd been thrashing the oats at the thrashing-floor, and they hadn't finished; they hadn't time to rake up the last heap; well, they 'd set two watch-men by it for the night, and they weren't the boldest-hearted of the chaps either. Well, they were sitting and gossiping, and Efrem takes and stuffs his shirt-sleeves full of straw, ties up the wrist-bands, and puts the shirt up over his head. And so he steals up in that shape to the thrashing-floor, and just pops out from behind the corner and gives them a peep of his horns. One chap says to the other: "Do you see?" "Yes," says the other, and didn't he give a screech all of a sudden ... and then the fences creaked and nothing more was seen of them. Efrem shovelled up the oats into a bag and dragged it off home. He told the story himself afterwards. He put them to shame, he did, the chaps.... He did really!'

Kondrat laughed again. And Yegor smiled. 'So the fences creaked and that was all?' he commented. 'There was nothing more seen of them,' Kondrat assented. 'They were simply gone in a flash.'

We were all silent again. Suddenly Kondrat started and sat up.

'Eh, mercy upon us!' he ejaculated; 'surely it's never a fire!'

'Where, where?' we asked.

'Yonder, see, in front, where we 're going.... A fire it is! Efrem there, Efrem--why, he foretold it! If it's not his doing, the damned fellow!...'

I glanced in the direction Kondrat was pointing. Two or three miles ahead of us, behind a green strip of low fir saplings, there really was a thick column of dark blue smoke slowly rising from the ground, gradually twisting and coiling into a cap-shaped cloud; to the right and left of it could be seen others, smaller and whiter.

A peasant, all red and perspiring, in nothing but his shirt, with his hair hanging dishevelled about his scared face, galloped straight towards us, and with difficulty stopped his hastily bridled horse.

'Mates,' he inquired breathlessly, 'haven't you seen the foresters?'

'No, we haven't. What is it? is the forest on fire?'

'Yes. We must get the people together, or else if it gets to Trosnoe ...'

The peasant tugged with his elbows, pounded with his heels on the horse's sides.... It galloped off.

Kondrat, too, whipped up his pair. We drove straight towards the smoke, which was spreading more and more widely; in places it suddenly grew black and rose up high. The nearer we moved to it, the more indefinite became its outlines; soon all the air was clouded over, there was a strong smell of burning, and here and there between the trees, with a strange, weird quivering in the sunshine, gleamed the first pale red tongues of flame.

'Well, thank God,' observed Kondrat, 'it seems it's an overground fire.'

'What's that?'

'Overground? One that runs along over the earth. With an underground fire, now, it's a difficult job to deal. What's one to do, when the earth's on fire for a whole yard's depth? There's only one means of safety--digging ditches,--and do you suppose that's easy? But an overground fire's nothing. It only scorches the grasses and burns the dry leaves! The forest will be all the better for it. Ouf, though, mercy on us, look how it flares!'

We drove almost up to the edge of the fire. I got down and went to meet it. It was neither dangerous nor difficult. The fire was running over the scanty pine-forest against the wind; it moved in an uneven line, or, to speak more accurately, in a dense jagged wall of curved tongues. The smoke was carried away by the wind. Kondrat had told the truth; it really was an overground fire, which only scorched the grass and passed on without finishing its work, leaving behind it a black and smoking, but not even smouldering, track. At times, it is true, when the fire came upon a hole filled with dry wood and twigs, it suddenly and with a kind of peculiar, rather vindictive roar, rose up in long, quivering points; but it soon sank down again and ran on as before, with a slight hiss and crackle. I even noticed, more than once, an oak-bush, with dry hanging leaves, hemmed in all round and yet untouched, except for a slight singeing at its base. I must own I could not understand why the dry leaves were not burned. Kondrat explained to me that it was owing to the fact that the fire was overground, 'that's to say, not angry.' 'But it's fire all the same,' I protested. 'Overground fire,' repeated Kondrat. However, overground as it was, the fire, none the less, produced its effect: hares raced up and down with a sort of disorder, running back with no sort of necessity into the neighbourhood of the fire; birds fell down in the smoke and whirled round and round; horses looked back and neighed, the forest itself fairly hummed--and man felt discomfort from the heat suddenly beating into his face....

'What are we looking at?' said Yegor suddenly, behind my back. 'Let's go on.'

'But where are we to go?' asked Kondrat.

'Take the left, over the dry bog; we shall get through.'

We turned to the left, and got through, though it was sometimes difficult for both the horses and the cart.

The whole day we wandered over the Charred Wood. At evening--the sunset had not yet begun to redden in the sky, but the shadows from the trees already lay long and motionless, and in the grass one could feel that chill that comes before the dew--I lay down by the roadside near the cart in which Kondrat, without haste, was harnessing the horses after their feed, and I recalled my cheerless reveries of the day before. Everything around was as still as the previous evening, but there was not the forest, stifling and weighing down the spirit. On the dry moss, on the crimson grasses, on the soft dust of the road, on the slender stems and pure little leaves of the young birch-trees, lay the clear soft light of the no longer scorching, sinking sun. Everything was resting, plunged in soothing coolness; nothing was yet asleep, but everything was getting ready for the restoring slumber of evening and night-time. Everything seemed to be saying to man: 'Rest, brother of ours; breathe lightly, and grieve not, thou too, at the sleep close before thee.' I raised my head and saw at the very end of a delicate twig one of those large flies with emerald head, long body, and four transparent wings, which the fanciful French call 'maidens,' while our guileless people has named them 'bucket-yokes.' For a long while, more than an hour, I did not take my eyes off her. Soaked through and through with sun-shine, she did not stir, only from time to time turning her head from side to side and shaking her lifted wings ... that was all. Looking at her, it suddenly seemed to me that I understood the life of nature, understood its clear and unmistakable though, to many, still mysterious significance. A subdued, quiet animation, an unhasting, restrained use of sensations and powers, an equilibrium of health in each separate creature--there is her very basis, her unvarying law, that is what she stands upon and holds to. Everything that goes beyond this level, above or below--it makes no difference--she flings away as worthless. Many insects die as soon as they know the joys of love, which destroy the equilibrium. The sick beast plunges into the thicket and expires there alone: he seems to feel that he no longer has the right to look upon the sun that is common to all, nor to breathe the open air; he has not the right to live;--and the man who from his own fault or from the fault of others is faring ill in the world--ought, at least, to know how to keep silence.

'Well, Yegor!' cried Kondrat all at once. He had already settled himself on the box of the cart and was shaking and playing with the reins. 'Come, sit down. What are you so thoughtful about? Still about the cow?'

'About the cow? What cow?' I repeated, and looked at Yegor: calm and stately as ever, he certainly did seem thoughtful, and was gazing away into the distance towards the fields already beginning to get dark.

'Don't you know?' answered Kondrat; 'his last cow died last night. He has no luck.--What are you going to do?'....

Yegor sat down on the box, without speaking, and we drove off. 'That man knows how to bear in silence,' I thought.

YAKOV PASINKOV

I

It happened in Petersburg, in the winter, on the first day of the carnival. I had been invited to dinner by one of my schoolfellows, who enjoyed in his youth the reputation of being as modest as a maiden, and turned out in the sequel a person by no means over rigid in his conduct. He is dead now, like most of my schoolfellows. There were to be present at the dinner, besides me, Konstantin Alexandrovitch Asanov, and a literary celebrity of those days. The literary celebrity kept us waiting for him, and finally sent a note that he was not coming, and in place of him there turned up a little light-haired gentleman, one of the everlasting uninvited guests with whom Petersburg abounds.

The dinner lasted a long while; our host did not spare the wine, and by degrees our heads were affected. Everything that each of us kept hidden in his heart--and who is there that has not something hidden in his heart?--came to the surface. Our host's face suddenly lost its modest and reserved expression; his eyes shone with a brazen-faced impudence, and a vulgar grin curved his lips; the light-haired gentleman laughed in a feeble way, with a senseless crow; but Asanov surprised me more than any one. The man had always been conspicuous for his sense of propriety, but now he began by suddenly rubbing his hand over his forehead, giving himself airs, boasting of his connections, and continually alluding to a certain uncle of his, a very important personage.... I positively should not have known him; he was unmistakably jeering at us ... he all but avowed his contempt for our society. Asanov's insolence began to exasperate me.

'Listen,' I said to him; 'if we are such poor creatures to your thinking, you'd better go and see your illustrious uncle. But possibly he's not at home to you.'

Asanov made me no reply, and went on passing his hand across his forehead.

'What a set of people!' he said again; 'they've never been in any decent society, never been acquainted with a single decent woman, while I have here,' he cried, hurriedly pulling a pocket-book out of his side-pocket and tapping it with his hand, 'a whole pack of letters from a girl whom you wouldn't find the equal of in the whole world.'

Our host and the light-haired gentleman paid no attention to Asanov's last words; they were holding each other by their buttons, and both relating something; but I pricked up my ears.

'Oh, you 're bragging, Mr. nephew of an illustrious personage,' I said, going up to Asanov; 'you haven't any letters at all.'

'Do you think so?' he retorted, and he looked down loftily at me; 'what's this, then?' He opened the pocket-book, and showed me about a dozen letters addressed to him…. A familiar handwriting, I fancied…. I feel the flush of shame mounting to my cheeks … my self-love is suffering horribly…. No one likes to own to a mean action…. But there is nothing for it: when I began my story, I knew I should have to blush to my ears in the course of it. And so, I am bound to harden my heart and confess that….

Well, this was what passed: I took advantage of the intoxicated condition of Asanov, who had carelessly dropped the letters on the champagne-stained table-cloth (my own head was dizzy enough too), and hurriedly ran my eyes over one of the letters….

My heart stood still…. Alas! I was myself in love with the girl who had written to Asanov, and I could have no doubt now that she loved him. The whole letter, which was in French, expressed tenderness and devotion….

'Mon cher ami Constantin!' so it began … and it ended with the words: 'be careful as before, and I will be yours or no one's.'

Stunned as by a thunderbolt, I sat for a few instants motionless; at last I regained my self-possession, jumped up, and rushed out of the room.

A quarter of an hour later I was back at home in my own lodgings.

*   *   *   *   *

The family of the Zlotnitskys was one of the first whose acquaintance I made on coming to Petersburg from Moscow. It consisted of a father and mother, two daughters, and a son. The father, a man already grey, but still vigorous, who had been in the army, held a fairly important position, spent the morning in a government office, went to sleep after dinner, and in the evening played cards at his club.... He was seldom at home, spoke little and unwillingly, looked at one from under his eyebrows with an expression half surly, half indifferent, and read nothing except books of travels and geography. Sometimes he was unwell, and then he would shut himself up in his own room, and paint little pictures, or tease the old grey parrot, Popka. His wife, a sickly, consumptive woman, with hollow black eyes and a sharp nose, did not leave her sofa for days together, and was always embroidering cushion-covers in canvas. As far as I could observe, she was rather afraid of her husband, as though she had somehow wronged him at some time or other. The elder daughter, Varvara, a plump, rosy, fair-haired girl of eighteen, was always sitting at the window, watching the people that passed by. The son, who was being educated in a government school, was only seen at home on Sundays, and he, too, did not care to waste his words. Even the younger daughter, Sophia, the girl with whom I was in love, was of a silent disposition. In the Zlotnitskys' house there reigned a perpetual stillness; it was only broken by the piercing screams of Popka, but visitors soon got used to these, and were conscious again of the burden and oppression of the eternal stillness. Visitors, however, seldom looked in upon the Zlotnitskys; their house was a dull one. The very furniture, the red paper with yellow patterns in the drawing-room, the numerous rush-bottomed chairs in the dining-room, the faded wool-work cushions, embroidered with figures of girls and dogs, on the sofa, the branching lamps, and the gloomy-looking portraits on the walls--everything inspired an involuntary melancholy, about everything there clung a sense of chill and flatness. On my arrival in Petersburg, I had thought it my duty to call on the Zlotnitskys. They were relations of my mother's. I managed with difficulty to sit out an hour with them, and it was a long while before I went there again. But by degrees I took to going oftener and oftener. I was drawn there by Sophia, whom I had not cared for at first, and with whom I finally fell in love.

She was a slender, almost thin, girl of medium height, with a pale face, thick black hair, and big brown eyes, always half closed. Her severe and well-defined features, especially her tightly shut lips, showed determination and strength of will. At home they knew her to be a girl with a will of her own....

'She's like her eldest sister, like Katerina,' Madame Zlotnitsky said one day, as she sat alone with me (in her husband's presence she did not dare to mention the said Katerina). 'You don't know her; she's in the Caucasus, married. At thirteen, only fancy, she fell in love with her husband, and announced to us at the time that she would never marry any one else. We did everything we could--nothing was of any use. She waited till she was three-and-twenty, and braved her father's anger, and so married her idol. There is no saying what Sonitchka might not do! The Lord preserve her from such stubbornness! But I am afraid for her; she's only sixteen now, and there's no turning her....'

Mr. Zlotnitsky came in, and his wife was instantly silent.

What had captivated me in Sophia was not her strength of will--no; but with all her dryness, her lack of vivacity and imagination, she had a special charm of her own, the charm of straightforwardness, genuine sincerity, and purity of heart. I respected her as much as I loved her.... It seemed to me that she too looked with friendly eyes on me; to have my illusions as to her feeling for me shattered, and her love for another man proved conclusively, was a blow to me.

The unlooked-for discovery I had made astonished me the more as Asanov was not often at the Zlotnitskys' house, much less so than I, and had shown no marked preference for Sonitchka. He was a handsome, dark fellow, with expressive but rather heavy features, with brilliant, prominent eyes, with a large white forehead, and full red lips under fine moustaches. He was very discreet, but severe in his behaviour, confident in his criticisms and utterances, and dignified in his silence. It was obvious that he thought a great deal of himself. Asanov rarely laughed, and then with closed teeth, and he never danced. He was rather loosely and clumsily built. He had at one time served in the --th regiment, and was spoken of as a capable officer.

'A strange thing!' I ruminated, lying on the sofa; 'how was it I noticed nothing?' ... 'Be careful as before': those words in Sophia's letter suddenly recurred to my memory. 'Ah!' I thought: 'that's it! What a sly little hussy! And I thought her open and sincere…. Wait a bit, that's all; I'll let you know….'

But at this point, if I can trust my memory, I began weeping bitterly, and could not get to sleep all night.

*   *   *   *   *

Next day at two o'clock I set off to the Zlotnitskys'. The father was not at home, and his wife was not sitting in her usual place; after the pancake festival of the preceding day, she had a headache, and had gone to lie down in her bedroom. Varvara was standing with her shoulder against the window, looking into the street; Sophia was walking up and down the room with her arms folded across her bosom; Popka was shrieking.

'Ah! how do you do?' said Varvara lazily, directly I came into the room, and she added at once in an undertone, 'There goes a peasant with a tray on his head.' … (She had the habit of keeping up a running commentary on the passers-by to herself.)

'How do you do?' I responded; 'how do you do, Sophia Nikolaevna? Where is Tatiana Vassilievna?'

'She has gone to lie down,' answered Sophia, still pacing the room.

'We had pancakes,' observed Varvara, without turning round. 'Why didn't you come? … Where can that clerk be going?' 'Oh, I hadn't time.' ('Present arms!' the parrot screeched shrilly.) 'How Popka is shrieking to-day!'

'He always does shriek like that,' observed Sophia.

We were all silent for a time.

'He has gone in at the gate,' said Varvara, and she suddenly got up on the window-sill and opened the window.

'What are you about?' asked Sophia.

'There's a beggar,' responded Varvara. She bent down, picked up a five-copeck piece from the window; the remains of a fumigating pastille still stood in a grey heap of ashes on the copper coin, as she flung it into the street; then she slammed the window to and jumped heavily down to the floor….

'I had a very pleasant time yesterday,' I began, seating myself in an arm-chair.

'I dined with a friend of mine; Konstantin Alexandritch was there.... (I looked at Sophia; not an eyebrow quivered on her face.) 'And I must own,' I continued, 'we'd a good deal of wine; we emptied eight bottles between the four of us.'

'Really!' Sophia articulated serenely, and she shook her head.

'Yes,' I went on, slightly irritated at her composure: 'and do you know what, Sophia Nikolaevna, it's a true saying, it seems, that in wine is truth.'

'How so?'

'Konstantin Alexandritch made us laugh. Only fancy, he began all at once passing his hand over his forehead like this, and saying: "I'm a fine fellow! I've an uncle a celebrated man!"....'

'Ha, ha!' came Varvara's short, abrupt laugh.

....'Popka! Popka! Popka!' the parrot dinned back at her.

Sophia stood still in front of me, and looked me straight in the face.

'And you, what did you say?' she asked; 'don't you remember?'

I could not help blushing.

'I don't remember! I expect I was pretty absurd too. It certainly is dangerous to drink,' I added with significant emphasis; 'one begins chattering at once, and one's apt to say what no one ought to know. One's sure to be sorry for it afterwards, but then it's too late.'

'Why, did you let out some secret?' asked Sophia.

'I am not referring to myself.'

Sophia turned away, and began walking up and down the room again. I stared at her, raging inwardly. 'Upon my word,' I thought, 'she is a child, a baby, and how she has herself in hand! She's made of stone, simply. But wait a bit....'

'Sophia Nikolaevna ...' I said aloud.

Sophia stopped.

'What is it?'

'Won't you play me something on the piano? By the way, I've something I want to say to you,' I added, dropping my voice.

Sophia, without saying a word, walked into the other room; I followed her. She came to a standstill at the piano.

'What am I to play you?' she inquired.

'What you like ... one of Chopin's nocturnes.'

Sophia began the nocturne. She played rather badly, but with feeling. Her sister played nothing but polkas and waltzes, and even that very seldom. She would go sometimes with her indolent step to the piano, sit down, let her coat slip from her shoulders down to her elbows (I never saw her without a coat), begin playing a polka very loud, and without finishing it, begin another, then she would suddenly heave a sigh, get up, and go back again to the window. A queer creature was that Varvara!

I sat down near Sophia.

'Sophia Nikolaevna,' I began, watching her intently from one side. 'I ought to tell you a piece of news, news disagreeable to me.'

'News? what is it?'

'I'll tell you.... Up till now I have been mistaken in you, completely mistaken.'

'How was that?' she rejoined, going on playing, and keeping her eyes fixed on her fingers.

'I imagined you to be open; I imagined that you were incapable of hypocrisy, of hiding your feelings, deceiving....'

Sophia bent her face closer over the music.

'I don't understand you.'

'And what's more,' I went on; 'I could never have conceived that you, at your age, were already quite capable of acting a part in such masterly fashion.'

Sophia's hands faintly trembled above the keys. 'Why are you saying this?' she said, still not looking at me; 'I play a part?'

'Yes, you do.' (She smiled ... I was seized with spiteful fury.) ... 'You pretend to be indifferent to a man and ... and you write letters to him,' I added in a whisper.

Sophia's cheeks grew white, but she did not turn to me: she played the nocturne through to the end, got up, and closed the piano.

'Where are you going?' I asked her in some perplexity. 'You have no answer to make me?'

'What answer can I make you? I don't know what you 're talking about.... And I am not good at pretending....'

She began putting by the music.

The blood rushed to my head. 'No; you know what I am talking about,' I said, and I too got up from my seat; 'or if you like, I will remind you directly of some of your expressions in one letter: "be as careful as before"....'

Sophia gave a faint start.

'I never should have expected this of you,' she said at last.

'I never should have expected,' I retorted, 'that you, Sophia Nikolaevna, would have deigned to notice a man who ...'

Sophia turned with a rapid movement to me; I instinctively stepped back a little from her; her eyes, always half closed, were so wide open that they looked immense, and they glittered wrathfully under her frowning brows.

'Oh! if that's it,' she said, 'let me tell you that I love that man, and that it's absolutely no consequence to me what you think about him or about my love for him. And what business is it of yours? ... What right have you to speak of this? If I have made up my mind ...'

She stopped speaking, and went hurriedly out of the room. I stood still. I felt all of a sudden so uncomfortable and so ashamed that I hid my face in my hands. I realised all the impropriety, all the baseness of my behaviour, and, choked with shame and remorse, I stood as it were in disgrace. 'Mercy,' I thought, 'what I've done!'

'Anton Nikititch,' I heard the maid-servant saying in the outer-room, 'get a glass of water, quick, for Sophia Nikolaevna.'

'What's wrong?' answered the man.

'I fancy she's crying....'

I started up and went into the drawing-room for my hat.

'What were you talking about to Sonitchka?' Varvara inquired indifferently, and after a brief pause she added in an undertone, 'Here's that clerk again.'

I began saying good-bye.

'Why are you going? Stay a little; mamma is coming down directly.'

'No; I can't now,' I said: 'I had better call and see her another time.'

At that instant, to my horror, to my positive horror, Sophia walked with resolute steps into the drawing-room. Her face was paler than usual, and her eyelids were a little red. She never even glanced at me.

'Look, Sonia,' observed Varvara; 'there's a clerk keeps continually passing our house.'

'A spy, perhaps...' Sophia remarked coldly and contemptuously.

This was too much. I went away, and I really don't know how I got home.

I felt very miserable, wretched and miserable beyond description. In twenty-four hours two such cruel blows! I had learned that Sophia loved another man, and I had for ever forfeited her respect. I felt myself so utterly annihilated and disgraced that I could not even feel indignant with myself. Lying on the sofa with my face turned to the wall, I was revelling in the first rush of despairing misery, when I suddenly heard footsteps in the room. I lifted my head and saw one of my most intimate friends, Yakov Pasinkov.

I was ready to fly into a rage with any one who had come into my room that day, but with Pasinkov I could never be angry. Quite the contrary; in spite of the sorrow devouring me, I was inwardly rejoiced at his coming, and I nodded to him. He walked twice up and down the room, as his habit was, clearing his throat, and stretching out his long limbs; then he stood a minute facing me in silence, and in silence he seated himself in a corner.

I had known Pasinkov a very long while, almost from childhood. He had been brought up at the same private school, kept by a German, Winterkeller, at which I had spent three years. Yakov's father, a poor major on the retired list, a very honest man, but a little deranged mentally, had brought him, when a boy of seven, to this German; had paid for him for a year in advance, and had then left Moscow and been lost sight of completely.... From time to time there were dark, strange rumours about him. Eight years later it was known as a positive fact that he had been drowned in a flood when crossing the Irtish. What had taken him to Siberia, God knows. Yakov had no other relations; his mother had long been dead. He was simply left stranded on Winterkeller's hands. Yakov had, it is true, a distant relation, a great-aunt; but she was so poor, that she was afraid at first to go to her nephew, for fear she should have the care of him thrust upon her. Her fears turned out to be groundless; the kind-hearted German kept Yakov with him, let him study with his other pupils, fed him (dessert, however, was not offered him except on Sundays), and rigged him out in clothes cut out of the cast-off morning-gowns--usually snuff-coloured--of his mother, an old Livonian lady, still alert and active in spite of her great age. Owing to all these circumstances, and owing generally to Yakov's inferior position in the school, his schoolfellows treated him in rather a casual fashion, looked down upon him, and used to call him 'mammy's dressing-gown,' the 'nephew of the mob-cap' (his aunt invariably wore a very peculiar mob-cap with a bunch of yellow ribbons sticking straight upright, like a globe artichoke, upon it), and sometimes the 'son of Yermak' (because his father had, like that hero, been drowned in the Irtish). But in spite of those nicknames, in spite of his ridiculous garb, and his absolute destitution, every one was fond of him, and indeed it was impossible not to be fond of him; a sweeter, nobler nature, I imagine, has never existed upon earth. He was very good at lessons too.

When I saw him first, he was sixteen years old, and I was only just thirteen. I was an exceedingly selfish and spoilt boy; I had grown up in a rather wealthy house, and so, on entering the school, I lost no time in making friends with a little prince, an object of special solicitude to Winterkeller, and with two or three other juvenile aristocrats; while I gave myself great airs with all the rest. Pasinkov I did not deign to notice at all. I regarded the long, gawky lad, in a shapeless coat and short trousers, which showed his coarse thread stockings, as some sort of page-boy, one of the house-serfs--at best, a person of the working class. Pasinkov was extremely courteous and gentle to everybody, though he never sought the society of any one. If he were rudely treated, he was neither humiliated nor sullen; he simply withdrew and held himself aloof, with a sort of regretful look, as it were biding his time. This was just how he behaved with me. About two months passed. One bright summer day I happened to go out of the playground after a noisy game of leap-frog, and walking into the garden I saw Pasinkov sitting on a bench under a high lilac-bush. He was reading. I glanced at the cover of the book as I passed, and read **Schiller's Werke** on the back. I stopped short.

'Do you mean to say you know German?' I questioned Pasinkov....

I feel ashamed to this day as I recall all the arrogance there was in the very sound of my voice.... Pasinkov softly raised his small but expressive eyes and looked at me.

'Yes,' he answered; 'do you?'

'I should hope so!' I retorted, feeling insulted at the question, and I was about to go on my way, but something held me back.

'What is it you are reading of Schiller?' I asked, with the same haughty insolence.

'At this moment I am reading "Resignation," a beautiful poem. Would you like me to read it to you? Come and sit here by me on the bench.'

I hesitated a little, but I sat down. Pasinkov began reading. He knew German far better than I did. He had to explain the meaning of several lines for me. But already I felt no shame at my ignorance and his superiority to me. From that day, from the very hour of our reading together in the garden, in the shade of the lilac-bush, I loved Pasinkov with my whole soul, I attached myself to him and fell completely under his sway.

I have a vivid recollection of his appearance in those days. He changed very little, however, later on. He was tall, thin, and rather awkwardly built, with a long back, narrow shoulders, and a hollow chest, which made him look rather frail and delicate, although as a fact he had nothing to complain of on the score of health. His large, dome-shaped head was carried a little on one side; his soft, flaxen hair straggled in lank locks about his slender neck. His face was not handsome, and might even have struck one as absurd, owing to the long, full, and reddish nose, which seemed almost to overhang his wide, straight mouth. But his open brow was splendid; and when he smiled, his little grey eyes gleamed with such mild and affectionate goodness, that every one felt warmed and cheered at heart at the very sight of him. I remember his voice too, soft and even, with a peculiar sort of sweet huskiness in it. He spoke, as a rule, little, and with noticeable difficulty. But when he warmed up, his words flowed freely, and--strange to say!--his voice grew still softer, his glance seemed turned inward and lost its fire, while his whole face faintly glowed. On his lips the words 'goodness,' 'truth,' 'life,' 'science,' 'love,' however enthusiastically they were uttered, never rang with a false note. Without strain, without effort, he stepped into the realm of the ideal; his pure soul was at any moment ready to stand before the 'holy shrine of beauty'; it awaited only the welcoming call, the contact of another soul.... Pasinkov was an idealist, one of the last idealists whom it has been my lot to come across. Idealists, as we all know, are all but extinct in these days; there are none of them, at any rate, among the young people of to day. So much the worse for the young people of to-day!

About three years I spent with Pasinkov, 'soul in soul,' as the saying is.

I was the confidant of his first love. With what grateful sympathy and intentness I listened to his avowal! The object of his passion was a niece of Winterkeller's, a fair-haired, pretty little German, with a chubby, almost childish little face, and confidingly soft blue eyes. She was very kind and sentimental: she loved Mattison,

Uhland, and Schiller, and repeated their verses very sweetly in her timid, musical voice. Pasinkov's love was of the most platonic. He only saw his beloved on Sundays, when she used to come and play at forfeits with the Winterkeller children, and he had very little conversation with her. But once, when she said to him, 'mein lieber, lieber Herr Jacob!' he did not sleep all night from excess of bliss. It never even struck him at the time that she called all his schoolfellows 'mein lieber.' I remember, too, his grief and dejection when the news suddenly reached us that Fraeulein Frederike--that was her name--was going to be married to Herr Kniftus, the owner of a prosperous butcher's shop, a very handsome man, and well educated too; and that she was marrying him, not simply in submission to parental authority, but positively from love. It was a bitter blow for Pasinkov, and his sufferings were particularly severe on the day of the young people's first visit. The former Fraeulein, now Frau, Frederike presented him, once more addressing him as 'lieber Herr Jacob,' to her husband, who was all splendour from top to toe; his eyes, his black hair brushed up into a tuft, his forehead and his teeth, and his coat buttons, and the chain on his waistcoat, everything, down to the boots on his rather large, turned-out feet, shone brilliantly. Pasinkov pressed Herr Kniftus's hand, and wished him (and the wish was sincere, that I am certain) complete and enduring happiness. This took place in my presence. I remember with what admiration and sympathy I gazed at Yakov. I thought him a hero!.... And afterwards, what mournful conversations passed between us. 'Seek consolation in art,' I said to him. 'Yes,' he answered me; 'and in poetry.' 'And in friendship,' I added. 'And in friendship,' he repeated. Oh, happy days!...

It was a grief to me to part from Pasinkov. Just before I left school, he had, after prolonged efforts and difficulties, after a correspondence often amusing, succeeded in obtaining his certificates of birth and baptism and his passport, and had entered the university. He still went on living at Winterkeller's expense; but instead of home-made jackets and breeches, he was provided now with ordinary attire, in return for lessons on various subjects, which he gave the younger pupils. Pasinkov was unchanged in his behaviour to me up to the end of my time at the school, though the difference in our ages began to be more noticeable, and I, I remember, grew jealous of some of his new student friends. His influence on me was most beneficial. It was a pity it did not last longer. To give a single instance: as a child I was in the habit of telling lies.... In Yakov's presence I could not bring my tongue to utter an untruth. What I particularly loved was walking alone with him, or pacing by his side up and down the room, listening while he, not looking at me, read poetry in his soft, intense voice. It positively seemed to me that we were slowly, gradually, getting away from the earth, and soaring away to some radiant, glorious land of mystery.... I remember one night. We were sitting together under the same lilac-bush; we were fond of that spot. All our companions were asleep; but we had softly got up, dressed, fumbling in the dark, and stealthily stepped out 'to dream.' It was fairly warm out of doors, but a fresh breeze blew now and then and made us huddle closer together. We talked, we talked a lot, and with much warmth--so much so, that we positively interrupted each other, though we did not argue. In the sky gleamed stars innumerable. Yakov raised his eyes, and pressing my hand he softly cried out:

'Above our heads
The sky with the eternal stars....
Above the stars their Maker....'

A thrill of awe ran through me; I felt cold all over, and sank on his shoulder.... My heart was full.... Where are those raptures? Alas! where youth is.

In Petersburg I met Yakov again eight years after. I had only just been appointed to a position in the service, and some one had got him a little post in some department. Our meeting was most joyful. I shall never forget the moment when, sitting alone one day at home, I suddenly heard his voice in the passage....

How I started; with what throbbing at the heart I leaped up and flung myself on his neck, without giving him time to take off his fur overcoat and unfasten his scarf! How greedily I gazed at him through bright, involuntary tears of tenderness! He had grown a little older during those seven years; lines, delicate as if they had been traced by a needle, furrowed his brow here and there, his cheeks were a little more hollow, and his hair was thinner; but he had hardly more beard, and his smile was just the same as ever; and his laugh, a soft, inward, as it were breathless laugh, was the same too....

Mercy on us! what didn't we talk about that day! ... The favourite poems we read to one another! I began begging him to move and come and live with me, but he would not consent. He promised, however, to come every day to see me, and he kept his word.

In soul, too, Pasinkov was unchanged. He showed himself just the same idealist as I had always known him. However rudely life's chill, the bitter chill of experience, had closed in about him, the tender flower that had bloomed so early in my friend's heart had kept all its pure beauty untouched. There was no trace of sadness even, no trace even of melancholy in him; he was quiet, as he had always been, but everlastingly glad at heart.

In Petersburg he lived as in a wilderness, not thinking of the future, and knowing scarcely any one. I took him to the Zlotnitskys'. He used to go and see them rather often. Not being self-conscious, he was not shy, but in their house, as everywhere, he said very little; they liked him, however. Even the tedious old man, Tatiana Vassilievna's husband, was friendly to him, and both the silent girls were soon quite at home with him.

Sometimes he would arrive, bringing with him in the back pocket of his coat some book that had just come out, and for a long time would not make up his mind to read, but would keep stretching his neck out on one side, like a bird, looking about him as though inquiring, 'could he?' At last he would establish himself in a corner (he always liked sitting in corners), would pull out a book and set to reading, at first in a whisper, then louder and louder, occasionally interrupting himself with brief criticisms or exclamations. I noticed that Varvara was readier to sit by him and listen than her sister, though she certainly did not understand much; literature was not in her line. She would sit opposite Pasinkov, her chin in her hands, staring at him--not into his eyes, but into his whole face--and would not utter a syllable, but only heave a noisy, sudden sigh. Sometimes in the evenings we used to play forfeits, especially on Sundays and holidays. We were joined on these occasions by two plump, short young ladies, sisters, and distant relations of the Zlotnitskys, terribly given to giggling, and a few lads from the military school, very good-natured, quiet fellows. Pasinkov always used to sit beside Tatiana Vassilievna, and with her, judge what was to be done to the one who had to pay a forfeit.

Sophia did not like the kisses and such demonstrations, with which forfeits are often paid, while Varvara used to be cross if she had to look for anything or guess something. The young ladies giggled incessantly--laughter seemed to bubble up by some magic in them,--I sometimes felt positively irritated as I looked at them, but Pasinkov only smiled and shook his head. Old Zlotnitsky took no part in our games, and even looked at us rather disapprovingly from the door of his study. Only once, utterly unexpectedly, he came in to us, and proposed that whoever had next to pay a forfeit should waltz with him; we, of course, agreed. It happened to be Tatiana Vassilievna who had to pay the forfeit. She crimsoned all over, and was confused and abashed like a girl of fifteen; but her husband at once told Sophia to go to the piano, while he went up to his wife, and waltzed two rounds with her of the old-fashioned *trois temps* waltz. I remember how his bilious, gloomy face, with its never-smiling eyes, kept appearing and disappearing as he slowly turned round, his stern expression never relaxing. He waltzed with a long step and a hop, while his wife pattered rapidly with her feet, and huddled up with her face close to his chest, as though she were in terror. He led her to her place, bowed to her, went back to his room and shut the door. Sophia was just getting up, but Varvara asked her to go on, went up to Pasinkov, and holding out her hand, with an awkward smile, said, 'Will you like a turn?' Pasinkov was surprised, but he jumped up--he was always distinguished by the most delicate courtesy--and took Varvara by the waist, but he slipped down at the first step, and leaving hold of his partner at once, rolled right under the pedestal on which the parrot's cage was standing.... The cage fell, the parrot was frightened and shrieked, 'Present arms!' Every one laughed.... Zlotnitsky appeared at his study door, looked grimly at us, and slammed the door to. From that time forth, one had only to allude to this incident before Varvara, and she would go off into peals of laughter at once, and look at Pasinkov, as though anything cleverer than his behaviour on that occasion it was impossible to conceive.

Pasinkov was very fond of music. He used often to beg Sophia to play him something, and to sit on one side listening, and now and then humming in a thin voice the most pathetic passages. He was particularly fond of Schubert's Constellation. He used to declare that when he heard the air played he could always fancy that with the sounds long rays of azure light came pouring down from on high, straight upon him. To this day, whenever I look upon a cloudless sky at night, with the softly quivering stars, I always recall Schubert's melody and Pasinkov.... An excursion into the country comes back to my mind. We set out, a whole party of us, in two hired four-wheel carriages, to Pargolovo. I remember we took the carriages from the Vladimirsky; they were very old, and painted blue, with round springs, and a wide box-seat, and bundles of hay inside; the brown, broken-winded horses that drew us along at a slow trot were each lame in a different leg. We strolled a long while about the pinewoods round Pargolovo, drank milk out of earthenware pitchers, and ate wild strawberries and sugar. The weather was exquisite. Varvara did not care for long walks: she used soon to get tired; but this time she did not lag behind us. She took off her hat, her hair came down, her heavy features lighted up, and her cheeks were flushed. Meeting two peasant girls in the wood, she sat down suddenly on the ground, called them to her, did not patronise them, but made them sit down beside her. Sophia looked at them from some distance with a cold smile, and did not go up to them. She was walking with Asanov. Zlotnitsky observed that Varvara was a regular hen for sitting. Varvara got up and walked away. In the course of the walk she several times went up to Pasinkov, and said to him, 'Yakov Ivanitch, I want to tell you something,' but what she wanted to tell him--remained unknown.

But it's high time for me to get back to my story.

*   *   *   *   *

I was glad to see Pasinkov; but when I recalled what I had done the day before, I felt unutterably ashamed, and I hurriedly turned away to the wall again. After a brief pause, Yakov asked me if I were unwell.

'I'm quite well,' I answered through my teeth; 'only my head aches.'

Yakov made no reply, and took up a book. More than an hour passed by; I was just coming to the point of confessing everything to Yakov ... suddenly there was a ring at the outer bell of my flat.

The door on to the stairs was opened.... I listened.... Asanov was asking my servant if I were at home.

Pasinkov got up; he did not care for Asanov, and telling me in a whisper that he would go and lie down on my bed, he went into my bedroom.

A minute later Asanov entered.

From the very sight of his flushed face, from his brief, cool bow, I guessed that he had not come to me without some set purpose in his mind. 'What is going to happen?' I wondered.

'Sir,' he began, quickly seating himself in an armchair, 'I have come to you for you to settle a matter of doubt for me.'

'And that is?'

'That is: I wish to know whether you are an honest man.'

I flew into a rage. 'What's the meaning of that?' I demanded.

'I'll tell you what's the meaning of it,' he retorted, underlining as it were each word. 'Yesterday I showed you a pocket-book containing letters from a certain person to me.... To-day you repeated to that person, with reproach--with reproach, observe--some expressions from those letters, without having the slightest right to do so. I should like to know what explanation you can give of this?'

'And I should like to know what right you have to cross-examine me,' I answered, trembling with fury and inward shame.

'You chose to boast of your uncle, of your correspondence; I'd nothing to do with it. You've got all your letters all right, haven't you?'

'The letters are all right; but I was yesterday in a condition in which you could easily----'

'In short, sir,' I began, speaking intentionally as loud as I could, 'I beg you to leave me alone, do you hear? I don't want to know anything about it, and I'm not going to give you any explanation. You can go to that person for explanations!' I felt that my head was beginning to go round.

Asanov turned upon me a look to which he obviously tried to impart an air of scornful penetration, pulled his moustaches, and got up slowly.

'I know now what to think,' he observed; 'your face is the best evidence against you. But I must tell you that that's not the way honourable people behave.... To read a letter on the sly, and then to go and worry an honourable girl....'

'Will you go to the devil!' I shouted, stamping, 'and send me a second; I don't mean to talk to you.'

'Kindly refrain from telling me what to do,' Asanov retorted frigidly; 'but I certainly will send a second to you.'

He went away. I fell on the sofa and hid my face in my hands. Some one touched me on the shoulder; I moved my hands--before me was standing Pasinkov.

'What's this? is it true?' ... he asked me. 'You read another man's letter?'

I had not the strength to answer, but I nodded in assent.

Pasinkov went to the window, and standing with his back to me, said slowly: 'You read a letter from a girl to Asanov. Who was the girl?'

'Sophia Zlotnitsky,' I answered, as a prisoner on his trial answers the judge.

For a long while Pasinkov did not utter a word.

'Nothing but passion could to some extent excuse you,' he began at last. 'Are you in love then with the younger Zlotnitsky?'

'Yes.'

Pasinkov was silent again for a little.

'I thought so. And you went to her to-day and began reproaching her?...'

'Yes, yes, yes!...' I articulated desperately. 'Now you can despise me....'

Pasinkov walked a couple of times up and down the room.

'And she loves him?' he queried.

'She loves him....'

Pasinkov looked down, and gazed a long while at the floor without moving.

'Well, it must be set right,' he began, raising his head,' things can't be left like this.'

And he took up his hat.

'Where are you going?'

'To Asanov.'

I jumped up from the sofa.

'But I won't let you. Good heavens! how can you! what will he think?'

Pasinkov looked at me.

'Why, do you think it better to keep this folly up, to bring ruin on yourself, and disgrace on the girl?'

'But what are you going to say to Asanov?'

'I'll try and explain things to him, I'll tell him you beg his forgiveness ...'

'But I don't want to apologise to him!'

'You don't? Why, aren't you in fault?'

I looked at Pasinkov; the calm and severe, though mournful, expression of his face impressed me; it was new to me. I made no reply, and sat down on the sofa.

Pasinkov went out.

In what agonies of suspense I waited for his return! With what cruel slowness the time lingered by! At last he came back--late.

'Well?' I queried in a timid voice.

'Thank goodness!' he answered; 'it's all settled.'

'You have been at Asanov's?'

'Yes.'

'Well, and he?--made a great to-do, I suppose?' I articulated with an effort.

'No, I can't say that. I expected more ... He ... he's not such a vulgar fellow as I thought.'

'Well, and have you seen any one else besides?' I asked, after a brief pause.

'I've been at the Zlotnitskys'.'

'Ah!...' (My heart began to throb. I did not dare look Pasinkov in the face.) 'Well, and she?'

'Sophia Nikolaevna is a reasonable, kind-hearted girl.... Yes, she is a kind-hearted girl. She felt awkward at first, but she was soon at ease. But our whole conversation only lasted five minutes.'

'And you ... told her everything ... about me ... everything?'

'I told her what was necessary.'

'I shall never be able to go and see them again now!' I pronounced dejectedly....

'Why? No, you can go occasionally. On the contrary, you are absolutely bound to go and see them, so that nothing should be thought....'

'Ah, Yakov, you will despise me now!' I cried, hardly keeping back my tears.

'Me! Despise you? ...' (His affectionate eyes glowed with love.) 'Despise you ... silly fellow! Don't I see how hard it's been for you, how you're suffering?'

He held out his hand to me; I fell on his neck and broke into sobs.

After a few days, during which I noticed that Pasinkov was in very low spirits, I made up my mind at last to go to the Zlotnitskys'. What I felt, as I stepped into their drawing-room, it would be difficult to convey in words; I remember that I could hardly distinguish the persons in the room, and my voice failed me. Sophia was no less ill at ease; she obviously forced herself to address me, but her eyes avoided mine as mine did hers, and every movement she made, her whole being, expressed constraint, mingled ... why conceal the truth? with secret aversion. I tried, as far as possible, to spare her and myself from such painful sensations. This meeting was happily our last--before her marriage. A sudden change in my fortunes carried me off to the other end of Russia, and I bade a long farewell to Petersburg, to the Zlotnitsky family, and, what was most grievous of all for me, to dear Yakov Pasinkov.

II

Seven years had passed by. I don't think it necessary to relate all that happened to me during that period. I moved restlessly about over Russia, and made my way into the remotest wilds, and thank God I did! The wilds are not so much to be dreaded as some people suppose, and in the most hidden places, under the fallen twigs and rotting leaves in the very heart of the forest, spring up flowers of sweet fragrance.

One day in spring, as I was passing on some official duties through a small town in one of the outlying provinces of Eastern Russia, through the dim little window of my coach I saw standing before a shop in the square a man whose face struck me as exceedingly familiar. I looked attentively at the man, and to my great delight recognised him as Elisei, Pasinkov's servant.

I at once told the driver to stop, jumped out of the coach, and went up to Elisei.

'Hullo, friend!' I began, with difficulty concealing my excitement; 'are you here with your master?'

'Yes, I'm with my master,' he responded slowly, and then suddenly cried out: 'Why, sir, is it you? I didn't know you.'

'Are you here with Yakov Ivanitch?'

'Yes, sir, with him, to be sure ... whom else would I be with?'

'Take me to him quickly.'

'To be sure! to be sure! This way, please, this way ... we're stopping here at the tavern.' Elisei led me across the square, incessantly repeating--'Well, now, won't Yakov Ivanitch be pleased!'

This man, of Kalmuck extraction, and hideous, even savage appearance, but the kindest-hearted creature and by no means a fool, was passionately devoted to

Pasinkov, and had been his servant for ten years.

'Is Yakov Ivanitch quite well?' I asked him.

Elisei turned his dusky, yellow little face to me.

'Ah, sir, he's in a poor way ... in a poor way, sir! You won't know his honour.... He's not long for this world, I'm afraid. That's how it is we've stopped here, or we had been going on to Odessa for his health.'

'Where do you come from?'

'From Siberia, sir.'

'From Siberia?'

'Yes, sir. Yakov Ivanitch was sent to a post out there. It was there his honour got his wound.'

'Do you mean to say he went into the military service?'

'Oh no, sir. He served in the civil service.'

'What a strange thing!' I thought.

Meanwhile we had reached the tavern, and Elisei ran on in front to announce me. During the first years of our separation, Pasinkov and I had written to each other pretty often, but his last letter had reached me four years before, and since then I had heard nothing of him.

'Please come up, sir!' Elisei shouted to me from the staircase; 'Yakov Ivanitch is very anxious to see you.'

I ran hurriedly up the tottering stairs, went into a dark little room--and my heart sank.... On a narrow bed, under a fur cloak, pale as a corpse, lay Pasinkov, and he was stretching out to me a bare, wasted hand. I rushed up to him and embraced him passionately.

'Yasha!' I cried at last; 'what's wrong with you?'

'Nothing,' he answered in a faint voice; 'I'm a bit feeble. What chance brought you here?'

I sat down on a chair beside Pasinkov's bed, and, never letting his hands out of my hands, I began gazing into his face. I recognised the features I loved; the expression of the eyes and the smile were unchanged; but what a wreck illness had made of him!

He noticed the impression he was making on me.

'It's three days since I shaved,' he observed; 'and, to be sure, I've not been combed and brushed, but except for that ... I'm not so bad.'

'Tell me, please, Yasha,' I began; 'what's this Elisei's been telling me ... you were wounded?'

'Ah! yes, it's quite a history,' he replied. 'I'll tell you it later. Yes, I was wounded, and only fancy what by?--an arrow.'

'An arrow?'

'Yes, an arrow; only not a mythological one, not Cupid's arrow, but a real arrow of very flexible wood, with a sharply-pointed tip at one end.... A very unpleasant sensation is produced by such an arrow, especially when it sticks in one's lungs.'

'But however did it come about? upon my word!...'

'I'll tell you how it happened. You know there always was a great deal of the absurd in my life. Do you remember my comical correspondence about getting my passport? Well, I was wounded in an absurd fashion too. And if you come to think of it, what self-respecting person in our enlightened century would permit himself to be wounded by an arrow? And not accidentally--observe--not at sports of any sort, but in a battle.'

'But you still don't tell me ...'

'All right, wait a minute,' he interrupted. 'You know that soon after you left Petersburg I was transferred to Novgorod. I was a good time at Novgorod, and I must own I was bored there, though even there I came across one creature....' (He sighed.) ... 'But no matter about that now; two years ago I got a capital little berth, some way off, it's true, in the Irkutsk province, but what of that! It seems as though my father and I were destined from birth to visit Siberia. A splendid country, Siberia! Rich, fertile--every one will tell you the same. I liked it very much there. The natives were put under my rule; they're a harmless lot of people; but as my ill-luck would have it, they took it into their heads, a dozen of them, not more, to smuggle in contraband goods. I was sent to arrest them. Arrest them I did, but one of them, crazy he must have been, thought fit to defend himself, and treated me to the arrow.... I almost died of it; however, I got all right again. Now, here I am going to get completely cured.... The government--God give them all good health!--have provided the cash.'

Pasinkov let his head fall back on the pillow, exhausted, and ceased speaking. A faint flush suffused his cheeks. He closed his eyes.

'He can't talk much,' Elisei, who had not left the room, murmured in an undertone.

A silence followed; nothing was heard but the sick man's painful breathing.

'But here,' he went on, opening his eyes, 'I've been stopping a fortnight in this little town.... I caught cold, I suppose. The district doctor here is attending me--you'll see him; he seems to know his business. I'm awfully glad it happened so, though, or how should we have met?' (And he took my hand. His hand, which had just before been cold as ice, was now burning hot.) 'Tell me something about yourself,' he began again, throwing the cloak back off his chest. 'You and I haven't seen each other since God knows when.'

I hastened to carry out his wish, so as not to let him talk, and started giving an account of myself. He listened to me at first with great attention, then asked for drink, and then began closing his eyes again and turning his head restlessly on the pillow. I advised him to have a little nap, adding that I should not go on further till he was well again, and that I should establish myself in a room beside him. 'It's very nasty here ...' Pasinkov was beginning, but I stopped his mouth, and went softly out. Elisei followed me.

'What is it, Elisei? Why, he's dying, isn't he?' I questioned the faithful servant.

Elisei simply made a gesture with his hand, and turned away.

Having dismissed my driver, and rapidly moved my things into the next room, I went to see whether Pasinkov was asleep. At the door I ran up against a tall man, very fat and heavily built. His face, pock-marked and puffy, expressed laziness--and nothing else; his tiny little eyes seemed, as it were, glued up, and his lips looked polished, as though he were just awake.

'Allow me to ask,' I questioned him, 'are you not the doctor?'

The fat man looked at me, seeming with an effort to lift his overhanging forehead with his eyebrows.

'Yes, sir,' he responded at last.

'Do me the favour, Mr. Doctor, won't you, please, to come this way into my room? Yakov Ivanitch, is, I believe, now asleep. I am a friend of his and should like to have a little talk with you about his illness, which makes me very uneasy.'

'Very good,' answered the doctor, with an expression which seemed to try and say, 'Why talk so much? I'd have come anyway,' and he followed me.

'Tell me, please,' I began, as soon as he had dropped into a chair, 'is my friend's condition serious? What do you think?'

'Yes,' answered the fat man, tranquilly.

'And...is it very serious?'

'Yes, it's serious.'

'So that he may...even die?'

'He may.'

I confess I looked almost with hatred at the fat man.

'Good heavens!' I began; 'we must take some steps, call a consultation, or something. You know we can't...Mercy on us!'

'A consultation?--quite possible; why not? It's possible. Call in Ivan Efremitch....'

The doctor spoke with difficulty, and sighed continually. His stomach heaved perceptibly when he spoke, as it were emphasising each word.

'Who is Ivan Efremitch?'

'The parish doctor.'

'Shouldn't we send to the chief town of the province? What do you think? There are sure to be good doctors there.'

'Well! you might.'

'And who is considered the best doctor there?'

'The best? There was a doctor Kolrabus there ... only I fancy he's been transferred somewhere else. Though I must own there's no need really to send.'

'Why so?'

'Even the best doctor will be of no use to your friend.'

'Why, is he so bad?'

'Yes, he's run down.' 'In what way precisely is he ill?'

'He received a wound.... The lungs were affected in consequence ... and then he's taken cold too, and fever was set up ... and so on. And there's no reserve force; a man can't get on, you know yourself, with no reserve force.'

We were both silent for a while.

'How about trying homoeopathy?...' said the fat man, with a sidelong glance at me.

'Homoeopathy? Why, you're an allopath, aren't you?'

'What of that? Do you think I don't understand homoeopathy? I understand it as well as the other! Why, the chemist here among us treats people homeopathically, and he has no learned degree whatever.'

'Oh,' I thought, 'it's a bad look-out!...'

'No, doctor,' I observed, 'you had better treat him according to your usual method.'

'As you please.'

The fat man got up and heaved a sigh.

'You are going to him?' I asked.

'Yes, I must have a look at him.'

And he went out.

I did not follow him; to see him at the bedside of my poor, sick friend was more than I could stand. I called my man and gave him orders to drive at once to the chief town of the province, to inquire there for the best doctor, and to bring him without fail. There was a slight noise in the passage. I opened the door quickly.

The doctor was already coming out of Pasinkov's room.

'Well?' I questioned him in a whisper.

'It's all right. I have prescribed a mixture.'

'I have decided, doctor, to send to the chief town. I have no doubt of your skill, but as you're aware, two heads are better than one.'

'Well, that's very praiseworthy!' responded the fat man, and he began to descend the staircase. He was obviously tired of me.

I went in to Pasinkov.

'Have you seen the local Aesculapius?' he asked.

'Yes,' I answered.

'What I like about him,' remarked Pasinkov, 'is his astounding composure. A doctor ought to be phlegmatic, oughtn't he? It's so encouraging for the patient.'

I did not, of course, try to controvert this.

Towards the evening, Pasinkov, contrary to my expectations, seemed better. He asked Elisei to set the samovar, announced that he was going to regale me with tea, and drink a small cup himself, and he was noticeably more cheerful. I tried, though, not to let him talk, and seeing that he would not be quiet, I asked him if he would like me to read him something. 'Just as at Winterkeller's--do you remember?' he answered. 'If you will, I shall be delighted. What shall we read? Look, there are my books in the window.'...

I went to the window and took up the first book that my hand chanced upon....

'What is it?' he asked.

'Lermontov.'

'Ah, Lermontov! Excellent! Pushkin is greater, no doubt.... Do you remember: "Once more the storm-clouds gather close Above me in the perfect calm" ... or, "For the last time thy image sweet In thought I dare caress." Ah! marvellous! marvellous! But Lermontov's fine too. Well, I'll tell you what, dear boy: you take the book, open it by chance, and read what you find!'

I opened the book, and was disconcerted; I had chanced upon 'The Last Will.' I tried to turn over the page, but Pasinkov noticed my action and said hurriedly: 'No, no, no, read what turned up.'

There was no getting out of it; I read 'The Last Will.'[2]

2   THE LAST WILL

> Alone with thee, brother,
> I would wish to be;
> On earth, so they tell me,
> I have not long to stay,
> Soon you will go home:
> See that ... But nay! for my fate
> To speak the truth, no one
> Is very greatly troubled.
>
> But if any one asks ...
>
> Well, whoever may ask,
> Tell them that through the breast
> I was shot by a bullet;
> That I died honourably for the Tsar,
> That our doctors are not much good,
> And that to my native land
> I send a humble greeting.

'Splendid thing!' said Pasinkov, directly I had finished the last verse. 'Splendid thing!

But, it's queer,' he added, after a brief pause, 'it's queer you should have chanced just on that.... Queer.'

I began to read another poem, but Pasinkov was not listening to me; he looked away, and twice he repeated again: 'Queer!'

I let the book drop on my knees.

'"There is a girl, their neighbour,"' he whispered, and turning to me he asked--'I say, do you remember Sophia Zlotnitsky?'

I turned red.

'I should think I did!'

'She was married, I suppose?...'

'To Asanov, long, long ago. I wrote to you about it.'

*   *   *   *   *

But if either of them is living,
Say I am lazy about writing,
That our regiment has been sent forward,
And that they must not expect me home.

There is a girl, their neighbour....
As you remember, it's long
Since we parted.... She will not
Ask for me.... All the same,
You tell her all the truth,
Don't spare her empty heart--
Let her weep a little....
It will not hurt her much!

My father and mother, hardly
Will you find living....
I'll own I should be sorry
That they should grieve for me.

'To be sure, to be sure, so you did. Did her father forgive her in the end?'

'He forgave her; but he would not receive Asanov.'

'Obstinate old fellow! Well, and are they supposed to be happy?'

'I don't know, really...I fancy they 're happy. They live in the country, in ----province. I've never seen them, though I have been through their parts.'

'And have they any children?'

'I think so.... By the way, Pasinkov?...' I began questioningly.

He glanced at me.

'Confess--do you remember, you were unwilling to answer my question at the time--did you tell her I cared for her?'

'I told her everything, the whole truth.... I always told her the truth. To be hypocritical with her would have been a sin!'

Pasinkov was silent for a while.

'Come, tell me,' he began again: 'did you soon get over caring for her, or not?'

'Not very soon, but I got over it. What's the good of sighing in vain?'

Pasinkov turned over, facing me.

'Well, I, brother,' he began--and his lips were quivering--'am no match for you there; I've not got over caring for her to this day.'

'What!' I cried in indescribable amazement; 'did you love her?'

'I loved her,' said Pasinkov slowly, and he put both hands behind his head. 'How I loved her, God only knows. I've never spoken of it to any one, to any one in the world, and I never meant to ... but there! "On earth, so they tell me, I have not long to stay." ... What does it matter?'

Pasinkov's unexpected avowal so utterly astonished me that I could positively say nothing. I could only wonder, 'Is it possible? how was it I never suspected it?'

'Yes,' he went on, as though speaking to himself, 'I loved her. I never ceased to love her even when I knew her heart was Asanov's. But how bitter it was for me to know that! If she had loved you, I should at least have rejoiced for you; but Asanov.... How did he make her care for him? It was just his luck! And change her feelings, cease to care, she could not! A true heart does not change....'

I recalled Asanov's visit after the fatal dinner, Pasinkov's intervention, and I could not help flinging up my hands in astonishment.

'You learnt it all from me, poor fellow!' I cried; 'and you undertook to go and see her then!'

'Yes,' Pasinkov began again; 'that explanation with her ... I shall never forget it.' It was then I found out, then I realised the meaning of the word I had chosen for myself long before: resignation. But still she has remained my constant dream, my ideal.... And he's to be pitied who lives without an ideal!'

I looked at Pasinkov; his eyes, fastened, as it were, on the distance, shone with feverish brilliance.

'I loved her,' he went on, 'I loved her, her, calm, true, unapproachable, incorruptible; when she went away, I was almost mad with grief.... Since then I have never cared for any one.'...

And suddenly turning, he pressed his face into the pillow, and began quietly weeping.

I jumped up, bent over him, and began trying to comfort him....

'It's no matter,' he said, raising his head and shaking back his hair; 'it's nothing; I felt a little bitter, a little sorry ... for myself, that is.... But it's all no matter. It's all the fault of those verses. Read me something else, more cheerful.'

I took up Lermontov and began hurriedly turning over the pages; but, as fate would have it, I kept coming across poems likely to agitate Pasinkov again. At last I read him 'The Gifts of Terek.'

'Jingling rhetoric!' said my poor friend, with the tone of a preceptor; 'but there are fine passages. Since I saw you, brother, I've tried my hand at poetry, and began one poem--"The Cup of Life"--but it didn't come off! It's for us, brother, to appreciate, not to create.... But I'm rather tired; I'll sleep a little--what do you say? What a splendid thing sleep is, come to think of it! All our life's a dream, and the best thing in it is dreaming too.'

'And poetry?' I queried.

'Poetry's a dream too, but a dream of paradise.'

Pasinkov closed his eyes.

I stood for a little while at his bedside. I did not think he would get to sleep quickly, but soon his breathing became more even and prolonged. I went away on tiptoe, turned into my own room, and lay down on the sofa. For a long while I mused on what Pasinkov had told me, recalled many things, wondered; at last I too fell asleep....

Some one touched me; I started up; before me stood Elisei.

'Come in to my master,' he said.

I got up at once.

'What's the matter with him?'

'He's delirious.'

'Delirious? And hasn't it ever been so before with him?'

'Yes, he was delirious last night, too; only to-day it is something terrible.'

I went to Pasinkov's room. He was not lying down, but sitting up in bed, his whole body bent forward. He was slowly gesticulating with his hands, smiling and talking, talking all the time in a weak, hollow voice, like the whispering of rushes. His eyes were wandering. The gloomy light of a night light, set on the floor, and shaded off by a book, lay, an unmoving patch on the ceiling; Pasinkov's face seemed paler than ever in the half darkness.

I went up to him, called him by his name--he did not answer. I began listening to his whispering: he was talking of Siberia, of its forests. From time to time there was sense in his ravings.

'What trees!' he whispered; 'right up to the sky. What frost on them! Silver ... snowdrifts.... And here are little tracks ... that's a hare's leaping, that's a white weasel... No, it's my father running with my papers. Here he is!... Here he is! Must go; the moon is shining. Must go, look for my papers.... Ah! A flower, a crimson flower--there's Sophia.... Oh, the bells are ringing, the frost is crackling.... Ah, no; it's the stupid bullfinches hopping in the bushes, whistling.... See, the redthroats! Cold.... Ah! here's Asanov.... Oh yes, of course, he's a cannon, a copper cannon, and his gun-carriage is green. That's how it is he's liked. Is it a star has fallen? No, it's an arrow flying.... Ah, how quickly, and straight into my heart!... Who shot it? You, Sonitchka?'

He bent his head and began muttering disconnected words. I glanced at Elisei; he was standing, his hands clasped behind his back, gazing ruefully at his master.

'Ah, brother, so you've become a practical person, eh?' he asked suddenly, turning upon me such a clear, such a fully conscious glance, that I could not help starting and was about to reply, but he went on at once: 'But I, brother, have not become a practical person, I haven't, and that's all about it! A dreamer I was born, a dreamer! Dreaming, dreaming.... What is dreaming? Sobakevitch's peasant--that's dreaming. Ugh!...'

Almost till morning Pasinkov wandered in delirium; at last he gradually grew quieter, sank back on the pillow, and dozed off. I went back into my room. Worn out by the cruel night, I slept soundly.

Elisei again waked me.

'Ah, sir!' he said in a shaking voice, 'I do believe Yakov Ivanitch is dying....'

I ran in to Pasinkov. He was lying motionless. In the light of the coming day he looked already a corpse. He recognised me.

'Good-bye,' he whispered; 'greet her for me, I'm dying....'

'Yasha!' I cried; 'nonsense! you are going to live....'

'No, no! I am dying.... Here, take this as a keepsake.' ... (He pointed to his breast.) ...

'What's this?' he began suddenly; 'look: the sea ... all golden, and blue isles upon it, marble temples, palm-trees, incense....'

He ceased speaking ... stretched....

Within half an hour he was no more. Elisei flung himself weeping at his feet. I closed his eyes.

On his neck there was a little silken amulet on a black cord. I took it.

Three days afterwards he was buried.... One of the noblest hearts was hidden for ever in the grave. I myself threw the first handful of earth upon him.

III

Another year and a half passed by. Business obliged me to visit Moscow. I took up my quarters in one of the good hotels there. One day, as I was passing along the corridor, I glanced at the black-board with the list of visitors staying in the hotel, and almost cried out aloud with astonishment. Opposite the number 12 stood, distinctly written in chalk, the name, Sophia Nikolaevna Asanova. Of late I had chanced to hear a good deal that was bad about her husband. I had learned that he was addicted to drink and to gambling, had ruined himself, and was generally misconducting himself. His wife was spoken of with respect.... In some excitement I went back to my room. The passion, that had long long ago grown cold, began as it were to stir within my heart, and it throbbed. I resolved to go and see Sophia Nikolaevna. 'Such a long time has passed since the day we parted,' I thought, 'she has, most likely, forgotten everything there was between us in those days.'

I sent Elisei, whom I had taken into my service after the death of Pasinkov, with my visiting-card to her door, and told him to inquire whether she was at home, and whether I might see her. Elisei quickly came back and announced that Sophia Nikolaevna was at home and would see me.

I went at once to Sophia Nikolaevna. When I went in, she was standing in the middle of the room, taking leave of a tall stout gentleman.

'As you like,' he was saying in a rich, mellow voice; 'he is not a harmless person, he's a useless person; and every useless person in a well-ordered society is harmful, harmful, harmful!'

With those words the tall gentleman went out. Sophia Nikolaevna turned to me.

'How long it is since we met!' she said. 'Sit down, please....'

We sat down. I looked at her.... To see again after long absence the features of a face once dear, perhaps beloved, to recognise them, and not recognise them, as though across the old, unforgotten countenance a new one, like, but strange, were looking out at one; instantaneously, almost unconsciously, to note the traces time has laid upon it;--all this is rather melancholy. 'I too must have changed in the same way,' each is inwardly thinking....

Sophia Nikolaevna did not, however, look much older; though, when I had seen her last, she was sixteen, and that was nine years ago.

Her features had become still more correct and severe; as of old, they expressed sincerity of feeling and firmness; but in place of her former serenity, a sort of secret ache and anxiety could be discerned in them. Her eyes had grown deeper and darker. She had begun to show a likeness to her mother....

Sophia Nikolaevna was the first to begin the conversation.

'We are both changed,' she began. 'Where have you been all this time?'

'I've been a rolling stone,' I answered. 'And have you been living in the country all the while?'

'For the most part I've been in the country. I'm only here now for a little time.'

'How are your parents?'

'My mother is dead, but my father is still in Petersburg; my brother's in the service; Varia lives with him.'

'And your husband?'

'My husband,' she said in a rather hurried voice--'he's just now in South Russia for the horse fairs. He was always very fond of horses, you know, and he has started stud stables ... and so, on that account ... he's buying horses now.'

At that instant there walked into the room a little girl of eight years old, with her hair in a pigtail, with a very keen and lively little face, and large dark grey eyes. On seeing me, she at once drew back her little foot, dropped a hasty curtsey, and went up to Sophia Nikolaevna.

'This is my little daughter; let me introduce her to you,' said Sophia Nikolaevna, putting one finger under the little girl's round chin; 'she would not stop at home--she persuaded me to bring her with me.'

The little girl scanned me with her rapid glance and faintly dropped her eye-lids.

'She is a capital little person,' Sophia Nikolaevna went on: 'there's nothing she's afraid of. And she's good at her lessons; I must say that for her.'

'Comment se nomme monsieur?' the little girl asked in an undertone, bending over to her mother.

Sophia Nikolaevna mentioned my name.

The little girl glanced at me again.

'What is your name?' I asked her.

'My name is Lidia,' answered the little girl, looking me boldly in the face.

'I expect they spoil you,' I observed.

'Who spoil me?'

'Who? everyone, I expect; your parents to begin with.'

(The little girl looked, without a word, at her mother.) 'I can fancy Konstantin Alexandritch,' I was going on ...

'Yes, yes,' Sophia Nikolaevna interposed, while her little daughter kept her attentive eyes fastened upon her; 'my husband, of course--he is very fond of children....'

A strange expression flitted across Lidia's clever little face. There was a slight pout about her lips; she hung her head.

'Tell me,' Sophia Nikolaevna added hurriedly; 'you are here on business, I expect?'

'Yes, I am here on business.... And are you too?'

'Yes.... In my husband's absence, you understand, I'm obliged to look after business matters.'

'Maman!' Lidia was beginning.

'Quoi, mon enfant?'

'Non--rien.... Je te dirai apres.'

Sophia Nikolaevna smiled and shrugged her shoulders.

'Tell me, please,' Sophia Nikolaevna began again; 'do you remember, you had a friend ... what was his name? he had such a good-natured face ... he was always reading poetry; such an enthusiastic--'

'Not Pasinkov?'

'Yes, yes, Pasinkov ... where is he now?'

'He is dead.'

'Dead?' repeated Sophia Nikolaevna; 'what a pity!...'

'Have I seen him?' the little girl asked in a hurried whisper.

'No, Lidia, you've never seen him.--What a pity!' repeated Sophia Nikolaevna.

'You regret him ...' I began; 'what if you had known him, as I knew him?... But, why did you speak of him, may I ask?'

'Oh, I don't know....' (Sophia Nikolaevna dropped her eyes.) 'Lidia,' she added; 'run away to your nurse.'

'You'll call me when I may come back?' asked the little girl.

'Yes.'

The little girl went away. Sophia Nikolaevna turned to me.

'Tell me, please, all you know about Pasinkov.' I began telling her his story. I sketched in brief words the whole life of my friend; tried, as far as I was able, to give an idea of his soul; described his last meeting with me and his end.

'And a man like that,' I cried, as I finished my story--'has left us, unnoticed, almost unappreciated! But that's no great loss. What is the use of man's appreciation? What pains me, what wounds me, is that such a man, with such a loving and devoted heart, is dead without having once known the bliss of love returned, without having awakened interest in one woman's heart worthy of him!... Such as I may well know nothing of such happiness; we don't deserve it; but Pasinkov!... And yet haven't I met thousands of men in my life, who could not compare with him in any respect, who were loved? Must one believe that some faults in a man--conceit, for instance, or frivolity--are essential to gain a woman's devotion? Or does love fear perfection, the perfection possible on earth, as something strange and terrible?'

Sophia Nikolaevna heard me to the end, without taking her stern, searching eyes off me, without moving her lips; only her eyebrows contracted from time to time.

'What makes you suppose,' she observed after a brief silence, 'that no woman ever loved your friend?'

'Because I know it, know it for a fact.'

Sophia Nikolaevna seemed about to say something, but she stopped. She seemed to be struggling with herself.

'You are mistaken,' she began at last; 'I know a woman who loved your dead friend passionately; she loves him and remembers him to this day ... and the news of his death will be a fearful blow for her.'

'Who is this woman? may I know?'

'My sister, Varia.'

'Varvara Nikolaevna!' I cried in amazement.

'Yes.'

'What? Varvara Nikolaevna?' I repeated, 'that...'

'I will finish your sentence,' Sophia Nikolaevna took me up; 'that girl you thought so cold, so listless and indifferent, loved your friend; that is why she has never married and never will marry. Till this day no one has known of this but me; Varia would die before she would betray her secret. In our family we know how to suffer in silence.'

I looked long and intently at Sophia Nikolaevna, involuntarily pondering on the bitter significance of her last words.

'You have surprised me,' I observed at last. 'But do you know, Sophia Niko-laevna, if I were not afraid of recalling disagreeable memories, I might surprise you too....'

'I don't understand you,' she rejoined slowly, and with some embarrassment.

'You certainly don't understand me,' I said, hastily getting up; 'and so allow me, instead of verbal explanation, to send you something ...'

'But what is it?' she inquired.

'Don't be alarmed, Sophia Nikolaevna, it's nothing to do with me.'

I bowed, and went back to my room, took out the little silken bag I had taken off Pasinkov, and sent it to Sophia Nikolaevna with the following note--

'This my friend wore always on his breast and died with it on him. In it is the only note you ever wrote him, quite insignificant in its contents; you can read it. He wore it because he loved you passionately; he confessed it to me only the day before his death. Now, when he is dead, why should you not know that his heart too was yours?'

Elisei returned quickly and brought me back the relic.

'Well?' I queried; 'didn't she send any message?'

'No.'

I was silent for a little.

'Did she read my note?'

'No doubt she did; the maid took it to her.'

'Unapproachable,' I thought, remembering Pasinkov's last words. 'All right, you can go,' I said aloud.

Elisei smiled somewhat queerly and did not go.

'There's a girl ...' he began, 'here to see you.'

'What girl?'

Elisei hesitated.

'Didn't my master say anything to you?'

'No.... What is it?'

'When my master was in Novgorod,' he went on, fingering the door-post, 'he made acquaintance, so to say, with a girl. So here is this girl, wants to see you. I met her the other day in the street. I said to her, "Come along; if the master allows it, I'll let you see him."'

'Ask her in, ask her in, of course. But ... what is she like?'

'An ordinary girl...working class...Russian.'

'Did Yakov Ivanitch care for her?'

'Well, yes ... he was fond of her. And she...when she heard my master was dead, she was terribly upset. She's a good sort of girl.'

'Ask her in, ask her in.'

Elisei went out and at once came back. He was followed by a girl in a striped cotton gown, with a dark kerchief on her head, that half hid her face. On seeing me, she was much taken aback and turned away.

'What's the matter?' Elisei said to her; 'go on, don't be afraid.'

I went up to her and took her by the hand.

'What is your name?' I asked her.

'Masha,' she replied in a soft voice, stealing a glance at me.

She looked about two- or three-and-twenty; she had a round, rather simple-looking, but pleasant face, soft cheeks, mild blue eyes, and very pretty and clean little hands. She was tidily dressed.

'You knew Yakov Ivanitch?' I pursued.

'I used to know him,' she said, tugging at the ends of her kerchief, and the tears stood in her eyes.

I asked her to sit down.

She sat down at once on the edge of a chair, without any affectation of ceremony. Elisei went out.

'You became acquainted with him in Novgorod?'

'Yes, in Novgorod,' she answered, clasping her hands under her kerchief. 'I only heard the day before yesterday, from Elisei Timofeitch, of his death. Yakov Ivanitch, when he went away to Siberia, promised to write to me, and twice he did write, and then he wrote no more. I would have followed him out to Siberia, but he didn't wish it.'

'Have you relations in Novgorod?'

'Yes.'

'Did you live with them?'

'I used to live with mother and my married sister; but afterwards mother was cross with me, and my sister was crowded up, too; she has a lot of children: and so I moved. I always rested my hopes on Yakov Ivanitch, and longed for nothing but to see him, and he was always good to me--you can ask Elisei Timofeitch.'

Masha paused.

'I have his letters,' she went on. 'Here, look.' She took several letters out of her pocket, and handed them to me. 'Read them,' she added.

I opened one letter and recognised Pasinkov's hand.

'Dear Masha!' (he wrote in large, distinct letters) 'you leaned your little head against my head yesterday, and when I asked why you do so, you told me--"I want to hear what you are thinking." I'll tell you what I was thinking; I was thinking how nice it would be for Masha to learn to read and write! She could make out this letter ...'

Masha glanced at the letter.

'That he wrote me in Novgorod,' she observed, 'when he was just going to teach me to read. Look at the others. There's one from Siberia. Here, read this.'

I read the letters. They were very affectionate, even tender. In one of them, the first one from Siberia, Pasinkov called Masha his best friend, promised to send her the money for the journey to Siberia, and ended with the following words--'I kiss your pretty little hands; the girls here have not hands like yours; and their heads are no match for yours, nor their hearts either.... Read the books I gave you, and think of me, and I'll not forget you. You are the only, only girl that ever cared for me; and so I want to belong only to you....'

'I see he was very much attached to you,' I said, giving the letters back to her.

'He was very fond of me,' replied Masha, putting the letters carefully into her pocket, and the tears flowed slowly down her cheeks. 'I always trusted in him; if the Lord had vouchsafed him long life, he would not have abandoned me. God grant him His heavenly peace!'...

She wiped her eyes with a corner of her kerchief.

'Where are you living now?' I inquired.

'I'm here now, in Moscow; I came here with my mistress, but now I'm out of a place. I did go to Yakov Ivanitch's aunt, but she is very poor herself. Yakov Ivanitch used often to talk of you,' she added, getting up and bowing; 'he always loved you and thought of you. I met Elisei Timofeitch the day before yesterday, and wondered whether you wouldn't be willing to assist me, as I'm out of a place just now....'

'With the greatest pleasure, Maria ... let me ask, what's your name from your father?'

'Petrovna,' answered Masha, and she cast down her eyes.

'I will do anything for you I can, Maria Petrovna,' I continued; 'I am only sorry that I am a visitor here, and know few good families.'

Masha sighed.

'If I could get a situation of some sort ... I can't cut out, but I can sew, so I'm always doing sewing ... and I can look after children too.'

'Give her money,' I thought; 'but how's one to do it?'

'Listen, Maria Petrovna,' I began, not without faltering; 'you must, please, excuse me, but you know from Pasinkov's own words what a friend of his I was ... won't you allow me to offer you--for the immediate present--a small sum?' ...

Masha glanced at me.

'What?' she asked.

'Aren't you in want of money?' I said.

Masha flushed all over and hung her head.

'What do I want with money?' she murmured; 'better get me a situation.'

'I will try to get you a situation, but I can't answer for it for certain; but you ought not to make any scruple, really ... I'm not like a stranger to you, you know.... Accept this from me, in memory of our friend....'

I turned away, hurriedly pulled a few notes out of my pocket-book, and handed them to her.

Masha was standing motionless, her head still more downcast.

'Take it,' I persisted.

She slowly raised her eyes to me, looked me in the face mournfully, slowly drew her pale hand from under her kerchief and held it out to me.

I laid the notes in her cold fingers. Without a word, she hid the hand again under her kerchief, and dropped her eyes.

'In future, Maria Petrovna,' I resumed, 'if you should be in want of anything, please apply directly to me. I will give you my address.'

'I humbly thank you,' she said, and after a short pause she added: 'He did not speak to you of me?'

'I only met him the day before his death, Maria Petrovna. But I'm not sure ... I believe he did say something.'

Masha passed her hand over her hair, pressed her cheek lightly, thought a moment, and saying 'Good-bye,' walked out of the room.

I sat at the table and fell into bitter musings. This Masha, her relations with

Pasinkov, his letters, the hidden love of Sophia Nikolaevna's sister for him.... 'Poor fellow! poor fellow!' I whispered, with a catching in my breath. I thought of all Pasinkov's life, his childhood, his youth, Fraeulein Frederike.... 'Well,' I thought, 'much fate gave to thee! much cause for joy!'

Next day I went again to see Sophia Nikolaevna. I was kept waiting in the ante-room, and when I entered, Lidia was already seated by her mother. I understood that Sophia Nikolaevna did not wish to renew the conversation of the previous day.

We began to talk--I really don't remember what about--about the news of the town, public affairs.... Lidia often put in her little word, and looked slily at me. An amusing air of importance had suddenly become apparent on her mobile little visage.... The clever little girl must have guessed that her mother had intentionally stationed her at her side.

I got up and began taking leave. Sophia Nikolaevna conducted me to the door.

'I made you no answer yesterday,' she said, standing still in the doorway; 'and, indeed, what answer was there to make? Our life is not in our own hands; but we all have one anchor, from which one can never, without one's own will, be torn--a sense of duty.'

Without a word I bowed my head in sign of assent, and parted from the youthful Puritan.

All that evening I stayed at home, but I did not think of her; I kept thinking and thinking of my dear, never-to-be-forgotten Pasinkov--the last of the idealists; and emotions, mournful and tender, pierced with sweet anguish into my soul, rousing echoes on the strings of a heart not yet quite grown old.... Peace to your ashes, unpractical man, simple-hearted idealist! and God grant to all practical men--to whom you were always incomprehensible, and who, perhaps, will laugh even now over you in the grave--God grant to them to experience even a hundredth part of those pure delights in which, in spite of fate and men, your poor and unambitious life was so rich!

ANDREI KOLOSOV

In a small, decently furnished room several young men were sitting before the fire. The winter evening was only just beginning; the samovar was boiling on the table, the conversation had hardly taken a definite turn, but passed lightly from one subject to another. They began discussing exceptional people, and in what way they differed from ordinary people. Every one expounded his views to the best of his abilities; they raised their voices and began to be noisy. A small, pale man, after listening long to the disquisitions of his companions, sipping tea and smoking a cigar the while, suddenly got up and addressed us all (I was one of the disputants) in the following words:--

'Gentlemen! all your profound remarks are excellent in their own way, but unprofitable.

Every one, as usual, hears his opponent's views, and every one retains his own convictions. But it's not the first time we have met, nor the first time we have argued, and so we have probably by now had ample opportunity for expressing our own views and learning those of others. Why, then, do you take so much trouble?'

Uttering these words, the small man carelessly flicked the ash off his cigar into the fireplace, dropped his eyelids, and smiled serenely. We all ceased speaking.

'Well, what are we to do then, according to you?' said one of us; 'play cards, or what? go to sleep? break up and go home?'

'Playing cards is agreeable, and sleep's always salutary,' retorted the small man; 'but it's early yet to break up and go home. You didn't understand me, though. Listen: I propose, if it comes to that, that each of you should describe some exceptional personality, tell us of any meeting you may have had with any remarkable man. I can assure you even the feeblest description has far more sense in it than the finest argument.'

We pondered.

'It's a strange thing,' observed one of us, an inveterate jester; 'except myself I don't know a single exceptional person, and with my life you are all, I fancy, familiar already. However, if you insist--'

'No!' cried another, 'we don't! But, I tell you what,' he added, addressing the small man, 'you begin. You have put a stopper on all of us, you're the person to fill the gap. Only mind, if we don't care for your story, we shall hiss you.'

'If you like,' answered the small man. He stood close to the fire; we sat round him and kept quiet. The small man looked at all of us, glanced at the ceiling, and began as follows:--

'Ten years ago, my dear friends, I was a student at Moscow. My father, a virtuous landowner of the steppes, had handed me over to a retired German professor, who, for a hundred roubles a month, undertook to lodge and board me, and to watch over my morals. This German was the fortunate possessor of an exceedingly solemn and decorous manner; at first I went in considerable awe of him. But on returning home one evening, I saw, with indescribable emotion, my preceptor sitting with three or four companions at a round table, on which there stood a fair-sized collection of empty bottles and half-full glasses. On seeing me, my revered preceptor got up, and, waving his arms and stammering, presented me to the honourable company, who all promptly offered me a glass of punch. This agreeable spectacle had a most illuminating effect on my intelligence; my future rose before me in the most seductive images. And, as a fact, from that memorable day I enjoyed unbounded freedom, and all but worried my preceptor to death. He had a wife who always smelt of smoke and pickled cucumbers; she was still youngish, but had not a single front tooth in her head. All German women, as we know, very quickly lose those indispensable ornaments of the human frame. I mention her, solely because she fell passionately in love with me and fed me almost into my grave.'

'To the point, to the point,' we shouted. 'Surely it's not your own adventures you're going to tell us?'

'No, gentlemen!' the small man replied composedly. 'I am an ordinary mortal. And so I lived at my German's, as the saying is, in clover. I did not attend lectures with too much assiduity, while at home I did positively nothing. In a very short time, I had got to know all my comrades and was on intimate terms with all of them.

Among my new friends was one rather decent and good-natured fellow, the son of a town provost on the retired list. His name was Bobov. This Bobov got in the habit of coming to see me, and seemed to like me. I, too ... do you know, I didn't like him, nor dislike him; I was more or less indifferent.... I must tell I hadn't in all Moscow a single relation, except an old uncle, who used sometimes to ask me for money. I never went anywhere, and was particularly afraid of women; I also avoided all acquaintance with the parents of my college friends, ever after one such parent (in my presence) pulled his son's hair--because a button was off his uniform, while at the very time I hadn't more than six buttons on my whole coat. In comparison with many of my comrades, I passed for being a person of wealth; my father used to send me every now and then small packets of faded blue notes, and consequently I not only enjoyed a position of independence, but I was continually surrounded by toadies and flatterers.... What am I saying?--why, for that matter, so was my bobtail dog Armishka, who, in spite of his setter pedigree, was so frightened of a shot, that the very sight of a gun reduced him to indescribable misery. Like every young man, however, I was not without that vague inward fermentation which usually, after bringing forth a dozen more or less shapeless poems, passes off in a peaceful and propitious manner. I wanted something, strove towards something, and dreamed of something; I'll own I didn't know precisely what it was I dreamed of. Now I understand what was lacking:--I felt my loneliness, thirsted for the society of so-called live people; the word Life waked echoes in my heart, and with a vague ache I listened to the sound of it.... Valerian Nikitich, pass me a cigarette.'

Lighting the cigarette, the small man continued:

'One fine morning Bobov came running to me, out of breath: "Do you know, old man, the great news? Kolosov has arrived." "Kolosov? and who on earth is Mr. Kolosov?"

'"You don't know him? Andriusha Kolosov! Come, old boy, let's go to him directly. He came back last night from a holiday engagement." "But what sort of fellow is he?" "An exceptional man, my boy, let me assure you!" "An exceptional man," I answered; "then you go alone. I'll stop at home. I know your exceptional men! A half-tipsy rhymester with an everlastingly ecstatic smile!" ... "Oh no! Kolosov's not like that." I was on the point of observing that it was for Mr. Kolosov to call on me; but, I don't know why, I obeyed Bobov and went. Bobov conducted me to one of the very dirtiest, crookedest, and narrowest streets in Moscow.... The house in which Kolosov lodged was built in the old-fashioned style, rambling and uncomfortable. We went into the courtyard; a fat peasant woman was hanging out clothes on a line stretched from the house to the fence.... Children were squalling on the wooden staircase...'

'Get on! get on!' we objected plaintively.

'I see, gentlemen, you don't care for the agreeable, and cling solely to the profitable. As you please! We groped our way through a dark and narrow passage to Kolosov's room; we went in. You have most likely an approximate idea of what a poor student's room is like. Directly facing the door Kolosov was sitting on a chest of drawers, smoking a pipe. He gave his hand to Bobov in a friendly way, and greeted me affably. I looked at Kolosov and at once felt irresistibly drawn to him. Gentlemen! Bobov was right: Kolosov really was a remarkable person. Let me describe a little more in detail.... He was rather tall, slender, graceful, and exceedingly goodlooking. His face...I find it very difficult to describe his face. It is easy to describe all the features one by one; but how is one to convey to any one else what constitutes the distinguishing characteristic, the essence of just *that* face?'

'What Byron calls "the music of the face,"' observed a tightly buttoned-up, pallid gentleman.

'Quite so.... And therefore I will confine myself to a single remark: the especial "something" to which I have just referred consisted in Kolosov's case in a carelessly gay and fearless expression of face, and also in an exceedingly captivating smile. He did not remember his parents, and had had a wretched bringing-up in the house of a distant relative, who had been degraded from the service for taking bribes. Up to the age of fifteen, he had lived in the country; then he found his way into Moscow, and after two years spent in the care of an old deaf priest's wife, he entered the university and began to get his living by lessons. He gave instruction in history, geography, and Russian grammar, though he had only a dim notion of these branches of science; but in the first place, there is an abundance of 'textbooks' among us in Russia, of the greatest usefulness to teachers; and secondly, the requirements of the respectable merchants, who confided their children's education to Kolosov, were exceedingly limited. Kolosov was neither a wit nor a humorist; but you cannot imagine how readily we all fell under that fellow's sway. We felt a sort of instinctive admiration of him; his words, his looks, his gestures were all so full of the charm of youth that all his comrades were head over ears in love with him. The professors considered him as a fairly intelligent lad, but 'of no marked abilities,' and lazy.

Kolosov's presence gave a special harmony to our evening reunions. Before him, our liveliness never passed into vulgar riotousness; if we were all melancholy--this half childlike melancholy, in his presence, led on to quiet, sometimes fairly sensible, conversation, and never ended in dejected boredom. You are smiling, gentlemen--I understand your smile; no doubt, many of us since then have turned out pretty cads! But youth ... youth....'

'Oh, talk not to me of a name great in story!
The days of our youth are the days of our glory....'

commented the same pallid gentleman.
'By Jove, what a memory he's got! and all from Byron!' observed the storyteller. 'In one word, Kolosov was the soul of our set. I was attached to him by a feeling stronger than any I have ever felt for any woman. And yet, I don't feel ashamed even now to remember that strange love--yes, love it was, for I recollect I went through at that time all the tortures of that passion, jealousy, for instance. Kolosov liked us all equally, but was particularly friendly with a silent, flaxen-haired, and unobtrusive youth, called Gavrilov. From Gavrilov he was almost inseparable; he would often speak to him in a whisper, and used to disappear with him out of Moscow, no one knew where, for two or three days at a time.... Kolosov did not care to be questioned, and I was lost in surmises. It was not simple curiosity that disturbed me. I longed to become the friend, the attendant squire of Kolosov; I was jealous of Gavrilov; I envied him; I could never find an explanation to satisfy me of Kolosov's strange absences. Meanwhile he had none of that air of mysteriousness about him, which is the proud possession of youths endowed with vanity, pallor, black hair, and 'expressive' eyes, nor had he anything of that studied carelessness under which we are given to understand that vast forces are slumbering; no, he was quite open and free; but when he was possessed by passion, an intense, impulsive energy was apparent in everything about him; only he did not waste his energies in vain, and

never under any circumstances became high-flown or affected. By the way ... tell me the truth, hasn't it happened to you to sit smoking a pipe with an air of as weary solemnity as if you had just resolved on a grand achievement, while you were simply pondering on what colour to choose for your next pair of trousers?... But the point is, that I was the first to observe in Kolosov, always cheerful and friendly as he was, these instinctive, passionate impulses.... They may well say that love is penetrating. I made up my mind at all hazards to get into his confidence. It was no use for me to lay myself out to please Kolosov; I had such a childlike adoration for him that he could have no doubt of my devotion ... but to my indescribable vexation, I had, at last, to yield to the conviction that Kolosov avoided closer intimacy with me, that he was as it were oppressed by my uninvited attachment. Once, when with obvious displeasure he asked me to lend him money--the very next day he returned me the loan with ironical gratitude. During the whole winter my relations with Kolosov were utterly unchanged; I often compared myself with Gavrilov, and could not make out in what respect he was better than I.... But suddenly everything was changed. In the middle of April, Gavrilov fell ill, and died in the arms of Kolosov, who never left his room for an instant, and went nowhere for a whole week afterwards. We were all grieved for poor Gavrilov; the pale, silent lad seemed to have had a foreboding of his end. I too grieved sincerely for him, but my heart ached with expectation of something.... One ever memorable evening ... I was alone, lying on the sofa, gazing idly at the ceiling ... some one rapidly opened the door of my room and stood still in the doorway; I raised my head; before me stood Kolosov.

He slowly came in and sat down beside me. 'I have come to you,' he began in a rather thick voice, 'because you care more for me than any of the others do.... I have lost my best friend'--his voice shook a little--'and I feel lonely.... None of you knew Gavrilov ... none of you knew....' He got up, paced up and down the room, came rapidly towards me again.... 'Will you take his place?' he said, and gave me his hand. I leaped up and flung myself on his breast. My genuine delight touched him.... I did not know what to say, I was choking.... Kolosov looked at me and softly laughed. We had tea. At tea he talked of Gavrilov; I heard that that timid, gentle boy had saved Kolosov's life, and I could not but own to myself that in Gavrilov's place I couldn't have resisted chattering about it--boasting of my luck. It struck eight. Kolosov got up, went to the window, drummed on the panes, turned swiftly round to me, tried to say something ... and sat down on a chair without a word. I took his hand. 'Kolosov, truly, truly I deserve your confidence!' He looked straight into my eyes. 'Well, if so,' he brought out at last, 'take your cap and come along.' 'Where to?' 'Gavrilov did not ask me.' I was silent at once. 'Can you play at cards?' 'Yes.'

We went out, took a cab to one of the gates of the town. At the gate we got out. Kolosov went on in front very quickly; I followed him. We walked along the high-road. After we had gone three-quarters of a mile, Kolosov turned off. Meanwhile night had come on. On the right in the fog were the twinkling lights, the innumerable church-spires of the immense city; on the left, two white horses were grazing in a meadow skirting the forest: before us stretched fields covered with greyish mists. I followed Kolosov in silence. He stopped all at once, stretched his hand out in front of him, and said: 'Here, this is where we are going.' I saw a small dark house; two little windows showed a dim light in the fog. 'In this house,' Kolosov went on, 'lives a man called Sidorenko, a retired lieutenant, with his sister, an old maid, and his daughter. I shall pass you off as a relation of mine--you must sit down and play at cards with him.' I nodded without a word.

I wanted to show Kolosov that I could be as silent as Gavrilov.... But I will own I was suffering agonies of curiosity. As we went up to the steps of the house, I caught sight, at a lighted window, of the slender figure of a girl.... She seemed waiting for us and vanished at once. We went into a dark and narrow passage. A crooked, hunchback old woman came to meet us, and looked at me with astonishment. 'Is Ivan Semyonitch at home?' inquired Kolosov. 'He is at home.'... 'He is at home!' called a deep masculine voice from within. We went into the dining-room, if dining-room one can call the long, rather dirty room; a small old piano huddled unassumingly in a corner beside the stove; a few chairs stood out along the walls which had once been yellow. In the middle of the room stood a tall, stooping man of fifty, in a greasy dressing-gown. I looked at him more attentively: a morose looking countenance, hair standing up like a brush, a low forehead, grey eyes, immense whiskers, thick lips.... 'A nice customer!' I thought. 'It's a longish time since we've seen you, Andrei Nikolaevitch,' he observed, holding out his hideous red hand, 'a longish time it is! And where's Sevastian Sevastianovitch?' 'Gavrilov is dead,' answered Kolosov mournfully. 'Dead! you don't say so! And who's this?' 'My relation--I have the honour to present to you Nikolai Alexei....' 'All right, all right,' Ivan

Semyonitch cut him short, 'delighted, delighted. And does he play cards?' 'Play, of course he does!' 'Ah, then, that's capital; we'll sit down directly. Hey! Matrona Semyonovna--where are you? the card-table--quick!... And tea!' With these words Mr. Sidorenko walked into the next room. Kolosov looked at me. 'Listen,' he said, 'you can't think how ashamed I am!'... I shut him up. 'Come, you there, what's your name, this way,' called Ivan Semyonitch. I went into the drawing-room. The drawing-room was even smaller than the dining-room. On the walls hung some monstrosities of portraits; in front of the sofa, of which the stuffing protruded in several places, stood a green table; on the sofa sat Ivan Semyonitch, already shuffling the cards. Near him on the extreme edge of a low chair sat a spare woman in a white cap and a black gown, yellow and wrinkled, with short-sighted eyes and thin cat-like lips. 'Here,' said Ivan Semyonitch, 'let me introduce him; the first man's dead; Andrei Nikolaevitch has brought us another; let's see how he plays!' The old lady bowed awkwardly and cleared her throat. I looked round; Kolosov was no longer in the room. 'Stop that coughing, Matrona Semyonovna; sheep cough,' grumbled Sidorenko. I sat down; the game began. Mr. Sidorenko got fearfully hot and furious at my slightest mistake; he pelted his sister with abusive epithets, but she had apparently had time to get used to her brother's amenities, and only blinked in response. But when he announced to Matrona Semyonovna that she was 'Antichrist,' the poor old woman fired up. 'Ivan Semyonitch,' she protested with heat, 'you were the death of your wife, Anfisa Karpovna, but you shan't worry me into my grave!' 'Indeed?' 'No! you shan't.' 'Indeed?' 'No! you shan't.' They kept it up in this fashion for some time. My position was, as you perceive, not merely an unenviable one: it was positively idiotic. I couldn't conceive what had induced Kolosov to bring me.... I have never been a good card-player; but on that occasion I was aware myself that I was playing excruciatingly badly. 'No!' the retired lieutenant repeated continually,' you can't hold a candle to Sevastianovitch! No! you play carelessly!' I, you may be sure, was inwardly wishing him at the devil. This torture continued for two hours; they beat me hollow. Before the end of the last rubber, I heard a slight sound behind my chair--I looked round and saw Kolosov; beside him stood a girl of seventeen, who was watching me with a scarcely perceptible smile. 'Fill me my pipe, Varia,' muttered Ivan Semyonitch. The girl promptly flew off into the other room. She was not very pretty, rather pale, rather thin; but never before or since have I seen such hair, such eyes. We finished the rubber somehow; I paid up, Sidorenko lighted his pipe and grumbled:

'Well, now it's time for supper!' Kolosov presented me to Varia, that is, to Varvara Ivanovna, the daughter of Ivan Semyonitch. Varia was embarrassed; I too was embarrassed. But in a few minutes Kolosov, as usual, had got everything and everyone into full swing; he sat Varia down to the piano, begged her to play a dance tune, and proceeded to dance a Cossack dance in competition with Ivan Semyonitch. The lieutenant uttered little shrieks, stamped and cut such incredible capers that even Matrona Semyonovna burst out laughing and retreated to her own room upstairs. The hunchback old woman laid the table; we sat down to supper. At supper Kolosov told all sorts of nonsensical stories; the lieutenant's guffaws were deafening; I peeped from under my eyelids at Varia. She never took her eyes off Kolosov ... and from the expression of her face alone, I could divine that she both loved him and was loved by him. Her lips were slightly parted, her head bent a little forward, a faint colour kept flitting across her whole face; from time to time she sighed deeply, suddenly dropped her eyes, and softly laughed to herself.... I rejoiced for Kolosov.... But at the same time, deuce take it, I was envious....

After supper, Kolosov and I promptly took up our caps, which did not, however, prevent the lieutenant from saying, with a yawn: 'You've paid us a long visit, gentlemen; it's time to say good-bye.' Varia accompanied Kolosov into the passage: 'When are you coming, Andrei Nikolaevitch?' she whispered to him. 'In a few days, for certain.' 'Bring him too,' she added, with a very sly smile. 'Of course, of course.' ... 'Your humble servant!' thought I....

On the way home, I heard the following story. Six months before, Kolosov had become acquainted with Mr. Sidorenko in a rather queer way. One rainy evening, Kolosov was returning home from shooting, and had reached the gate of the city, when suddenly, at no great distance from the highroad, he heard groans, interspersed with curses. He had a gun; without thinking long, he made straight for the sound, and found a man lying on the ground with a dislocated ankle. This man was Mr. Sidorenko. With great difficulty he got him home, handed him over to the care of his frightened sister and his daughter, and ran for the doctor.... Meantime it was nearly morning; Kolosov was almost dropping with fatigue. With the permission of Matrona Semyonovna, he lay down on the sofa in the parlour, and slept till eight o'clock. On waking up he would at once have gone home; but they kept him and gave him some tea. In the night he had twice succeeded in catching a glimpse of the pale face of Varvara Ivanovna; he had not particularly noticed her, but in the morning she made a decidedly agreeable impression on him. Matrona Semyonovna garrulously praised and thanked Kolosov; Varvara sat silent, pouring out the tea, glanced at him now and then, and with timid shame-faced attentiveness handed him first a cup of tea, then the cream, then the sugar-basin. Meanwhile the lieutenant waked up, loudly called for his pipe, and after a short pause bawled: 'Sister! hi, sister!' Matrona Semyonovna went to his bedroom. 'What about that... what the devil's his name? is he gone?' 'No, I'm still here,' answered Kolosov, going up to the door; 'are you better now?' 'Yes,' answered the lieutenant; 'come in here, my good sir.' Kolosov went in. Sidorenko looked at him, and reluctantly observed: 'Well, thanks; come sometimes and see me--what's your name? who the devil's to know?' 'Kolosov,' answered Andrei. 'Well, well, come and see us; but it's no use your sticking on here now, I daresay they're expecting you at home.' Kolosov retreated, said good-bye to Matrona Semyonovna, bowed to Varvara Ivanovna, and returned home. From that day he began to visit Ivan Semyonitch, at first at long intervals, then more and more frequently. The summer came on; he would sometimes take his gun, put on his knapsack, and set off as if he were going shooting. He would go to the retired lieutenant's, and stay on there till evening.

Varvara Ivanovna's father had served twenty-five years in the army, had saved a small sum of money, and bought himself a few acres of land a mile and a half from Moscow. He could scarcely read and write; but in spite of his external clumsiness and coarseness, he was shrewd and cunning, and even, on occasion, capable of sharp practice, like many Little Russians. He was a fearful egoist, obstinate as an ox, and in general exceedingly impolite, especially with strangers; I even detected in him something like a contempt for the whole human race. He indulged himself in every caprice, like a spoilt child; would know no one, and lived for his own pleasure. We were once somehow or other talking about marriages with him; 'Marriage ... marriage,' said he; 'whom the devil would I let my daughter marry? Eh? what should I do it for? for her husband to knock her about as I used to my wife? Besides, whom should I be left with?' Such was the retired lieutenant, Ivan Semyonitch. Kolosov used to go and see him, not on his account, of course, but for the sake of his daughter. One fine evening, Andrei was sitting in the garden with her, chatting about something; Ivan Semyonitch went up to him, looked sullenly at Varia, and called Andrei away. 'Listen, my dear fellow,' he said to him; 'you find it good fun, I see, gossiping with my only child, but I'm dull in my old age; bring some one with you, or I've nobody to deal a card to; d'ye hear? I shan't give admittance to you by yourself.' The next day Kolosov turned up with Gavrilov, and poor Sevastian Sevastianovitch had for a whole autumn and winter been playing cards in the evenings with the retired lieutenant; that worthy treated him without ceremony, as it is called--in other words, fearfully rudely. You now probably realise why it was that, after Gavrilov's death, Kolosov took me with him to Ivan Semyonitch's. As he communicated all these details, Kolosov added, 'I love Varia, she is the dearest girl; she liked you.'

I have forgotten, I fancy, to make known to you that up to that time I had been afraid of women and avoided them, though I would sometimes, in solitude, spend whole hours in dreaming of tender interviews, of love, of mutual love, and so on. Varvara Ivanovna was the first girl with whom I was forced to talk, by necessity--by necessity it really was. Varia was an ordinary girl, and yet there are very few such girls in holy Russia. You will ask me--why so? Because I never noticed in her anything strained, unnatural, affected; because she was a simple, candid, rather melancholy creature, because one could never call her 'a young lady.' I liked her soft smile; I liked her simple-hearted, ringing little voice, her light and mirthful laugh, her attentive though by no means 'profound' glances. The child promised nothing; but you could not help admiring her, as you admire the sudden, soft cry of the oriole at evening, in the lofty, dark birch-wood. I must confess that at the present time I should pass by such a creature with some indifference; I've no taste now for solitary evening strolls, and orioles; but in those days ...

I've no doubt, gentlemen, that, like all well-educated persons, you have been in love at least once in the course of your life, and have learnt from your own experience how love springs up and develops in the human heart, and therefore I'm not going to enlarge too much on what took place with me at that time. Kolosov and I used to go pretty often to Ivan Semyonitch's; and though those damned cards often drove me to utter despair, still, in the mere proximity of the woman one loves (I had fallen in love with Varia) there is a sort of strange, sweet, tormenting joy. I made no effort to suppress this growing feeling; besides, by the time I had at last brought my-self to call the emotion by its true name, it was already too strong.... I cherished my love in silence, and jealously and shyly concealed it. I myself enjoyed this agonising ferment of silent passion. My sufferings did not rob me of my sleep, nor of my appe-tite; but for whole days together I was conscious of that peculiar physical sensation in my breast which is a symptom of the presence of love. I am incapable of depicting the conflict of various sensations which took place within me when, for example, Kolosov came in from the garden with Varia, and her whole face was aglow with ecstatic devotion, exhaustion from excess of bliss.... She so completely lived in his life, was so completely taken up with him, that unconsciously she adopted his ways, looked as he looked, laughed as he laughed.... I can imagine the moments she passed with Andrei, the raptures she owed to him.... While he ... Kolosov did not lose his freedom; in her absence he did not, I suppose, even think of her; he was still the same unconcerned, gay, and happy fellow we had always known him.

And, as I have already told you, we used, Kolosov and I, to go pretty often to Ivan Semyonitch's. Sometimes, when he was out of humour, the retired lieutenant did not make me sit down to cards; on such occasions, he would shrink into a corner in silence, scowling and looking crossly at every one. The first time I was delighted at his letting me off so easily; but afterwards I would sometimes begin myself beg-ging him to sit down to whist, the part of third person was so insupportable! I was so unpleasantly in Kolosov's and Varia's way, though they did assure each other that there was no need to mind me!...

Meanwhile time went on.... They were happy.... I have no great fondness for describing other people's happiness. But then I began to notice that Varia's childish ecstasy had gradually given way to a more womanly, more restless feeling. I began to surmise that the new song was being sung to the old tune--that is, that Kolosov was...little by little...cooling. This discovery, I must own, delighted me; I did not feel, I must confess, the slightest indignation against Andrei.

The intervals between our visits became longer and longer.... Varia began to meet us with tear-stained eyes. Reproaches were heard ... Sometimes I asked Ko-losov with affected indifference, 'Well, shall we go to Ivan Semyonitch's to-day?' ... He looked coldly at me, and answered quietly, 'No, we're not going.' I sometimes fancied that he smiled slily when he spoke to me of Varia.... I failed generally to fill

Gavrilov's place with him.... Gavrilov was a thousand times more good-natured and foolish than I.

Now allow me a slight digression.... When I spoke of my university comrades, I did not mention a certain Mr. Shtchitov. He was five-and-thirty; he had been a student for ten years already. I can see even now his rather long pale face, his little brown eyes, his long hawk nose crooked at the end, his thin sarcastic lips, his solemn upstanding shock of hair, and his chin that lost itself complacently in the wide striped cravat of the colour of a raven's wing, the shirt front with bronze buttons, the open blue frock-coat and striped waistcoat.... I can hear his unpleasantly jarring laugh.... He went everywhere, was conspicuous at all possible kinds of 'dancing classes.' ... I remember I could not listen to his cynical stories without a peculiar shudder.... Kolosov once compared him to an unswept Russian refreshment bar ... a horrible comparison! And with all that, there was a lot of intelligence, common sense, observation, and wit in the man.... He sometimes impressed us by some saying so apt, so true and cutting, that we were all involuntarily reduced to silence and looked at him with amazement. But, to be sure, it is just the same to a Russian whether he has uttered an absurdity or a clever thing. Shtchitov was especially dreaded by those self-conscious, dreamy, and not particularly gifted youths who spend whole days in painfully hatching a dozen trashy lines of verse and reading them in sing-song to their 'friends,' and who despise every sort of positive science. One such he simply drove out of Moscow, by continually repeating to him two of his own lines. Yet all the while Shtchitov himself did nothing and learnt nothing.... But that's all in the natural order of things. Well, Shtchitov, God only knows why, began jeering at my romantic attachment to Kolosov. The first time, with noble indignation, I told him to go to the devil; the second time, with chilly contempt, I informed him that he was not capable of judging of our friendship--but I did not send him away; and when, on taking leave of me, he observed that without Kolosov's permission I didn't even dare to praise him, I felt annoyed; Shtchitov's last words sank into my heart.--For more than a fortnight I had not seen Varia.... Pride, love, a vague anticipation, a number of different feelings were astir within me ... with a wave of the hand and a fearful sinking at my heart, I set off alone to Ivan Semyonitch's.

I don't know how I made my way to the familiar little house; I remember I sat down several times by the road to rest, not from fatigue, but from emotion. I went into the passage, and had not yet had time to utter a single word when the door of the drawing-room flew open and Varia ran to meet me. 'At last,' she said, in a quavering voice; 'where's Andrei Nikolaevitch?' 'Kolosov has not come,' I muttered with an effort. 'Not come!' she repeated. 'Yes ... he told me to tell you that ... he was detained....' I positively did not know what I was saying, and I did not dare to raise my eyes. Varia stood silent and motionless before me. I glanced at her: she turned away her head; two big tears rolled slowly down her cheeks. In the expression of her face there was such sudden, bitter suffering; the conflict between bashfulness, sorrow, and confidence in me was so simply, so touchingly apparent in the unconscious movement of her poor little head that it sent a pang to my heart. I bent a little forward ... she gave a hurried start and ran away. In the parlour I was met by Ivan Semyonitch. 'How's this, my good sir, are you alone?' he asked me, with a queer twitch of his left eyelid. 'Yes, I've come alone,' I stammered. Sidorenko went off into a sudden guffaw and departed into the next room.

I had never been in such a foolish position; it was too devilishly disgusting! But there was nothing to be done. I began walking up and down the room. 'What was the fat pig laughing at?' I wondered. Matrona Semyonovna came into the room with a stocking in her hands and sat down in the window. I began talking to her. Meanwhile tea was brought in. Varia came downstairs, pale and sorrowful. The retired lieutenant made jokes about Kolosov. 'I know,' said he, 'what sort of customer he is; you couldn't tempt him here with lollipops now, I expect!' Varia hurriedly got up and went away. Ivan Semyonitch looked after her and gave a sly whistle. I glanced at him in perplexity. 'Can it be,' I wondered, 'that he knows all about it?' And the lieutenant, as though divining my thoughts, nodded his head affirmatively. Directly after tea I got up and took leave. 'You, my good sir, we shall see again,' observed the lieutenant. I did not say a word in reply.... I began to feel simply frightened of the man.

On the steps a cold and trembling hand clutched at mine; I looked round: Varia. 'I must speak to you,' she whispered. 'Come to-morrow rather earlier, straight into the garden. After dinner papa is asleep; no one will interfere with us.' I pressed her hand without a word, and we parted.

Next day, at three o'clock in the afternoon, I was in Ivan Semyonitch's garden.

In the morning I had not seen Kolosov, though he had come to see me. It was a grey autumn day, but soft and warm. Delicate yellow blades of grass nodded over the blanching turf; the nimble tomtits were hopping about the bare dark-brown twigs; some belated larks were hurriedly running about the paths; a hare was creeping cautiously about among the greens; a herd of cattle wandered lazily over the stubble. I found Varia in the garden under the apple-tree on the little garden-seat; she was wearing a dark dress, rather creased; her weary eyes, the dejected droop of her hair, seemed to express genuine suffering.

I sat down beside her. We were both silent. For a long while she kept twisting a twig in her hand; she bent her head, and uttered: 'Andrei Nikolaevitch....' I noticed at once, by the twitching of her lips, that she was getting ready to cry, and began consoling her, assuring her hotly of Andrei's devotion.... She heard me, nodded her head mournfully, articulated some indistinct words, and then was silent but did not cry. The first moments I had dreaded most of all had gone off fairly well. She began little by little to talk about Andrei. 'I know that he does not love me now,' she repeated: 'God be with him! I can't imagine how I am to live without him.... I don't sleep at nights, I keep weeping.... What am I to do! What am I to do! ...' Her eyes filled with tears. 'I thought him so kind ... and here ...' Varia wiped her eyes, cleared her throat, and sat up. 'It seems such a little while ago,' she went on: 'he was reading to me out of Pushkin, sitting with me on this bench....' Varia's naive communicativeness touched me. I listened in silence to her confessions; my soul was slowly filled with a bitter, torturing bliss; I could not take my eyes off that pale face, those long, wet eyelashes, and half-parted, rather parched lips.... And meanwhile I felt ... Would you care to hear a slight psychological analysis of my emotions at that moment? in the first place I was tortured by the thought that it was not I that was loved, not I that as making Varia suffer: secondly, I was delighted at her confidence; I knew she would be grateful to me for giving her an opportunity of expressing her sorrow: thirdly, I was inwardly vowing to myself to bring Kolosov and Varia together again, and was deriving consolation from the consciousness of my magnanimity ... in the fourth place, I hoped, by my self-sacrifice, to touch Varia's heart; and then ... You see I do not spare myself; no, thank God! it's high time!

But from the bell-tower of the monastery near it struck five o'clock; the evening was coming on rapidly. Varia got up hastily, thrust a little note into my hand,

and went off towards the house. I overtook her, promised to bring Andrei to her, and stealthily, like a happy lover, crept out by the little gate into the field. On the note was written in an unsteady hand the words: To Andrei Nikolaevitch.

Next day I set off early in the morning to Kolosov's. I'm bound to confess that, although I assured myself that my intentions were not only honourable, but positively brimful of great-hearted self-sacrifice, I was yet conscious of a certain awkwardness, even timidity. I arrived at Kolosov's. There was with him a fellow called Puzyritsin, a former student who had never taken his degree, one of those authors of sensational novels of the so-called 'Moscow' or 'grey' school. Puzyritsin was a very good-natured and shy person, and was always preparing to be an hussar, in spite of his thirty-three years. He belonged to that class of people who feel it absolutely necessary, once in the twenty-four hours, to utter a phrase after the pattern of, 'The beautiful always falls into decay in the flower of its splendour; such is the fate of the beautiful in the world,' in order to smoke his pipe with redoubled zest all the rest of the day in a circle of 'good comrades.' On this account he was called an idealist. Well, so Puzyritsin was sitting with Kolosov reading him some 'fragment.' I began to listen; it was all about a youth, who loves a maiden, kills her, and so on. At last Puzyritsin finished and retreated. His absurd production, solemnly bawling voice, his presence altogether, had put Kolosov into a mood of sarcastic irritability. I felt that I had come at an unlucky moment, but there was nothing to be done for it; without any kind of preface, I handed Andrei Varia's note.

Kolosov looked at me in perplexity, tore open the note, ran his eyes over it, said nothing, but smiled composedly. 'Oh, ho!' he said at last; 'so you've been at Ivan Semyonitch's?'

'Yes, I was there yesterday, alone,' I answered abruptly and resolutely.

'Ah!...' observed Kolosov ironically, and he lighted his pipe. 'Andrei,' I said to him, 'aren't you sorry for her?... If you had seen her tears...'

And I launched into an eloquent description of my visit of the previous day. I was genuinely moved. Kolosov did not speak, and smoked his pipe.

'You sat with her under the apple-tree in the garden,' he said at last. 'I remember in May I, too, used to sit with her on that seat.... The apple-tree was in blossom, the fresh white flowers fell upon us sometimes; I held both Varia's hands... we were happy then.... Now the apple-blossom is over, and the apples on the tree are sour.'

I flew into a passion of noble indignation, began reproaching Andrei for coldness, for cruelty, argued with him that he had no right to abandon a girl so suddenly, after awakening in her a multitude of new emotions; I begged him at least to go and say good-bye to Varia. Kolosov heard me to the end.

'Admitting,' he said to me, when, agitated and exhausted, I flung myself into an armchair, 'that you, as my friend, may be allowed to criticise me. But hear my defence, at least, though...'

Here he paused for a little while and smiled curiously. 'Varia's an excellent girl,' he went on, 'and has done me no wrong whatever.... On the contrary, I am greatly, very greatly indebted to her. I have left off going to see her for a very simple reason--I have left off caring for her....'

'But why? why?' I interrupted him.

'Goodness knows why. While I loved her, I was entirely hers; I never thought of the future, and everything, my whole life, I shared with her ... now this passion has died out in me.... Well, you would tell me to be a humbug, to play at being in love, wouldn't you? But what for? from pity for her? If she's a decent girl, she won't care for such charity herself, but if she is glad to be consoled by my ... my sympathy, well, she's not good for much!'

Kolosov's carelessly offhand expressions offended me, perhaps, the more because they were applied to the woman with whom I was secretly in love.... I fired up. 'Stop,' I said to him; 'stop! I know why you have given up going to see Varia.'

'Why?'

'Taniusha has forbidden you to.'

In uttering these words, I fancied I was dealing a most cutting blow at Andrei. Taniusha was a very 'easy-going' young lady, black-haired, dark, five-and-twenty, free in her manners, and devilishly clever, a Shtchitov in petticoats. Kolosov quarrelled with her and made it up again half a dozen times in a month. She was passionately fond of him, though sometimes, during their misunderstandings, she would vow and declare that she thirsted for his blood.... And Andrei, too, could not get on without her. Kolosov looked at me, and responded serenely, 'Perhaps so.'

'Not perhaps so,' I shouted, 'but certainly!'

Kolosov at last got sick of my reproaches.... He got up and put on his cap.

'Where are you going?'

'For a walk; you and Puzyritsin have given me a headache between you.'

'You are angry with me?'

'No,' he answered, smiling his sweet smile, and holding out his hand to me.

'Well, anyway, what do you wish me to tell Varia?'

'Eh?' ... He thought a little. 'She told you,' he said, 'that we had read Pushkin together.... Remind her of one line of Pushkin's.' 'What line? what line?' I asked impatiently. 'This one:

   "What has been will not be again."'

With those words he went out of the room. I followed him; on the stairs he stopped.

'And is she very much upset?' he asked me, pulling his cap over his eyes.

'Very, very much!...'

'Poor thing! Console her, Nikolai; you love her, you know.'

'Yes, I have grown fond of her, certainly....'

'You love her,' repeated Kolosov, and he looked me straight in the face. I turned away without a word, and we separated.

On reaching home, I was in a perfect fever.

'I have done my duty,' I thought; 'I have overcome my own egoism; I have urged Andrei to go back to Varia!... Now I am in the right; he that will not when he may...!' At the same time Andrei's indifference wounded me. He had not been jealous of me, he told me to console her.... But is Varia such an ordinary girl, is she not even worthy of sympathy?... There are people who know how to appreciate what you despise, Andrei Nikolaitch!... But what's the good? She does not love me.... No, she does not love me now, while she has not quite lost hope of Kolosov's return.... But afterwards...who knows, my devotion will touch her. I will make no claims.... I will give myself up to her wholly, irrevocably.... Varia! is it possible you will not love me?...never!...never!...

Such were the speeches your humble servant was rehearsing in the city of Moscow, in the year 1833, in the house of his revered preceptor. I wept...I felt faint... The weather was horrible...a fine rain trickled down the window panes with a persistent, thin, little patter; damp, dark-grey storm-clouds hung stationary over the town. I dined hurriedly, made no response to the anxious inquiries of the kind German woman, who whimpered a little herself at the sight of my red, swollen eyes

(Germans--as is well known--are always glad to weep). I behaved very ungraciously to my preceptor...and at once after dinner set off to Ivan Semyonitch... Bent double in a jolting droshky, I kept asking myself whether I should tell Varia all as it was, or go on deceiving her, and little by little turn her heart from Andrei... I reached Ivan Semyonitch's without knowing what to decide upon... I found all the family in the parlour. On seeing me, Varia turned fearfully white, but did not move from her place; Sidorenko began talking to me in a peculiarly jeering way. I responded as best I could, looking from time to time at Varia, and almost unconsciously giving a dejected and pensive expression to my features. The lieutenant started whist again. Varia sat near the window and did not stir. 'You're dull now, I suppose?' Ivan Semyonitch asked her twenty times over.

At last I succeeded in seizing a favourable opportunity.

'You are alone again,' Varia whispered to me.

'Yes,' I answered gloomily; 'and probably for long.'

She swiftly drew in her head.

'Did you give him my letter?' she asked in a voice hardly audible.

'Yes.'

'Well?'... she gasped for breath. I glanced at her.... There was a sudden flash of spiteful pleasure within me.

'He told me to tell you,' I pronounced deliberately, 'that "what has been will not be again...."'

Varia pressed her left hand to her heart, stretched her right hand out in front, staggered, and went quickly out of the room. I tried to overtake her.... Ivan Semyonitch stopped me. I stayed another two hours with him, but Varia did not appear. On the way back I felt ashamed ... ashamed before Varia, before Andrei, before myself; though they say it is better to cut off an injured limb at once than to keep the patient in prolonged suffering; but who gave me a right to deal such a merciless blow at the heart of a poor girl?... For a long while I could not sleep ... but I fell asleep at last. In general I must repeat that 'love' never once deprived me of sleep.

I began to go pretty often to Ivan Semyonitch's. I used to see Kolosov as before, but neither he nor I ever referred to Varia. My relations with her were of a rather curious kind. She became attached to me with that sort of attachment which excludes every possibility of love. She could not help noticing my warm sympathy, and talked eagerly with me ... of what, do you suppose?... of Kolosov, nothing but Kolosov! The man had taken such possession of her that she did not, as it were, belong to herself. I tried in vain to arouse her pride ... she was either silent or, if she talked--chattered on about Kolosov. I did not even suspect in those days that sorrow of that kind--talkative sorrow--is in reality far more genuine than any silent suffering. I must own I passed many bitter moments at that time. I was conscious that I was not capable of filling Kolosov's place; I was conscious that Varia's past was so full, so rich ... and her present so poor.... I got to the point of an involuntary shudder at the words 'Do you remember' ... with which almost every sentence of hers began. She grew a little thinner during the first days of our acquaintance ... but afterwards got better again, and even grew cheerful; she might have been compared then with a wounded bird, not yet quite recovered. Meanwhile my position had become insupportable; the lowest passions gradually gained possession of my soul; it happened to me to slander Kolosov in Varia's presence. I resolved to cut short such unnatural relations. But how? Part from Varia--I could not.... Declare my love to her--I did not dare; I felt that I could not, as yet, hope for a return. Marry her.... This idea alarmed me; I was only eighteen; I felt a dread of putting all my future into bondage so early; I thought of my father, I could hear the jeering comments of Kolosov's comrades.... But they say every thought is like dough; you have only to knead it well--you can make anything you like of it. I began, for whole days together, to dream of marriage.... I imagined what gratitude would fill Varia's heart when I, the friend and confidant of Kolosov, should offer her my hand, knowing her to be hopelessly in love with another. Persons of experience, I remembered, had told me that marriage for love is a complete absurdity; I began to indulge my fancy; I pictured to myself our peaceful life together in some snug corner of South Russia; an mentally I traced the gradual transition in Varia's heart from gratitude to affection, from affection to love.... I vowed to myself at once to leave Moscow, the university, to forget everything and every one. I began to avoid meeting Kolosov.

At last, one bright winter day (Varia had been somehow peculiarly enchanting the previous evening), I dressed myself in my best, slowly and solemnly sallied out from my room, took a first-rate sledge, and drove down to Ivan Semyonitch's. Varia was sitting alone in the drawing-room reading Karamzin. On seeing me she softly laid the book down on her knees, and with agitated curiosity looked into my face; I had never been to see them in the morning before.... I sat down beside her; my heart beat painfully. 'What are you reading?' I asked her at last. 'Karamzin.' 'What, are you taking up Russian literature?...' She suddenly cut me short. 'Tell me, haven't you come from Andrei?' That name, that trembling, questioning voice, the half-joyful, half-timid expression of her face, all these unmistakable signs of persistent love, pierced to my heart like arrows. I resolved either to part from Varia, or to receive from her herself the right to chase the hated name of Andrei from her lips for ever. I do not remember what I said to her; at first I must have expressed myself in rather confused fashion, as for a long while she did not understand me; at last I could stand it no longer, and almost shouted, 'I love you, I want to marry you.' 'You love me?' said Varia in bewilderment. I fancied she meant to get up, to go away, to refuse me. 'For God's sake,' I whispered breathlessly, 'don't answer me, don't say yes or no; think it over; to-morrow I will come again for a final answer.... I have long loved you. I don't ask of you love, I want to be your champion, your friend; don't answer me now, don't answer.... Till to-morrow.' With these words I rushed out of the room. In the passage Ivan Semyonitch met me, and not only showed no surprise at my visit, but positively, with an agreeable smile, offered me an apple. Such unexpected amiability so struck me that I was simply dumb with amazement. 'Take the apple, it's a nice apple, really!' persisted Ivan Semyonitch. Mechanically I took the apple at last, and drove all the way home with it in my hand.

You may easily imagine how I passed all that day and the following morning. That night I slept rather badly. 'My God! my God!' I kept thinking; 'if she refuses me! ... I shall die.... I shall die....' I repeated wearily. 'Yes, she will certainly refuse me.... And why was I in such a hurry!'... Wishing to turn my thoughts, I began to write a letter to my father--a desperate, resolute letter. Speaking of myself, I used the expression 'your son.' Bobov came in to see me. I began weeping on his shoulder, which must have surprised poor Bobov not a little.... I afterwards learned that he had come to me to borrow money (his landlord had threatened to turn him out of the house); he had no choice but to hook it, as the students say....

At last the great moment arrived. On going out of my room, I stood still in the doorway. 'With what feelings,' thought I, 'shall I cross this threshold again to-day?' ... My emotion at the sight of Ivan Semyonitch's little house was so great that I got down, picked up a handful of snow and pressed it to my face. 'Oh, heavens!'

I thought, 'if I find Varia alone--I am lost!' My legs were giving way under me; I could hardly get to the steps. Things were as I had hoped. I found Varia in the parlour with Matrona Semyonovna. I made my bows awkwardly, and sat down by the old lady. Varia's face was rather paler than usual.... I fancied that she tried to avoid my eyes.... But what were my feelings when Matrona Semyonovna suddenly got up and went into the next room!... I began looking out of the window--I was trembling inwardly like an autumn leaf. Varia did not speak.... At last I mastered my timidity, went up to her, bent my head....

'What are you going to say to me?' I articulated in a breaking voice.

Varia turned away--the tears were glistening on her eyelashes.

'I see,' I went on, 'it's useless for me to hope.'...

Varia looked shyly round and gave me her hand without a word.

'Varia!' I cried involuntarily...and stopped, as though frightened at my own hopes.

'Speak to papa,' she articulated at last.

'You permit me to speak to Ivan Semyonitch?' ...

'Yes.'... I covered her hands with kisses.

'Don't, don't,' whispered Varia, and suddenly burst into tears.

I sat down beside her, talked soothingly to her, wiped away her tears.... Luckily, Ivan Semyonitch was not at home, and Matrona Semyonovna had gone up to her own little room. I made vows of love, of constancy to Varia.

...'Yes,' she said, suppressing her sobs and continually wiping her eyes; 'I know you are a good man, an honest man; you are not like Kolosov.'... 'That name again!' thought I. But with what delight I kissed those warm, damp little hands! with what subdued rapture I gazed into that sweet face!... I talked to her of the future, walked about the room, sat down on the floor at her feet, hid my eyes in my hands, and shuddered with happiness.... Ivan Semyonitch's heavy footsteps cut short our conversation. Varia hurriedly got up and went off to her own room--without, however, pressing my hand or glancing at me. Mr. Sidorenko was even more amiable than on the previous day: he laughed, rubbed his stomach, made jokes about Matrona Semyonovna, and so on. I was on the point of asking for his blessing there and then, but I thought better of it and deferred doing so till the next day. His ponderous jokes jarred upon me; besides I was exhausted.... I said good-bye to him and went away.

I am one of those persons who love brooding over their own sensations, though I cannot endure such persons myself. And so, after the first transport of heartfelt joy, I promptly began to give myself up to all sorts of reflections. When I had got half a mile from the house of the retired lieutenant, I flung my hat up in the air, in excessive delight, and shouted 'Hurrah!' But while I was being jolted through the long, crooked streets of Moscow, my thoughts gradually took another turn. All sorts of rather sordid doubts began to crowd upon my mind. I recalled my conversation with Ivan Semyonitch about marriage in general ... and unconsciously I murmured to myself, 'So he was putting it on, the old humbug!' It is true that I continually repeated, 'but then Varia is mine! mine!' ... Yet that 'but'--alas, that ***but***!--and then, too, the words, 'Varia is mine!' aroused in me not a deep, overwhelming rapture, but a sort of paltry, egoistic triumph.... If Varia had refused me point-blank, I should have been burning with furious passion; but having received her consent, I was like a man who has just said to a guest, 'Make yourself at home,' and sees the guest actually beginning to settle into his room, as if he were at home. 'If she had loved Kolosov,' I thought, 'how was it she consented so soon? It's clear she's glad to marry any one.... Well, what of it? all the better for me.'... It was with such vague and curious feelings that I crossed the threshold of my room. Possibly, gentlemen, my story does not strike you as sounding true.

I don't know whether it sounds true or not, but I know that all I have told is the absolute and literal truth. However, I gave myself up all that day to a feverish gaiety, assured myself that I simply did not deserve such happiness; but next morning....

A wonderful thing is sleep! It not only renews one's body: in a way it renews one's soul, restoring it to primaeval simplicity and naturalness. In the course of the day you succeed in *tuning* yourself, in soaking yourself in falsity, in false ideas ... sleep with its cool wave washes away all such pitiful trashiness; and on waking up, at least for the first few instants, you are capable of understanding and loving truth. I waked up, and, reflecting on the previous day, I felt a certain discomfort.... I was, as it were, ashamed of all my own actions. With instinctive uneasiness I thought of the visit to be made that day, of my interview with Ivan Semyonitch.... This uneasiness was acute and distressing; it was like the uneasiness of the hare who hears the barking of the dogs and is bound at last to run out of his native forest into the open country...and there the sharp teeth of the harriers are awaiting him.... 'Why was I in such a hurry?' I repeated, just as I had the day before, but in quite a different sense. I remember the fearful difference between yesterday and to-day struck myself; for the first time it occurred to me that in human life there lie hid secrets-- strange secrets.... With childish perplexity I gazed into this new, not fantastic, real world. By the word 'real' many people understand 'trivial.' Perhaps it sometimes is so; but I must own that the first appearance of **reality** before me shook me profoundly, scared me, impressed me....

What fine-sounding phrases all about love that didn't come off, to use Gogol's expression! ... I come back to my story. In the course of that day I assured myself again that I was the most blissful of mortals. I drove out of the town to Ivan Semyonitch's. He received me very gleefully; he had been meaning to go and see a neighbour, but I myself stopped him. I was afraid to be left alone with Varia. The evening was cheerful, but not reassuring. Varia was neither one thing nor the other, neither cordial nor melancholy ... neither pretty nor plain. I looked at her, as the philosophers say, objectively--that is to say, as the man who has dined looks at the dishes. I thought her hands were rather red. Sometimes, however, my heart warmed, and watching her I gave way to other dreams and reveries. I had only just made her an offer, as it is called, and here I was already feeling as though we were living as husband and wife ... as though our souls already made up one lovely whole, belonged to one another, and consequently were trying each to seek out a separate path for itself....

'Well, have you spoken to papa?' Varia said to me, as soon as we were left alone.

This inquiry impressed me most disagreeably.... I thought to myself, 'You're pleased to be in a desperate hurry, Varvara Ivanovna.'

'Not yet,' I answered, rather shortly, 'but I will speak to him.'

Altogether I behaved rather casually with her. In spite of my promise, I said nothing definite to Ivan Semyonitch. As I was leaving, I pressed his hand significantly, and informed him that I wanted to have a little talk with him ... that was all.... 'Good-bye!' I said to Varia.

'Till we meet!' said she.

I will not keep you long in suspense, gentlemen; I am afraid of exhausting your patience....We never met again. I never went back to Ivan Semyonitch's. The first days, it is true, of my voluntary separation from Varia did not pass without tears, self-reproach, and emotion; I was frightened myself at the rapid drooping of my love; twenty times over I was on the point of starting off to see her. Vividly I pictured to myself her amazement, her grief, her wounded feelings; but--I never went to Ivan Semyonitch's again. In her absence I begged her forgiveness, fell on my knees before her, assured her of my profound repentance--and once, when I met a girl in the street slightly resembling her, I took to my heels without looking back, and only breathed freely in a cook-shop after the fifth jam-puff. The word 'to-morrow' was invented for irresolute people, and for children; like a baby, I lulled myself with that magic word. 'To-morrow I will go to her, whatever happens,' I said to myself, and ate and slept well to-day. I began to think a great deal more about Kolosov than about Varia ... everywhere, continually, I saw his open, bold, careless face. I began going to see him as before. He gave me the same welcome as ever. But how deeply I felt his superiority to me! How ridiculous I thought all my fancies, my pensive melancholy, during the period of Kolosov's connection with Varia, my magnanimous resolution to bring them together again, my anticipations, my raptures, my remorse!... I had played a wretched, drawn-out part of screaming farce, but he had passed so simply, so well, through it all....

You will say, 'What is there wonderful in that? your Kolosov fell in love with a girl, then fell out of love again, and threw her over.... Why, that happens with everybody....' Agreed; but which of us knows just when to break with our past? Which of us, tell me, is not afraid of the reproaches--I don't mean of the woman--the reproaches of every chance fool? Which of us is proof against the temptation of making a display of magnanimity, or of playing egoistically with another devoted heart? Which of us, in fact, has the force of character to be superior to petty vanity, to **_petty fine feelings_**, sympathy and self-reproach?... Oh, gentlemen, the man who leaves a woman at that great and bitter moment when he is forced to recognise that his heart is not altogether, not fully, hers, that man, believe me, has a truer and deeper comprehension of the sacredness of love than the faint-hearted creatures who, from dulness or weakness, go on playing on the half-cracked strings of their flabby and sentimental hearts! At the beginning of my story I told you that we all considered Andrei Kolosov an extraordinary man. And if a clear, simple outlook upon life, if the absence of every kind of cant in a young man, can be called an extraordinary thing, Kolosov deserved the name. At a certain age, to be natural is to be extraordinary.... It is time to finish, though. I thank you for your attention.... Oh, I forgot to tell you that three months after my last visit I met the old humbug Ivan Semyonitch. I tried, of course, to glide hurriedly and unnoticed by him, but yet I could not help overhearing the words, 'Feather-headed scoundrels!' uttered angrily.

'And what became of Varia?' asked some one.

'I don't know,' answered the story-teller.

We all got up and separated.

1864.

A CORRESPONDENCE

A few years ago I was in Dresden. I was staying at an hotel. From early morning till late evening I strolled about the town, and did not think it necessary to make acquaintance with my neighbours; at last it reached my ears in some chance way that there was a Russian in the hotel--lying ill. I went to see him, and found a man in galloping consumption. I had begun to be tired of Dresden; I stayed with my new acquaintance. It's dull work sitting with a sick man, but even dulness is sometimes agreeable; moreover, my patient was not low-spirited and was very ready to talk. We tried to kill time in all sorts of ways; We played 'Fools,' the two of us together, and made fun of the doctor. My compatriot used to tell this very bald-headed German all sorts of fictions about himself, which the doctor had always 'long ago anticipated.' He used to mimic his astonishment at any new, exceptional symptom, to throw his medicines out of window, and so on. I observed more than once, however, to my friend that it would be as well to send for a good doctor before it was too late, that his complaint was not to be trifled with, and so on. But Alexey (my new friend's name was Alexey Petrovitch S----) always turned off my advice with jests at the expense of doctors in general, and his own in particular; and at last one rainy autumn evening he answered my urgent entreaties with such a mournful look, he shook his head so sorrowfully and smiled so strangely, that I felt somewhat disconcerted. The same night Alexey was worse, and the next day he died. Just before his death his usual cheerfulness deserted him; he tossed about uneasily in his bed, sighed, looked round him in anguish ... clutched at my hand, and whispered with an effort, 'But it's hard to die, you know ... dropped his head on the pillow, and shed tears. I did not know what to say to him, and sat in silence by his bed. But Alexey soon got the better of these last, late regrets.... 'I say,' he said to me, 'our doctor'll come to-day and find me dead.... I can fancy his face.'... And the dying man tried to mimic him. He asked me to send all his things to Russia to his relations, with the exception of a small packet which he gave me as a souvenir.

This packet contained letters--a girl's letters to Alexey, and copies of his letters to her. There were fifteen of them. Alexey Petrovitch S---- had known Marya Alexandrovna B---- long before, in their childhood, I fancy. Alexey Petrovitch had a cousin, Marya Alexandrovna had a sister. In former years they had all lived together; then they had been separated, and had not seen each other for a long while. Later on, they had chanced one summer to be all together again in the country, and they had fallen in love--Alexey's cousin with Marya Alexandrovna, and Alexey with her sister. The summer had passed by, the autumn came; they parted. Alexey, like a sensible person, soon came to the conclusion that he was not in love at all, and had effected a very satisfactory parting from his charmer. His cousin had continued writing to Marya Alexandrovna for nearly two years longer ... but he too perceived at last that he was deceiving her and himself in an unconscionable way, and he too dropped the correspondence.

I could tell you something about Marya Alexandrovna, gentle reader, but you will find out what she was from her letters. Alexey wrote his first letter to her soon after she had finally broken with his cousin. He was at that time in Petersburg; he went suddenly abroad, fell ill, and died at Dresden. I resolved to print his correspondence with Marya Alexandrovna, and trust the reader will look at it with indulgence, as these letters are not love-letters--Heaven forbid! Love-letters are as a rule only read by two persons (they read them over a thousand times to make up), and to a third person they are unendurable, if not ridiculous.

I

FROM ALEXEY PETROVITCH TO MARYA ALEXANDROVNA
ST. PETERSBURG, *March* 7, 1840.
DEAR MARYA ALEXANDROVNA,--

I fancy I have never written to you before, and here I am writing to you now.... I have chosen a curious time to begin, haven't I? I'll tell you what gave me the impulse. Mon cousin Theodore was with me to-day, and...how shall I put it?...and he confided to me as the greatest secret (he never tells one anything except as a great secret), that he was in love with the daughter of a gentleman here, and that this time he is firmly resolved to be married, and that he has already taken the first step--he has declared himself! I made haste, of course, to congratulate him on an event so agreeable for him; he has been longing to declare himself for a great while...but inwardly, I must own, I was rather astonished. Although I knew that everything was over between you, still I had fancied.... In short, I was surprised. I had made arrangements to go out to see friends to-day, but I have stopped at home and mean to have a little gossip with you. If you do not care to listen to me, fling this letter forthwith into the fire. I warn you I mean to be frank, though I feel you are fully justified in taking me for a rather impertinent person. Observe, however, that I would not have taken up my pen if I had not known your sister was not with you; she is staying, so Theodore told me, the whole summer with your aunt, Madame B---. God give her every blessing!

And so, this is how it has all worked out.... But I am not going to offer you my friendship and all that; I am shy as a rule of high-sounding speeches and 'heartfelt' effusions. In beginning to write this letter, I simply obeyed a momentary impulse. If there is another feeling latent within me, let it remain hidden under a bushel for the time.

I'm not going to offer you sympathy either. In sympathising with others, people for the most part want to get rid, as quick as they can, of an unpleasant feeling of involuntary, egoistic regret.... I understand genuine, warm sympathy ... but such sympathy you would not accept from just any one.... Do, please, get angry with me.... If you're angry, you'll be sure to read my missive to the end.

But what right have I to write to you, to talk of my friendship, of my feelings, of consolation? None, absolutely none; that I am bound to admit, and I can only throw myself on your kindness.

Do you know what the preface of my letter's like? I'll tell you: some Mr. N. or M. walking into the drawing-room of a lady who doesn't in the least expect him, and who does, perhaps, expect some one else.... He realises that he has come at an unlucky moment, but there's no help for it.... He sits down, begins talking...goodness knows what about: poetry, the beauties of nature, the advantages of a good education...talks the most awful rot, in fact. But, meanwhile, the first five minutes have gone by, he has settled himself comfortably; the lady has resigned herself to the inevitable, and so Mr. N. or M. regains his self-possession, takes breath, and begins a real conversation--to the best of his ability.

In spite, though, of all this rigmarole, I don't still feel quite comfortable. I seem to see your bewildered--even rather wrathful--face; I feel that it will be almost impossible you should not ascribe to me some hidden motives, and so, like a Roman who has committed some folly, I wrap myself majestically in my toga, and await in silence your final sentence....

The question is: Will you allow me to go on writing to you?--I remain sincerely and warmly devoted to you,

ALEXEY S.

II

FROM MARYA ALEXANDROVNA TO ALEXEY PETROVITCH
VILLAGE OF X----, *March* 22, 1840.
DEAR SIR,
ALEXEY PETROVITCH,

I have received your letter, and I really don't know what to say to you. I should not even have answered you at all, if it had not been that I fancied that under your jesting remarks there really lies hid a feeling of some friendliness. Your letter made an unpleasant impression on me. In answer to your rigmarole, as you call it, let me too put to you one question: *What for?* What have I to do with you, or you with me? I do not ascribe to you any bad motives ... on the contrary, I'm grateful for your sympathy ... but we are strangers to each other, and I, just now at least, feel not the slightest inclination for greater intimacy with any one whatever.--With sincere esteem, I remain, etc.,

MARYA B.

III

FROM ALEXEY PETROVITCH TO MARYA ALEXANDROVNA
ST. PETERSBURG, *March* 30.

Thank you, Marya Alexandrovna, thank you for your note, brief as it was. All this time I have been in great suspense; twenty times a day I have thought of you and my letter. You can't imagine how bitterly I laughed at myself; but now I am in an excellent frame of mind, and very much pleased with myself. Marya Alexandrovna, I am going to begin a correspondence with you! Confess, this was not at all what you expected after your answer; I'm surprised myself at my boldness.... Well, I don't care, here goes! But don't be uneasy; I want to talk to you, not of you, but of myself. It's like this, do you see: it's absolutely needful for me, in the old-fashioned phraseology, to open my heart to some one. I have not the slightest right to select you for my confidant--agreed.

But listen: I won't demand of you an answer to my letters; I don't even want to know whether you read my 'rigmarole'; but, in the name of all that's holy, don't send my letters back to me!

Let me tell you, I am utterly alone on earth. In my youth I led a solitary life, though I never, I remember, posed as a Byronic hero; but first, circumstances, and secondly, a faculty of imaginative dreaming and a love for dreaming, rather cool blood, pride, indolence--a number of different causes, in fact, cut me off from the society of men. The transition from dream-life to real life took place in me late... perhaps too late, perhaps it has not fully taken place up to now. So long as I found entertainment in my own thoughts and feelings, so long as I was capable of abandoning myself to causeless and unuttered transports and so on, I did not complain of my solitude. I had no associates; I had what are called friends. Sometimes I needed their presence, as an electrical machine needs a discharger--and that was all. Love... of that subject we will not speak for the present. But now, I will own, now solitude weighs heavy on me; and at the same time, I see no escape from my position. I do not blame fate; I alone am to blame and am deservedly punished. In my youth I was absorbed by one thing--my precious self; I took my simple-hearted self-love for modesty; I avoided society--and here I am now, a fearful bore to myself. What am I to do with myself? There is no one I love; all my relations with other people are somehow strained and false.

And I've no memories either, for in all my past life I can find nothing but my own personality. Save me. To you I have made no passionate protestations of love. You I have never smothered in a flood of aimless babble. I passed by you rather coldly, and it is just for that reason I make up my mind to have recourse to you now. (I have had thoughts of doing so before this, but at that time you were not free....) Among all my self-created sensations, pleasures and sufferings, the one genuine feeling was the not great, but instinctive attraction to you, which withered up at the time, like a single ear of wheat in the midst of worthless weeds.... Let me just for once look into another face, into another soul--my own face has grown hateful to me. I am like a man who should have been condemned to live all his life in a room with walls of looking-glass.... I do not ask of you any sort of confessions--oh mercy, no! Bestow on me a sister's unspoken sympathy, or at least the simple curiosity of a reader. I will entertain you, I will really.

Meanwhile I have the honour to be your sincere friend,

A. S.

IV

FROM ALEXEY PETROVITCH TO MARYA ALEXANDROVNA
ST. PETERSBURG, *April* 7.

I am writing to you again, though I foresee that without your approval I shall soon cease writing. I must own that you cannot but feel some distrust of me. Well, perhaps you are right too. In old days I should have triumphantly announced to you (and very likely I should have quite believed my own words myself) that I had 'developed,' made progress, since the time when we parted. With condescending, almost affectionate, contempt I should have referred to my past, and with touching self-conceit have initiated you into the secrets of my real, present life ... but, now, I assure you, Marya Alexandrovna, I'm positively ashamed and sick to remember the capers and antics cut at times by my paltry egoism. Don't be afraid: I am not going to force upon you any great truths, any profound views. I have none of them--of those truths and views. I have become a simple good fellow--really. I am bored, Marya Alexandrovna, I'm simply bored past all enduring. That is why I am writing to you.... I really believe we may come to be friends....

But I'm positively incapable of talking to you, till you hold out a hand to me, till I get a note from you with the one word 'Yes.' Marya Alexandrovna, are you willing to listen to me? That's the question.--Yours devotedly,

A. S.

V

FROM MARYA ALEXANDROVNA TO ALEXEY PETROVITCH
VILLAGE OF X----, *April* 14.
What a strange person you are! Very well, then.--Yes!

MARYA B.

VI

FROM ALEXEY PETROVITCH TO MARYA ALEXANDROVNA
ST. PETERSBURG, *May* 2, 1840.
Hurrah! Thanks, Marya Alexandrovna, thanks! You are a very kind and indulgent creature.

I will begin according to my promise to talk about myself, and I shall talk with a relish approaching to appetite.... That's just it. Of anything in the world one may speak with fire, with enthusiasm, with ecstasy, but with appetite one talks only of oneself.

Let me tell you, during the last few days a very strange experience has befallen me. I have for the first time taken an all-round view of my past. You understand me. Every one of us often recalls what is over--with regret, or vexation, or simply from nothing to do. But to bend a cold, clear gaze over all one's past life--as a traveller turns and looks from a high mountain on the plain he has passed through--is only possible at a certain age ... and a secret chill clutches at a man's heart when it happens to him for the first time. Mine, anyway, felt a sick pang. While we are young, *such* an all-round view is impossible. But my youth is over, and, like one who has climbed on to a mountain, everything lies clear before me.

Yes, my youth is gone, gone never to return!... Here it lies before me, as it were in the palm of my hand.

A sorry spectacle! I will confess to you, Marya Alexandrovna, I am very sorry for myself. My God! my God! Can it be that I have myself so utterly ruined my life, so mercilessly embroiled and tortured myself!... Now I have come to my senses, but it's too late. Has it ever happened to you to save a fly from a spider? Has it? You remember, you put it in the sun; its wings and legs were stuck together, glued.... How awkwardly it moved, how clumsily it attempted to get clear!... After prolonged efforts, it somehow gets better, crawls, tries to open its wings ... but there is no more frolicking for it, no more light-hearted buzzing in the sunshine, as before, when it was flying through the open window into the cool room and out again, freely winging its way into the hot air.... The fly, at least, fell through none of its own doing into the dreadful web ... but I!

I have been my own spider!

And, at the same time, I cannot greatly blame myself. Who, indeed, tell me, pray, is ever to blame for anything--alone? Or, to put it better, we are all to blame, and yet we can't be blamed. Circumstances determine us; they shove us into one road or another, and then they punish us for it. Every man has his destiny.... Wait a bit, wait a bit! A cleverly worked-out but true comparison has just come into my head. As the clouds are first condensed from the vapours of earth, rise from out of her bosom, then separate, move away from her, and at last bring her prosperity or ruin: so, about every one of us, and out of ourselves, is fashioned--how is one to express it?--is fashioned a sort of element, which has afterwards a destructive or saving influence on us. This element I call destiny.... In other words, and speaking simply, every one makes his own destiny and destiny makes every one....

Every one makes his destiny--yes!... but people like us make it too much--that's what's wrong with us! Consciousness is awakened too early in us; too early we begin to keep watch on ourselves.... We Russians have set ourselves no other task in life but the cultivation of our own personality, and when we're children hardly grown-up we set to work to cultivate it, this luckless personality! Receiving no definite guidance from without, with no real respect for anything, no strong belief in anything, we are free to make what we choose of ourselves ... one can't expect every one to understand on the spot the uselessness of intellect 'seething in vain activity' ... and so we get again one monster the more in the world, one more of those worthless creatures in whom habits of self-ccnsciousness distort the very striving for truth, and a ludicrous simplicity exists side by side with a pitiful duplicity ... one of those beings of impotent, restless thought who all their lives know neither the satisfaction of natural activity, nor genuine suffering, nor the genuine thrill of conviction.... Mixing up together in ourselves the defects of all ages, we rob each defect of its good redeeming side ... we are as silly as children, but we are not sincere as they are; we are cold as old people, but we have none of the good sense of old age.... To make up, we are psychologists. Oh yes, we are great psychologists! But our psychology is akin to pathology; our psychology is that subtle study of the laws of morbid condition and morbid development, with which healthy people have nothing to do.... And, what is the chief point, we are not young, even in our youth we are not young!

And at the same time--why libel ourselves? Were we never young, did we never know the play, the fire, the thrill of life's forces? We too have been in Arcady, we too have strayed about her bright meadows!... Have you chanced, strolling about a copse, to come across those dark grasshoppers which, jumping up from under your very feet, suddenly with a whirring sound expand bright red wings, fly a few yards, and then drop again into the grass? So our dark youth at times spread its particoloured wings for a few moments and for no long flight.... Do you remember our silent evening walks, the four of us together, beside your garden fence, after some long, warm, spirited conversation? Do you remember those blissful moments? Nature, benign and stately, took us to her bosom. We plunged, swooning, into a flood of bliss. All around, the sunset with a sudden and soft flush, the glowing sky, the earth bathed in light, everything on all sides seemed full of the fresh and fiery breath of youth, the joyous triumph of some deathless happiness. The sunset flamed; and, like it, our rapturous hearts burned with soft and passionate fire, and the tiny leaves of the young trees quivered faintly and expectantly over our heads, as though in response to the inward tremor of vague feelings and anticipations in us. Do you remember the purity, the goodness and trustfulness of ideas, the softening of noble hopes, the silence of full hearts? Were we not really then worth something better than what life has brought us to? Why was it ordained for us only at rare moments to see the longed-for shore, and never to stand firmly on it, never to touch it:

       'Never to weep with joy, like the first Jew Upon the border of the promised land'!

These two lines of Fet's remind me of others, also his.... Do you remember once, as we stood in the highroad, we saw in the distance a cloud of pink dust, blown up by the light breeze against the setting sun? 'In an eddying cloud,' you began, and we were all still at once to listen:

'In an eddying cloud
Dust rises in the distance ...
Rider or man on foot
Is seen not in the dust.
I see some one trotting
On a gallant steed ...
Friend of mine, friend far away,
Think! oh, think of me!'

You ceased ... we all felt a shudder pass over us, as though the breath of love had flitted over our hearts, and each of us--I am sure of it--felt irresistibly drawn into the distance, the unknown distance, where the phantom of bliss rises and lures through the mist. And all the while, observe the strangeness; why, one wonders, should we have a yearning for the far away? Were we not in love with each other? Was not happiness 'so close, so possible'? As I asked you just now: why was it we did not touch the longed-for shore? Because falsehood walked hand in hand with us; because it poisoned our best feelings; because everything in us was artificial and strained; because we did not love each other at all, but were only trying to love, fancying we loved....

But enough, enough! why inflame one's wounds? Besides, it is all over and done with. What was good in our past moved me, and on that good I will take leave of you for a while. It's time to make an end of this long letter. I am going out for a breath here of the May air, in which spring is breaking through the dry fastness of winter with a sort of damp, keen warmth. Farewell.--Yours,

A. S.

VII

FROM MARYA ALEXANDROVNA TO ALEXEY PETROVITCH
VILLAGE OF X----,*May* 1840.

I have received your letter, Alexey Petrovitch, and do you know what feeling t
aroused in me?--indignation ... yes, indignation ... and I will explain to you at once
why it aroused just that feeling in me. It's only a pity I'm not a great hand with my
pen; I rarely write, and am not good at expressing my thoughts precisely and in few
words. But you will, I hope, come to my aid. You must try, on your side, to understand me, if only to find out why I am indignant with you.

Tell me--you have brains--have you ever asked yourself what sort of creature
a Russian woman is? what is her destiny? her position in the world--in short, what
is her life? I don't know if you have had time to put this question to yourself; I can't
picture to myself how you would answer it.... I should, perhaps, in conversation be
capable of giving you my ideas on the subject, but on paper I am scarcely equal to
it. No matter, though. This is the point: you will certainly agree with me that we
women, those of us at least who are not satisfied with the common interests of domestic life, receive our final education, in any case, from you men: you have a great
and powerful influence on us. Now, consider what you do to us. I am talking about
young girls, especially those who, like me, live in the wilds, and there are very many
such in Russia. Besides, I don't know anything of others and cannot judge of them.
Picture to yourself such a girl. Her education, suppose, is finished; she begins to
live, to enjoy herself. But enjoyment alone is not much to her. She demands much
from life, she reads, and dreams ... of love. Always nothing but love! you will say....
Suppose so; but that word means a great deal to her. I repeat that I am not speaking
of a girl to whom thinking is tiresome and boring.... She looks round her, is waiting
for the time when he will come for whom her soul yearns.... At last he makes his
appearance--she is captivated; she is wax in his hands. All--happiness and love and
thought--all have come with a rush together with him; all her tremors are soothed,
all her doubts solved by him. Truth itself seems speaking by his lips. She venerates
him, is over-awed at her own happiness, learns, loves. Great is his power over her

at that time!... If he were a hero, he would fire her, would teach her to sacrifice herself, and all sacrifices would be easy to her! But there are no heroes in our times.... Anyway, he directs her as he pleases. She devotes herself to whatever interests him, every word of his sinks into her soul. She has not yet learned how worthless and empty and false a word may be, how little it costs him who utters it, and how little it deserves belief! After these first moments of bliss and hope there usually comes--through circumstances--(circumstances are always to blame)--there comes a parting. They say there have been instances of two kindred souls, on getting to know one another, becoming at once inseparably united; I have heard it said, too, that things did not always go smoothly with them in consequence ... but of what I have not seen myself I will not speak,--and that the pettiest calculation, the most pitiful prudence, can exist in a youthful heart, side by side with the most passionate enthusiasm--of that I have to my sorrow had practical experience. And so, the parting comes.... Happy the girl who realises at once that it is the end of everything, who does not beguile herself with expectations! But you, valorous, just men, for the most part, have not the pluck, nor even the desire, to tell us the truth.... It is less disturbing for you to deceive us.... However, I am ready to believe that you deceive yourselves together with us.... Parting! To bear separation is both hard and easy. If only there be perfect, untouched faith in him whom one loves, the soul can master the anguish of parting.... I will say more. It is only then, when she is left alone, that she finds out the sweetness of solitude--not fruitless, but filled with memories and ideas. It is only then that she finds out herself, comes to her true self, grows strong.... In the letters of her friend far away she finds a support for herself; in her own, she, very likely for the first time, finds full self-expression.... But as two people who start from a stream's source, along opposite banks, at first can touch hands, then only communicate by voice, and finally lose sight of each other altogether; so two natures grow apart at last by separation. Well, what then? you will say; it's clear they were not destined to be together.... But herein the difference between a man and a woman comes out. For a man it means nothing to begin a new life, to shake off all his past; a woman cannot do this. No, she cannot fling off her past, she cannot break away from her roots--no, a thousand times no! And now begins a pitiful and ludicrous spectacle.... Gradually losing hope and faith in herself--and how bitter that is you cannot even imagine!--she pines and wears herself out alone, obstinately clinging to her memories and turning away from everything that the life around offers her.... But he? Look for him! where is he? And is it worth his while to stand still? When has he time to look round? Why, it's all a thing of the past for him. Or else this is what happens: it happens that he feels a sudden inclination to meet the former object of his feelings, that he even makes an excursion with that aim.... But, mercy on us! the pitiful conceit that leads him into doing that! In his gracious sympathy, in his would-be friendly advice, in his indulgent explanation of the past, such consciousness of his superiority is manifest! It is so agreeable and cheering for him to let himself feel every instant--what a clever person he is, and how kind! And how little he understands what he has done! How clever he is at not even guessing what is passing in a woman's heart, and how offensive is his compassion if he does guess it!... Tell me, please, where is she to get strength to bear all this? Recollect this, too: for the most part, a girl in whose brain--to her misfortune--thought has begun to stir, such a girl, when she begins to love, and falls under a man's influence, inevitably grows apart from her family, her circle of friends. She was not, even before then, satisfied with their life, though she moved in step with them, while she treasured all her secret dreams in her soul.... But the discrepancy soon becomes apparent.... They cease to comprehend her, and are ready to look askance at everything she does.... At first this is nothing to her, but afterwards, afterwards ... when she is left alone, when what she was striving towards, for which she had sacrificed everything--when heaven is not gained while everything near, everything possible, is lost--what is there to support her? Jeers, sly hints, the vulgar triumph of coarse commonsense, she could still endure somehow ... but what is she to do, what is to be her refuge, when an inner voice begins to whisper to her that all of them are right and she was wrong, that life, whatever it may be, is better than dreams, as health is better than sickness ... when her favourite pursuits, her favourite books, grow hateful to her, books out of which there is no reading happiness--what, tell me, is to be her support? Must she not inevitably succumb in such a struggle? how is she to live and to go on living in such a desert? To know oneself beaten and to hold out one's hand, like a beggar, to persons quite indifferent, for them to bestow the sympathy which the proud heart had once fancied it could well dispense with--all that would be nothing! But to feel yourself ludicrous at the very instant when you are shedding bitter, bitter tears ... O God, spare such suffering!...

My hands are trembling, and I am quite in a fever.... My face burns. It is time to stop.... I'll send off this letter quickly, before I'm ashamed of its feebleness. But for God's sake, in your answer not a word--do you hear?--not a word of sympathy, or I'll never write to you again. Understand me: I should not like you to take this letter as the outpouring of a misunderstood soul, complaining.... Ah! I don't care!--Good-bye.

M.

VIII

FROM ALEXEY PETROVITCH TO MARYA ALEXANDROVNA
ST. PETERSBURG, *May* 28, 1840.

Marya Alexandrovna, you are a splendid person ... you ... your letter revealed the truth to me at last! My God! what suffering! A man is constantly thinking that now at last he has reached simplicity, that he's no longer showing off, humbugging, lying ... but when you come to look at him more attentively, he's become almost worse than before. And this, too, one must remark: the man himself, alone that is, never attains this self-recognition, try as he will; his eyes cannot see his own defects, just as the compositor's wearied eyes cannot see the slips he makes; another fresh eye is needed for that. My thanks to you, Marya Alexandrovna.... You see, I speak to you of myself; of you I dare not speak.... Ah, how absurd my last letter seems to me now, so flowery and sentimental! I beg you earnestly, go on with your confession. I fancy you, too, will be the better for it, and it will do me great good. It's a true saying: 'A woman's wit's better than many a reason,' and a woman's heart's far and away--by God, yes! If women knew how much better, nobler, and wiser they are than men--yes, wiser--they would grow conceited and be spoiled. But happily they don't know it; they don't know it because their intelligence isn't in the habit of turning incessantly upon themselves, as with us. They think very little about themselves--that's their weakness and their strength; that's the whole secret--I won't say of our superiority, but of our power. They lavish their soul, as a prodigal heir does his father's gold, while we exact a percentage on every worthless morsel.... How are they to hold their own with us?... All this is not compliments, but the simple truth, proved by experience. Once more, I beseech you, Marya Alexandrovna, go on writing to me.... If you knew all that is coming into my brain! ... But I have no wish now to speak, I want to listen to you. My turn will come later. Write, write.--Your devoted,

A. S.

IX

FROM MARYA ALEXANDROVNA TO ALEXEY PETROVITCH
VILLAGE OF X----, *June* 12, 1840.
I had hardly sent off my last letter to you, Alexey Petrovitch, when I regretted it; but there was no help for it then. One thing reassures me somewhat: I am sure you realised that it was under the influence of feelings long ago suppressed that it was written, and you excused me. I did not even read through, at the time, what I had written to you; I remember my heart beat so violently that the pen shook in my fingers. However, though I should probably have expressed myself differently if I had allowed myself time to reflect, I don't mean, all the same, to disavow my own words, or the feelings which I described to you as best I could. To-day I am much cooler and far more self-possessed.

I remember at the end of my letter I spoke of the painful position of a girl who is conscious of being solitary, even among her own people.... I won't expatiate further upon them, but will rather tell you a few instances; I think I shall bore you less in that way. In the first place, then, let me tell you that all over the country-side I am never called anything but the female philosopher. The ladies especially honour me with that name. Some assert that I sleep with a Latin book in my hand, and in spectacles; others declare that I know how to extract cube roots, whatever they may be. Not a single one of them doubts that I wear manly apparel on the sly, and instead of 'good-morning', address people spasmodically with 'Georges Sand!'--and indignation grows apace against the female philosopher. We have a neighbour, a man of five-and-forty, a great wit ... at least, he is reputed a great wit ... for him my poor personality is an inexhaustible subject of jokes. He used to tell of me that directly the moon rose I could not take my eyes off it, and he will mimic the way in which I gaze at it; and declares that I positively take my coffee with moonshine instead of with milk--that's to say, I put my cup in the moonlight. He swears that I use phrases of this kind--'It is easy because it is difficult, though on the other hand it is difficult because it is easy'.... He asserts that I am always looking for a word, always striving 'thither,' and with comic rage inquires: 'whither-thither? whither?' He has also circulated a story about me that I ride at night up and down by the river, singing Schubert's Serenade, or simply moaning, 'Beethoven, Beethoven!' She is, he will say, such an impassioned old person, and so on, and so on. Of course, all this comes straight to me. This surprises you, perhaps. But do not forget that four years have passed since your stay in these parts. You remember how every one frowned upon us in those days. Their turn has come now. And all that, too, is no consequence. I have to hear many things that wound my heart more than that. I won't say anything about my poor, good mother's never having been able to forgive me for your cousin's indifference to me. But my whole life is burning away like a house on fire, as my nurse expresses it. 'Of course,' I am constantly hearing, 'we can't keep pace with you! we are plain people, we are guided by nothing but common-sense. Though, when you come to think of it, what have all these metaphysics, and books, and intimacies with learned folks brought you to?' You perhaps remember my sister--not the one to whom you were once not indifferent--but the other elder one, who is married. Her husband, if you recollect, is a simple and rather comic person; you often used to make fun of him in those days. But she's happy, after all; she's the mother of a family, she's fond of her husband, her husband adores her.... 'I am like every one else,' she says to me sometimes, 'but you!' And she's right; I envy her....

And yet, I feel I should not care to change with her, all the same. Let them call me a female philosopher, a queer fish, or what they choose--I will remain true to the end ... to what? to an ideal, or what? Yes, to my ideal. Yes, I will be faithful to the end to what first set my heart throbbing--to what I have recognised, and recognise still, as truth, and good.... If only my strength does not fail me, if only my divinity does not turn out to be a dumb and soulless idol!...

If you really feel any friendship for me, if you have really not forgotten me, you ought to aid me, you ought to solve my doubts, and strengthen my convictions....

Though after all, what help can you give me? 'All that's rubbish, fiddle-faddle,' was said to me yesterday by my uncle--I think you don't know him--a retired naval officer, a very sensible man; 'husband, children, a pot of soup; to look after the husband and children and keep an eye on the pot--that's what a woman wants.'... Tell me, is he right?

If he really is right, I can still make up for the past, I can still get into the common groove. Why should I wait any longer? what have I to hope for? In one of your letters you spoke of the wings of youth. How often--how long they are tied! And later on comes the time when they fall off, and there is no rising above earth, no flying to heaven any more. Write to me.--Yours,

M.

X

FROM ALEXEY PETROVITCH TO MARYA ALEXANDROVNA
ST. PETERSBURG, *June* 16, 1840.

I hasten to answer your letter, dear Marya Alexandrovna. I will confess to you that if it were not ... I can't say for business, for I have none ... if it were not that I am stupidly accustomed to this place, I should have gone off to see you again, and should have talked to my heart's content, but on paper it all comes out cold and dead....

Marya Alexandrovna, I tell you again, women are better than men, and you ought to prove this in practice. Let such as us fling away our convictions, like cast-off clothes, or abandon them for a crust of bread, or lull them into an untroubled sleep, and put over them--as over the dead, once dear to us--a gravestone, at which to come at rare intervals to pray--let us do all this; but you women must not be false to yourselves, you must not be false to your ideal.... That word has become ridiculous.... To fear being ridiculous--is not to love truth. It happens, indeed, that the senseless laughter of the fool drives even good men into giving up a great deal ... as, for instance, the defence of an absent friend.... I have been guilty of that myself. But, I repeat, you women are better than we.... In trifling matters you give in sooner than we; but you know how to face fearful odds better than we. I don't want to give you either advice or help--how should I? besides, you have no need of it. But I hold out my hand to you; I say to you, Have patience, struggle on to the end; and let me tell you, that, as a sentiment, the consciousness of an honestly sustained struggle is almost higher than the triumph of victory.... Victory does not depend on ourselves. Of course your uncle is right from a certain point of view; family life is everything for a woman; for her there is no other life.

But what does that prove? None but Jesuits will maintain that any means are good if only they attain the end. It's false! it's false! Feet sullied with the mud of the road are unworthy to go into a holy temple. At the end of your letter is a phrase I do not like; you want to get into the common groove; take care, don't make a false step! Besides--do not forget,--there is no erasing the past; and however much you try, whatever pressure you put on yourself, you will not turn into your sister. You have reached a higher level than she; but your soul has been scorched in the fire, hers is untouched. Descend to her level, stoop to her, you can; but nature will not give up her rights, and the burnt place will not grow again....

You are afraid--let us speak plainly--you are afraid of being left an old maid. You are, I know, already twenty-six. Certainly the position of old maids is an unenviable one; every one is so ready to laugh at them, every one comments with such ungenerous amusement on their peculiarities and weaknesses. But if you scrutinise with a little attention any old bachelor, one may just as well point the finger of scorn at him; one will find plenty in him, too, to laugh at. There's no help for it. There is no getting happiness by struggling for it. But we must not forget that it's not happiness, but human dignity, that's the chief aim in life.

You describe your position with great humour. I well understand all the bitterness of it; your position one may really call tragic. But let me tell you you are not alone in it; there is scarcely any quite modern person who isn't placed in it. You will say that that makes it no better for you; but I am of opinion that suffering in company with thousands is quite a different matter from suffering alone. It is not a matter of egoism, but a sense of a general inevitability which comes in.

All this is very fine, granted, you will say ... but not practicable in reality. Why not practicable? I have hitherto imagined, and I hope I shall never cease to imagine, that in God's world everything honest, good, and true is practicable, and will sooner or later come to pass, and not only will be realised, but is already being realised. Let each man only hold firm in his place, not lose patience, nor desire the impossible, but do all in his power. But I fancy I have gone off too much into abstractions. I will defer the continuation of my reflections till the next letter; but I cannot lay down my pen without warmly, most warmly, pressing your hand, and wishing you from my soul all that is good on earth.

Yours, A. S.

P.S.--By the way, you say it's useless for you to wait, that you have nothing to hope for; how do you know that, let me ask?

XI

FROM MARYA ALEXANDROVNA TO ALEXEY PETROVITCH
VILLAGE OF X----, *June* 30, 1840.
How grateful I am to you for your letter, Alexey Petrovitch! How much good it did me! I see you really are a good and trustworthy man, and so I shall not be reserved with you. I trust you. I know you would make no unkind use of my openness, and will give me friendly counsel. Here is the question.

You noticed at the end of my letter a phrase which you did not quite like. I will tell what it had reference to. There is one of the neighbours here ... he was not here when you were, and you have not seen him. He ... I could marry him if I liked; he is still young, well-educated, and has property. There are no difficulties on the part of my parents; on the contrary, they--I know for a fact--desire this marriage. He is a good man, and I think he loves me ... but he is so spiritless and narrow, his aspirations are so limited, that I cannot but be conscious of my superiority to him. He is aware of this, and as it were rejoices in it, and that is just what sets me against him. I cannot respect him, though he has an excellent heart. What am I to do? tell me! Think for me and write me your opinion sincerely.

But how grateful I am to you for your letter!... Do you know, I have been haunted at times by such bitter thoughts.... Do you know, I had come to the point of being almost ashamed of every feeling--not of enthusiasm only, but even of faith; I used to shut a book with vexation whenever there was anything about hope or happiness in it, and turned away from a cloudless sky, from the fresh green of the trees, from everything that was smiling and joyful. What a painful condition it was! I say, *was* ... as though it were over!

I don't know whether it is over; I know hat if it does not return I am indebted to you for it. Do you see, Alexey Petrovitch, how much good you have done, perhaps, without suspecting it yourself! By the way, do you know I feel very sorry for you? We are now in the full blaze of summer, the days are exquisite, the sky blue and brilliant.... It couldn't be lovelier in Italy even, and you are staying in the stifling, baking town, and walking on the burning pavement. What induces you to do so? You might at least move into some summer villa out of town. They say there are bright spots at Peterhof, on the sea-coast.

I should like to write more to you, but it's impossible. Such a sweet fragrance comes in from the garden that I can't stay indoors. I am going to put on my hat and go for a walk.

... Good-bye till another time, good Alexey Petrovitch. Yours devotedly, M. B.

P.S.--I forgot to tell you ... only fancy, that witty gentleman, about whom I wrote to you the other day, has made me a declaration of love, and in the most ardent terms. I thought at first he was laughing at me; but he finished up with a formal proposal--what do you think of him, after all his libels! But he is positively too old. Yesterday evening, to tease him, I sat down to the piano before the open window, in the moonlight, and played Beethoven. It was so nice to feel its cold light on my face, so delicious to fill the fragrant night air with the sublime music, through which one could hear at times the singing of a nightingale. It is long since I have been so happy. But write to me about what I asked you at the beginning of my letter; it is very important.

XII

FROM ALEXEY PETROVITCH TO MARYA ALEXANDROVNA
ST. PETERSBURG, *July* 8, 1840.
DEAR MARYA ALEXANDROVNA,--Here is my opinion in a couple of words: both the old bachelor and the young suitor--overboard with them both! There is no need even to consider it. Neither of them is worthy of you--that's as clear as that twice two makes four. The young neighbour is very likely a good-natured person, but that's enough about him! I am convinced that there is nothing in common between him and you, and you can fancy how amusing it would be for you to live together! Besides, why be in a hurry? Is it a possible thing that a woman like you--I don't want to pay compliments, and that's why I don't expatiate further--that such a woman should meet no one who would be capable of appreciating her? No, Marya Alexandrovna, listen to me, if you really believe that I am your friend, and that my advice is of use. But confess, it was agreeable to see the old scoffer at your feet.... If I had been in your place, I'd have kept him singing Beethoven's Adelaida and gazing at the moon the whole night long.

Enough of them, though,--your adorers! It's not of them I want to talk to you to-day. I am in a strange, half-irritated, half-emotional state of mind to-day, in consequence of a letter I got yesterday. I am enclosing a copy of it to you. This letter was written by one of my friends of long ago, a colleague in the service, a good-natured but rather limited person. He went abroad two years ago, and till now has not written to me once. Here is his letter.--*N.B.* He is very good-looking.

'CHER ALEXIS,--I am in Naples, sitting at the window in my room, in Chiaja. The weather is superb. I have been staring a long while at the sea, then I was seized with impatience, and suddenly the brilliant idea entered my head of writing a letter to you. I always felt drawn to you, my dear boy--on my honour I did. And so now I feel an inclination to pour out my soul into your bosom ... that's how one expresses it, I believe, in your exalted language. And why I've been overcome with impatience is this. I'm expecting a friend--a woman; we're going together to Baiae to eat oysters and oranges, and see the tanned shepherds in red caps dance the tarantella, to bask in the sun, like lizards--in short, to enjoy life to the utmost. My dear boy, I am more happy than I can possibly tell you.

If only I had your style--oh! what a picture I would draw for you! But unfortunately, as you are aware, I'm an illiterate person. The woman I am expecting, and who has kept me now more than a hour continually starting and looking at the door, loves me--but how I love her I fancy even your fluent pen could not describe.

'I must tell you that it is three months since I got to know her, and from the very first day of our acquaintance my love mounts continually ***crescendo***, like a chromatic scale, higher and higher, and at the present moment I am simply in the seventh heaven. I jest, but in reality my devotion to this woman is something extraordinary, supernatural. Fancy, I scarcely talk to her, I can do nothing but stare at her, and laugh like a fool. I sit at her feet, I feel that I'm awfully silly and happy, simply inexcusably happy. It sometimes happens that she lays her hand on my head.... Well, I tell you, simply ... But there, you can't understand it; you 're a philosopher and always were a philosopher. Her name is Nina, Ninetta, as you like; she's the daughter of a rich merchant here. Fine as any of your Raphaels; fiery as gunpowder, gay, so clever that it's amazing how she can care for a fool like me; she sings like a bird, and her eyes ...

'Please excuse this unintentional break.... I fancied the door creaked.... No, she's not coming yet, the heartless wretch! You will ask me how all this is going to end, and what I intend to do with myself, and whether I shall stay here long? I know nothing about it, my boy, and I don't want to. What will be, will be.... Why, if one were to be for ever stopping and considering ... 'She! ... she's running up the staircase, singing.... She is here. Well, my boy, good-bye.... I've no time for you now, I'm so sorry. She has bespattered the whole letter; she slapped a wet nosegay down on the paper. For the first moment, she thought I was writing to a woman; when she knew that it was to a friend, she told me to send her greetings, and ask you if you have any flowers, and whether they are sweet? Well, good-bye. ... If you could hear her laughing. Silver can't ring like it; and the good-nature in every note of it--you want to kiss her little feet for it. We are going, going. Don't mind the untidy smudges, and envy yours, M.'

The letter was in fact bespattered all over, and smelt of orange-blossom ... two white petals had stuck to the paper. This letter has agitated me.... I remember my stay in Naples.... The weather was magnificent then too--May was just beginning; I had just reached twenty-two; but I knew no Ninetta. I sauntered about alone, consumed with a thirst for bliss, at once torturing and sweet, so sweet that it was, as it were, like bliss itself. ... Ah, what is it to be young! ... I remember I went out once for a row in the bay. There were two of us; the boatman and I ... what did you imagine? What a night it was, and what a sky, what stars, how they quivered and broke on the waves! with what delicate flame the water flashed and glimmered under the oars, what delicious fragrance filled the whole sea--cannot describe this, 'eloquent' though my style may be. In the harbour was a French ship of the line. It was all red with lights; long streaks of red, the reflection of the lighted windows, stretched over the dark sea. The captain of the ship was giving a ball. The gay music floated across to me in snatches at long intervals. I recall in particular the trill of a little flute in the midst of the deep blare of the trumpets; it seemed to flit, like a butterfly, about my boat. I bade the man row to the ship; twice he took me round it. ... I caught glimpses at the windows of women's figures, borne gaily round in the whirl-wind of the waltz.... I told the boatman to row away, far away, straight into the darkness.... I remember a long while the music persistently pursued me.... At last the sounds died away. I stood up in the boat, and in the dumb agony of desire stretched out my arms to the sea.... Oh! how my heart ached at that moment! How bitter was my loneliness to me! With what rapture would I have abandoned myself utterly then, utterly ... utterly, if there had been any one to abandon myself to! With what a bitter emotion in my soul I flung myself down in the bottom of the boat and, like Repetilov, asked to be taken anywhere, anywhere away! But my friend here has experienced nothing like that. And why should he? He has managed things far more wisely than I. He is living ... while I ... He may well call me a philosopher.... Strange! they call you a philosopher too.... What has brought this calamity on both of us?

I am not living.... But who is to blame for that? Why am I staying on here, in Petersburg? what am I doing here? why am I wearing away day after day? why don't I go into the country? What is amiss with our steppes? has not one free breathing space in them? is one cramped in them? A strange craze to pursue dreams, when happiness is perhaps within reach! Resolved! I am going, going to-morrow, if I can. I am going home--that is, to you,--it's just the same; we're only twenty versts from one another. Why, after all, grow stale here! And how was it this idea did not strike me sooner? Dear Marya Alexadrovna, we shall soon see each other. It's extraordinary, though, that this idea never entered my head before! I ought to have gone long, long ago. Good-bye till we meet, Marya Alexandrovna.

July 9.

I purposely gave myself twenty-four hours for reflection, and am now absolutely convinced that I have no reason to stay here. The dust in the streets is so penetrating that my eyes are bad. To-day I am beginning to pack, the day after to-morrow I shall most likely start, and within ten days I shall have the pleasure of seeing you. I trust you will welcome me as in old days. By the way, your sister is still staying at your aunt's, isn't she?

Marya Alexandrovna, let me press your hand warmly, and say from my heart, Good-bye till we meet. I had been getting ready to go away, but that letter has hastened my project. Supposing the letter proves nothing, supposing even Ninetta would not please any one else, me for instance, still I am going; that's decided now. Till we meet, yours,

A. S.

XIII

FROM MARYA ALEXANDROVNA TO ALEXEY PETROVITCH
VILLAGE OF X-----, *July* 16, 1840.

You are coming here, Alexey Petrovitch, you will soon be with us, eh? I will not conceal from you that this news both rejoices and disturbs me.... How shall we meet? Will the spiritual tie persist which, as it seems to me, has sprung up between us? Will it not be broken by our meeting? I don't know; I feel somehow afraid. I will not answer your last letter, though I could say much; I am putting it all off till our meeting. My mother is very much pleased at your coming.... She knew I was corresponding with you. The weather is delicious; we will go a great many walks, and I will show you some new places I have discovered.... I especially like one long, narrow valley; it lies between hillsides covered with forest.... It seems to be hiding in their windings. A little brook courses through it, scarcely seeming to move through the thick grass and flowers.... You shall see. Come: perhaps you will not be bored.

M.B.

P.S.--I think you will not see my sister; she is still staying at my aunt's. I fancy (but this is between ourselves) she is going to marry a very agreeable young man--an officer. Why did you send me that letter from Naples? Life here cannot help seeming dingy and poor in contrast with that luxuriance and splendour. But Mademoiselle Ninetta is wrong; flowers grow and smell sweet--with us too.

XIV

FROM MARYA ALEXANDROVNA TO ALEXEY PETROVITCH
VILLAGE OF X----, *January* 1841.

I have written to you several times, Alexey Petrovitch ... you have not answered. Are you living? Or perhaps you are tired of our correspondence; perhaps you have found yourself some diversion more agreeable than what can be afforded for you by the letters of a provincial young lady. You remembered me, it is easy to see, simply from want of anything better to do. If that's so, I wish you all happiness. If you do not even now answer me, I will not trouble you further. It only remains for me to regret my indiscretion in having allowed myself to be agitated for nothing, in having held out a hand to a friend, and having come for one minute out of my lonely corner. I must remain in it for ever, must lock myself up--that is my apportioned lot, the lot of all old maids. I ought to accustom myself to this idea. It's useless to come out into the light of day, needless to wish for fresh air, when the lungs cannot bear it. By the way, we are now hemmed in all round by deadly drifts of snow. For the future I will be wiser.... People don't die of dreariness; but of misery, perhaps, one might perish. If I am wrong, prove it to me. But I fancy I am not wrong. In any case, good-bye. I wish you all happiness.

M. B.

XV

FROM ALEXEY PETROVITCH TO MARYA ALEXANDROVNA
DRESDEN, *September* 1842.

I am writing to you, my dear Marya Alexandrovna, and I am writing only because I do not want to die without saying good-bye to you, without recalling myself to your memory. I am given up by the doctors ... and I feel myself that my life is ebbing away. On my table stands a rose: before it withers, I shall be no more. This comparison is not, however, altogether an apt one. A rose is far more interesting than I.

I am, as you see, abroad. It is now six months since I have been in Dresden. I received your last letters--I am ashamed to confess--more than a year ago. I lost some of them and never answered them.... I will tell you directly why. But it seems you were always dear to me; to no one but you have I any wish to say good-bye, and perhaps I have no one else to take leave of.

Soon after my last letter to you (I was on the very point of going down to your neighbourhood, and had made various plans in advance) an incident occurred which had, one may truly say, a great influence on my fate, so great an influence that here I am dying, thanks to that incident. I went to the theatre to see a ballet. I never cared for ballets; and for every sort of actress, singer, and dancer I had always had a secret feeling of repulsion.... But it is clear there's no changing one's fate, and no one knows himself, and one cannot foresee the future. In reality, in life it's only the unexpected that happens, and we do nothing in a whole lifetime but accommodate ourselves to facts.... But I seem to be rambling off into philosophising again. An old habit! In brief, I fell in love with a dancing-girl.

This was the more curious as one could not even call her a beauty. It is true she had marvellous hair of ashen gold colour, and great clear eyes, with a dreamy, and at the same time daring, look in them.... Could I fail to know the expression of those eyes? For a whole year I was pining and swooning in the light--of them! She was splendidly well-made, and when she danced her national dance the audience would stamp and shout with delight.... But, I fancy, no one but I fell in love with her,--at least, no one was in love with her as I was. From the very minute when I saw her for the first time (would you believe it, I have only to close my eyes, and at once the theatre is before me, the almost empty stage, representing the heart of a forest, and she running in from the wing on the right, with a wreath of vine on her head and a tiger-skin over her shoulders)--from that fatal moment I have belonged to her utterly, just as a dog belongs to its master; and if, now that I am dying, I do not belong to her, it is only because she has cast me off.

To tell the truth, she never troubled herself particularly about me. She scarcely noticed me, though she was very good-natured in making use of my money. I was for her, as she expressed it in her broken French, 'oun Rousso, boun enfant,' and nothing more. But I ... I could not live where she was not living; I tore myself away once for all from everything dear to me, from my country even, and followed that woman.

You will suppose, perhaps, that she had brains. Not in the least! One had only to glance at her low brow, one needed only one glimpse of her lazy, careless smile, to feel certain at once of the scantiness of her intellectual endowments. And I never imagined her to be an exceptional woman. In fact, I never for one instant deceived myself about her. But that was of no avail to me. Whatever I thought of her in her absence, in her presence I felt nothing but slavish adoration.... In German fairy-tales, the knights often fall under such an enchantment. I could not take my eyes off her features, I could never tire of listening to her talk, of admiring all her gestures; I positively drew my breath as she breathed. However, she was good-natured, un-constrained--too unconstrained indeed,--did not give herself airs, as actresses gen-erally do. There was a lot of life in her--that is, a lot of blood, that splendid southern blood, into which the sun of those parts must have infused some of its beams. She slept nine hours out of the twenty-four, enjoyed her dinner, never read a single line of print, except, perhaps, the newspaper articles in which she was mentioned; and almost the only tender feeling in her life was her devotion to il Signore Carlino, a greedy little Italian, who waited on her in the capacity of secretary, and whom, later on, she married. And such a woman I could fall in love with--I, a man, versed in all sorts of intellectual subtleties, and no longer young! ... Who could have antici-pated it? I, at least, never anticipated it. I never anticipated the part I was to play. I never anticipated that I should come to hanging about rehearsals, waiting, bored and frozen, behind the scenes, breathing in the smut and grime of the theatre, making friends with all sorts of utterly unpresentable persons.... Making friends, did I say?-- cringing slavishly upon them. I never anticipated that I should carry a ballet-dancer's shawl; buy her her new gloves, clean her old ones with bread-crumbs (I did even that, alas!), carry home her bouquets, hang about the offices of journalists and editors, waste my substance, give serenades, catch colds, wear myself out.... I never expected in a little German town to receive the jeering nickname 'der Kunst-barbar.'... And all this for nothing, in the fullest sense of the word, for nothing. That's just it.

... Do you remember how we used, in talk and by letter, to reason together about love and indulge in all sort of subtleties? But in actual life it turns out that real love is a feeling utterly unlike what we pictured to ourselves. Love, indeed, is not a feeling at all, it's a malady, a certain condition of soul and body. It does not develop gradually. One cannot doubt about it, one cannot outwit it, though it does not always come in the same way. Usually it takes possession of a person without question, suddenly, against his will--for all the world like cholera or fever.... It clutches him, poor dear, as the hawk pounces on the chicken, and bears him off at its will, however he struggles or resists.... In love, there's no equality, none of the so-called free union of souls, and such idealisms, concocted at their leisure by German professors.... No, in love, one person is slave, and the other master; and well may the poets talk of the fetters put on by love. Yes, love is a fetter, and the heaviest to bear. At least I have come to this conviction, and have come to it by the path of experience; I have bought this conviction at the cost of my life, since I am dying in my slavery.

What a life mine has been, if you think of it! In my first youth nothing would satisfy me but to take heaven by storm for myself.... Then I fell to dreaming of the good of all humanity, of the good of my country. Then that passed too. I was thinking of nothing but making a home, family life for myself ... and so tripped over an ant-heap--and plop, down into the grave.... Ah, we're great hands, we Russians, at making such a finish!

But it's time to turn away from all that, it's long been time! May this burden be loosened from off my soul together with life! I want, for the last time, if only for an instant, to enjoy the sweet and gentle feeling which is shed like a soft light within me, directly I think of you. Your image is now doubly precious to me.... With it, rises up before me the image of my country, and I send to it and to you a farewell greeting. Live, live long and happily, and remember one thing: whether you remain in the wilds of the steppes--where you have sometimes been so sorrowful, but where I should so like to spend my last days--or whether you enter upon a different career, remember life deceives all but him who does not reflect upon her, and, demanding nothing of her, accepts serenely her few gifts and serenely makes the most of them. Go forward while you can. But if your strength fails you, sit by the wayside and watch those that pass by without anger or envy. They, too, have not far to go. In old days, I did not tell you this, but death will teach any one. Though who says what is life, what is truth? Do you remember who it was made no reply to that question? ... Farewell, Marya Alexandrovna, farewell for the last time, and do not remember evil against poor ALEXEY.

The Codes Of Hammurabi And Moses
W. W. Davies

QTY

The discovery of the Hammurabi Code is one of the greatest achievements of archaeology, and is of paramount interest, not only to the student of the Bible, but also to all those interested in ancient history...

Religion   ISBN: *1-59462-338-4*   Pages:132

MSRP $12.95

The Theory of Moral Sentiments
Adam Smith

QTY

This work from 1749. contains original theories of conscience amd moral judgment and it is the foundation for systemof morals.

Philosophy ISBN: *1-59462-777-0*   Pages:536

MSRP $19.95

Jessica's First Prayer
Hesba Stretton

QTY

In a screened and secluded corner of one of the many railway-bridges which span the streets of London there could be seen a few years ago, from five o'clock every morning until half past eight, a tidily set-out coffee-stall, consisting of a trestle and board, upon which stood two large tin cans, with a small fire of charcoal burning under each so as to keep the coffee boiling during the early hours of the morning when the work-people were thronging into the city on their way to their daily toil...

Pages:84

Childrens   ISBN: *1-59462-373-2*   *MSRP $9.95*

My Life and Work
Henry Ford

QTY

Henry Ford revolutionized the world with his implementation of mass production for the Model T automobile. Gain valuable business insight into his life and work with his own auto-biography... "We have only started on our development of our country we have not as yet, with all our talk of wonderful progress, done more than scratch the surface. The progress has been wonderful enough but..."

Pages:300

Biographies/ ISBN: *1-59462-198-5*   *MSRP $21.95*

The Art of Cross-Examination
Francis Wellman

QTY

I presume it is the experience of every author, after his first book is published upon an important subject, to be almost overwhelmed with a wealth of ideas and illustrations which could readily have been included in his book, and which to his own mind, at least, seem to make a second edition inevitable. Such certainly was the case with me; and when the first edition had reached its sixth impression in five months, I rejoiced to learn that it seemed to my publishers that the book had met with a sufficiently favorable reception to justify a second and considerably enlarged edition. ..

Pages:412

Reference   **ISBN:** *1-59462-647-2*   *MSRP $19.95*

On the Duty of Civil Disobedience
Henry David Thoreau

QTY

Thoreau wrote his famous essay, On the Duty of Civil Disobedience, as a protest against an unjust but popular war and the immoral but popular institution of slave-owning. He did more than write—he declined to pay his taxes, and was hauled off to gaol in consequence. Who can say how much this refusal of his hastened the end of the war and of slavery ?

Law   **ISBN:** *1-59462-747-9*   **Pages:48**

MSRP $7.45

Dream Psychology Psychoanalysis for Beginners
Sigmund Freud

QTY

Sigmund Freud, born Sigismund Schlomo Freud (May 6, 1856 - September 23, 1939), was a Jewish-Austrian neurologist and psychiatrist who co-founded the psychoanalytic school of psychology. Freud is best known for his theories of the unconscious mind, especially involving the mechanism of repression; his redefinition of sexual desire as mobile and directed towards a wide variety of objects; and his therapeutic techniques, especially his understanding of transference in the therapeutic relationship and the presumed value of dreams as sources of insight into unconscious desires.

Pages:196

Psychology   **ISBN:** *1-59462-905-6*   *MSRP $15.45*

The Miracle of Right Thought
Orison Swett Marden

QTY

Believe with all of your heart that you will do what you were made to do. When the mind has once formed the habit of holding cheerful, happy, prosperous pictures, it will not be easy to form the opposite habit. It does not matter how improbable or how far away this realization may see, or how dark the prospects may be, if we visualize them as best we can, as vividly as possible, hold tenaciously to them and vigorously struggle to attain them, they will gradually become actualized, realized in the life. But a desire, a longing without endeavor, a yearning abandoned or held indifferently will vanish without realization.

Pages:360

Self Help   **ISBN:** *1-59462-644-8*   *MSRP $25.45*

QTY

The Rosicrucian Cosmo-Conception Mystic Christianity *by Max Heindel*   ISBN: *1-59462-188-8* **$38.95**
The Rosicrucian Cosmo-conception is not dogmatic, neither does it appeal to any other authority than the reason of the student. It is: not controversial, but is: sent forth in the, hope that it may help to clear...   New Age/Religion Pages 646

Abandonment To Divine Providence *by Jean-Pierre de Caussade*   ISBN: *1-59462-228-0* **$25.95**
"The Rev. Jean Pierre de Caussade was one of the most remarkable spiritual writers of the Society of Jesus in France in the 18th Century. His death took place at Toulouse in 1751. His works have gone through many editions and have been republished...   Inspirational/Religion Pages 400

Mental Chemistry *by Charles Haanel*   ISBN: *1-59462-192-6* **$23.95**
Mental Chemistry allows the change of material conditions by combining and appropriately utilizing the power of the mind. Much like applied chemistry creates something new and unique out of careful combinations of chemicals the mastery of mental chemistry...   New Age Pages 354

The Letters of Robert Browning and Elizabeth Barret Barrett 1845-1846 vol II   ISBN: *1-59462-193-4* **$35.95**
by Robert Browning and *Elizabeth Barrett*   Biographies Pages 596

Gleanings In Genesis (volume I) *by Arthur W. Pink*   ISBN: *1-59462-130-6* **$27.45**
Appropriately has Genesis been termed "the seed plot of the Bible" for in it we have, in germ form, almost all of the great doctrines which are afterwards fully developed in the books of Scripture which follow...   Religion/Inspirational Pages 420

The Master Key *by L. W. de Laurence*   ISBN: *1-59462-001-6* **$30.95**
In no branch of human knowledge has there been a more lively increase of the spirit of research during the past few years than in the study of Psychology, Concentration and Mental Discipline. The requests for authentic lessons in Thought Control, Mental Discipline and...   New Age/Business Pages 422

The Lesser Key Of Solomon Goetia *by L. W. de Laurence*   ISBN: *1-59462-092-X* **$9.95**
This translation of the first book of the "Lemegton" which is now for the first time made accessible to students of Talismanic Magic was done, after careful collation and edition, from numerous Ancient Manuscripts in Hebrew, Latin, and French...   New Age/Occult Pages 92

Rubaiyat Of Omar Khayyam *by Edward Fitzgerald*   ISBN:*1-59462-332-5* **$13.95**
Edward Fitzgerald, whom the world has already learned, in spite of his own efforts to remain within the shadow of anonymity, to look upon as one of the rarest poets of the century, was born at Bredfield, in Suffolk, on the 31st of March, 1809. He was the third son of John Purcell...   Music Pages 172

Ancient Law *by Henry Maine*   ISBN: *1-59462-128-4* **$29.95**
The chief object of the following pages is to indicate some of the earliest ideas of mankind, as they are reflected in Ancient Law, and to point out the relation of those ideas to modern thought.   Religiom/History Pages 452

Far-Away Stories *by William J. Locke*   ISBN: *1-59462-129-2* **$19.45**
"Good wine needs no bush, but a collection of mixed vintages does. And this book is just such a collection. Some of the stories I do not want to remain buried for ever in the museum files of dead magazine-numbers an author's not unpardonable vanity..."   Fiction Pages 272

Life of David Crockett *by David Crockett*   ISBN: *1-59462-250-7* **$27.45**
"Colonel David Crockett was one of the most remarkable men of the times in which he lived. Born in humble life, but gifted with a strong will, an indomitable courage, and unremitting perseverance...   Biographies/New Age Pages 424

Lip-Reading *by Edward Nitchie*   ISBN: *1-59462-206-X* **$25.95**
Edward B. Nitchie, founder of the New York School for the Hard of Hearing, now the Nitchie School of Lip-Reading, Inc, wrote "LIP-READING Principles and Practice". The development and perfecting of this meritorious work on lip-reading was an undertaking...   How-to Pages 400

A Handbook of Suggestive Therapeutics, Applied Hypnotism, Psychic Science   ISBN: *1-59462-214-0* **$24.95**
by Henry Munro   Health/New Age/Health/Self-help Pages 376

A Doll's House: and Two Other Plays *by Henrik Ibsen*   ISBN: *1-59462-112-8* **$19.95**
Henrik Ibsen created this classic when in revolutionary 1848 Rome. Introducing some striking concepts in playwriting for the realist genre, this play has been studied the world over.   Fiction/Classics/Plays 308

The Light of Asia *by sir Edwin Arnold*   ISBN: *1-59462-204-3* **$13.95**
In this poetic masterpiece, Edwin Arnold describes the life and teachings of Buddha. The man who was to become known as Buddha to the world was born as Prince Gautama of India but he rejected the worldly riches and abandoned the reigns of power when...   Religion/History/Biographies Pages 170

The Complete Works of Guy de Maupassant *by Guy de Maupassant*   ISBN: *1-59462-157-8* **$16.95**
"For days and days, nights and nights, I had dreamed of that first kiss which was to consecrate our engagement, and I knew not on what spot I should put my lips..."   Fiction/Classics Pages 240

The Art of Cross-Examination *by Francis L. Wellman*   ISBN: *1-59462-309-0* **$26.95**
Written by a renowned trial lawyer, Wellman imparts his experience and uses case studies to explain how to use psychology to extract desired information through questioning.   How-to/Science/Reference Pages 408

Answered or Unanswered? *by Louisa Vaughan*   ISBN: *1-59462-248-5* **$10.95**
Miracles of Faith in China   Religion Pages 112

The Edinburgh Lectures on Mental Science (1909) *by Thomas*   ISBN: *1-59462-008-3* **$11.95**
This book contains the substance of a course of lectures recently given by the writer in the Queen Street Hall, Edinburgh. Its purpose is to indicate the Natural Principles governing the relation between Mental Action and Material Conditions...   New Age/Psychology Pages 148

Ayesha *by H. Rider Haggard*   ISBN: *1-59462-301-5* **$24.95**
Verily and indeed it is the unexpected that happens! Probably if there was one person upon the earth from whom the Editor of this, and of a certain previ-ous history, did not expect to hear again...   Classics Pages 380

Ayala's Angel *by Anthony Trollope*   ISBN: *1-59462-352-X* **$29.95**
The two girls were both pretty, but Lucy who was twenty-one who supposed to be simple and comparatively unattractive, whereas Ayala was credited, as her Bombwhat romantic name might show, with poetic charm and a taste for romance. Ayala when her father died was nineteen...   Fiction Pages 484

The American Commonwealth *by James Bryce*   ISBN: *1-59462-286-8* **$34.45**
An interpretation of American democratic political theory. It examines political mechanics and society from the perspective of Scotsman James Bryce   Politics Pages 572

Stories of the Pilgrims *by Margaret P. Pumphrey*   ISBN: *1-59462-116-0* **$17.95**
This book explores pilgrims religious oppression in England as well as their escape to Holland and eventual crossing to America on the Mayflower, and their early days in New England...   History Pages 268

QTY

The Fasting Cure *by Sinclair Upton*   ISBN: *1-59462-222-1*   **$13.95**
In the Cosmopolitan Magazine for May, 1910, and in the Contemporary Review (London) for April, 1910, I published an article dealing with my experiences in fasting. I have written a great many magazine articles, but never one which attracted so much attention...   New Age/Self Help/Health Pages 164

Hebrew Astrology *by Sepharial*   ISBN: *1-59462-308-2*   **$13.45**
In these days of advanced thinking it is a matter of common observation that we have left many of the old landmarks behind and that we are now pressing forward to greater heights and to a wider horizon than that which represented the mind-content of our progenitors...   Astrology Pages 144

Thought Vibration or The Law of Attraction in the Thought World   ISBN: *1-59462-127-6*   **$12.95**
by William Walker Atkinson   Psychology/Religion Pages 144

Optimism *by Helen Keller*   ISBN: *1-59462-108-X*   **$15.95**
Helen Keller was blind, deaf, and mute since 19 months old, yet famously learned how to overcome these handicaps, communicate with the world, and spread her lectures promoting optimism. An inspiring read for everyone...   Biographies/Inspirational Pages 84

Sara Crewe *by Frances Burnett*   ISBN: *1-59462-360-0*   **$9.45**
In the first place, Miss Minchin lived in London. Her home was a large, dull, tall one, in a large, dull square, where all the houses were alike, and all the sparrows were alike, and where all the door-knockers made the same heavy sound...   Childrens/Classic Pages 88

The Autobiography of Benjamin Franklin *by Benjamin Franklin*   ISBN: *1-59462-135-7*   **$24.95**
The Autobiography of Benjamin Franklin has probably been more extensively read than any other American historical work, and no other book of its kind has had such ups and downs of fortune. Franklin lived for many years in England, where he was agent...   Biographies/History Pages 332

Name	
Email	
Telephone	
Address	
City, State ZIP	

☐ **Credit Card**   ☐ **Check / Money Order**

Credit Card Number	
Expiration Date	
Signature	

Please Mail to: Book Jungle
PO Box 2226
Champaign, IL 61825
or Fax to: 630-214-0564

ORDERING INFORMATION

web: *www.bookjungle.com*
email: *sales@bookjungle.com*
fax: *630-214-0564*
mail: *Book Jungle PO Box 2226 Champaign, IL 61825*
or PayPal *to sales@bookjungle.com*

Please contact us for bulk discounts

DIRECT-ORDER TERMS

**20% Discount if You Order
Two or More Books**
Free Domestic Shipping!
Accepted: Master Card, Visa,
Discover, American Express

www.ingramcontent.com/pod-product-compliance
Lightning Source LLC
Chambersburg PA
CBHW080909020726
47502CB00008B/2394